FIRST YEAR

Kristina Ross is a writer and producer for the stage and screen. A graduate of the Victorian College of the Arts and a recipient of the Queensland Theatre's Young Playwrights Award, she has had the pleasure of working as an actor for the Melbourne Theatre Company, Red Stitch Actors' Theatre, the Artisan Collective and the ABC. Kristina currently lives on the Gold Coast with her husband and two children.

FIRST YEAR

KRISTINA ROSS

ALLEN&UNWIN
SYDNEY•MELBOURNE•AUCKLAND•LONDON

First published in 2024

Allen & Unwin
Cammeraygal Country
83 Alexander Street
Crows Nest NSW 2065
Australia
Phone: (61 2) 8425 0100
Email: info@allenandunwin.com
Web: www.allenandunwin.com

Allen & Unwin acknowledges the Traditional Owners of the Country on which we live and work. We pay our respects to all Aboriginal and Torres Strait Islander Elders, past and present.

 A catalogue record for this book is available from the National Library of Australia

ISBN 978 1 76147 065 3

Set in 12.8/17.7 pt Adobe Jenson Pro by Bookhouse, Sydney
Printed and bound in Australia by the Opus Group

10 9 8 7 6 5 4 3 2 1

The paper in this book is FSC® certified. FSC® promotes environmentally responsible, socially beneficial and economically viable management of the world's forests.

For Brewie and the Ross boys

—the purpose of playing, whose end, both at the first and now, was and is to hold as 'twere the mirror up to nature.

William Shakespeare, *Hamlet* (3.2.20–22)

PROLOGUE

The culture of our drama school was often referred to as cult-like. While I trained there, I ignored the whisperings of mental breakdowns and short-lived careers, certain I'd be the exception. Years later, I understood the warnings of our well-meaning alumni, and my reverence for the school dissolved. I'd allowed myself to become defined by it: the people, the place, the *work*.

It was vicious, cutthroat. A class of thirty, representing the best in the country. We were required to offer ourselves up to be dissected in the pursuit of becoming *artists*. To become malleable to the method. Terrified of being culled, we obliged, willingly donning the lives of others that would never truly leave us.

Worth the cost. Or so we were led to believe.

TERM ONE

TERM ONE

I

MELBOURNE, MID-2000s

The drama school stood defiantly between brick buildings on a cobblestoned street south of the city. Clad in square aluminium panels that twitched in the wind, the giant, garish structure resembled a trio of Rubik's Cubes, haphazardly stacked. It seemed to pique the interest of passers-by, who craned their necks to look up it, as if curious to what it might contain.

From the footpath I watched the smokers loitering on the wide cement steps beside the entrance, the glass doors sliding open as students filtered in and out. Their reflections contorted in the mirror-like panelling; extreme, funhouse versions of themselves, emphatic with their laughter and cries of recognition. They all seemed to know one another, and I realised my error in not attending Buddy Day the week before. Daunted, but unable to stall my arrival any longer, I made my way inside, smiling at no one in particular.

The foyer was packed. It was far more subdued than the building's exterior—high ceilings, a polished concrete floor and a handful of thoughtfully placed linen sofas. To my right, a staircase with deep steps of bleached wood rose through the centre of an atrium. Directly opposite, a partitioned wall served as a counter for reception, which opened into a large room full of desks and sleek computer monitors. On a shelf beside the counter, reverentially placed, black-and-white portraits of the training staff peered from within gilded frames. *Head of Acting. Head of Voice. Head of Movement.* Beyond that, the foyer was obscured by a sea of floral and double denim. Arms moved wildly. Heads flung back. Voices at fever pitch.

—

The student body was made up of three companies named after the year they would complete their training, the intent being that upon graduation the actors could assemble themselves into a theatre company of their own. But until then, we were known to one another simply as first, second or third years.

From the periphery, I managed to differentiate the students by the intensity of their enthusiasm. Indifferent to their surroundings, with little interest in conversation, were the third years, preparing to dedicate themselves to the work. Sprawled over the furniture, casually colluding with one another, were the second years. And those attempting to make their presence felt with overzealous introductions were the newcomers, my fellow first years.

—

The audition process was notoriously rigorous. Seventeen-year-old girls like myself were not usually accepted. The school rarely

6

took on anyone younger than twenty-one; the staff wanted their students to have lived a little first. I would soon find out that most of my peers had been auditioning for years. Some wore that like a badge of honour; others skirted around the truth, not wanting to admit to themselves that they'd spent so much time in an in-between place, waiting to solidify their futures by attending a prestigious drama school.

I had been encouraged by my high school drama teacher to apply; she considered the institution the best in the country for how physical methods were used as an entry point to the work. I trusted her implicitly and often stayed back after class to listen to her talk about her days as an actress in London. She sparked an interest in me, about a life in the theatre, that grew to become an obsession.

We chose my Shakespeare piece together from the pamphlet of monologues that became available three months before auditions were held in each capital city. Then I asked her to schedule a meeting with my parents, to help me break the news to them that I would not be following my father into law as expected.

'Is she any good?' my father asked.

'Yes,' the drama teacher replied.

My mother turned to me and smiled. 'What a shame.'

No one in my family worked in the arts. My parents pleaded with me to reconsider, knowing more about the industry than I gave them credit for. But I was determined. Rather than fight the inevitable, they sat in on rehearsals and helped me pick apart my Shakespeare monologue, setting aside the conversation about luck and nepotism for one about how I'd defy the odds.

—

My audition was held at the Queensland Theatre Company rehearsal rooms. My mother dropped me at the gate and waited in the car. I emerged two hours later utterly spent.

'How was it?' she asked.

I recalled the studio, standing on the floor alone before strangers. How I'd trembled with adrenaline but somehow managed to summon the courage to speak, my voice becoming increasingly hoarse as I recited the lines over until the men behind the desk were satisfied with my *delivery*.

I wanted to crawl into my mother's lap, cry at the humiliating terror of it all.

'Fine,' I said instead. To admit to insecurity would be tantamount to defeat.

'So, that's it?'

I shook my head. 'Call-backs are tomorrow.'

The following day, hopefuls were scattered around the foyer, talking to themselves under their breath like a scene from *One Flew Over the Cuckoo's Nest*. Every seat was taken, every wall paced along. The stakes were too high to allow myself to be affected by the energy of others. To calm my nerves, I stepped outside into the courtyard.

I shielded my eyes against the sun and saw the outline of a man perched on the edge of a metre-high garden bed. He wore black jeans, a black t-shirt and no shoes, and was muttering to himself between drags of a cigarette, eyes fixed on his feet. Intimidated, I attempted to walk past him.

'Juliet?' he asked, his face averted.

'Maeve,' I corrected quietly.

He looked at me directly. 'You'll do Juliet, right?'

His intensity dissolved my surroundings. 'That obvious?'

'Nah, wild guess.' He brought the cigarette to his lips and spoke again after a long, slow exhalation. '*Gallop apace, you fiery-footed steeds . . .*' He gestured the rest with his free hand.

I played along. 'You doing Juliet too?'

He laughed with appealing ease. 'Hamlet.'

I mentally scanned the pages of the audition booklet. '*O, what a rogue and peasant slave am I!*'

He clapped, the cigarette caught between his teeth.

'Fitting, I think,' I said.

He raised his eyebrows. 'Perceptive.'

'It's a compliment.'

'Don't know about that.'

'The piece is . . . difficult.'

'It can be. Sometimes.'

A latecomer ran through the gap between us, releasing me from his gaze. He stubbed out his cigarette and began walking towards the foyer.

'Good luck today,' I called, sinking beneath a want I couldn't yet name.

He considered me a moment. 'You too.' The door clicked softly behind him.

'Fuck.' I dropped onto a bench. *Fuck, fuck, fuck.* I inhaled, closed my eyes and attempted to steady myself with the text.

'*Gallop apace, you fiery-footed steeds,*
Towards Phoebus' lodging. Such a waggoner
As Phaëton would whip you to the west
And bring in cloudy night immediately.'

'Maeve?'

I shot up as if caught in the act of something illicit. 'Yes?'

9

'We're making our way inside now.' I'd met Oliver—a burly man with a shaved head and very kind eyes—at the first round of auditions. He was a third-year student, volunteering his time.

'Right, thank you.'

Gallop apace, gallop apace, gallop apace.

I walked across the sunny courtyard and into the empty foyer, following the echo of voices from within the rehearsal studio.

The call-backs were nothing like my initial audition. I had expected to take a seat beside the other auditionees and wait to be called on to deliver my first monologue. For that monologue to be pulled apart, my creative choices questioned. To be asked to perform it again, for the critique to cut deeply. But the table where the two men had sat the day before was abandoned, and the chairs along the furthest wall were all empty. Instead, I joined a circle of eight standing in the centre of the space.

'Close your eyes,' a man intoned. 'Feel the breath enter your chest, your diaphragm, your kidneys, your sex. Now release it.'

Jeremy Ford was an eccentric. Lecoq-trained, he'd enjoyed a successful career as a director in Europe before emigrating to Australia and settling into a permanent role at the drama school I was auditioning for. Dressed in black linen pants and a t-shirt, he had the body of a yogi and greying, shoulder-length hair.

Ford moved with purpose. Barefoot, he swung his arms back and forth, throwing his voice around the room with each exhalation. We mimicked him. He stopped now and then to observe someone, to place his hands on their back and encourage them to *breathe*. It took time for us to fall into a rhythm of our own, aware as we were of being watched, scrutinised.

Standing outside the circle were Oliver and the celebrated actor Rhett Lambert, a round man of sixty, overdressed for the

Queensland heat in a collared shirt and suit pants. A close friend of the head of school, he took a keen interest in nurturing the next generation of artists and blocked out eight weeks every year to direct the second-year students in Shakespeare.

'Who will begin?' Ford asked when the warm-up was complete.

One, two, three seconds passed.

'Anyone?'

'*Gallop apace*—' My voice was thin, tentative.

Ford gestured for me to stop. 'Maeve.'

'Yes?'

'Run.'

I rolled my shoulders, shook my limbs. '*Gallop apace*—'

'No.'

'What?'

'*Run.*'

I stared at him. 'And speak?'

'If the movement draws it from you.'

I was alone suddenly; the other auditionees had retreated to the walls. '*Run,*' I heard again. '*Run!*'

On the inward breath I tore towards a clump of bodies, a blur that parted to allow for my collision against cement. The words released on impact: '*Gallop apace.*' Startled by the sound of my own voice, I sprinted to the opposite end of the space, searching for a proper beginning.

'*Gallop apace, you fiery-footed steeds,*
Towards Phoebus' lodging.'

'Keep running!'

I did as Ford commanded, criss-crossing the floor, delivering the lines, my breath becoming embarrassingly loud from the effort.

'Go with her,' Ford called. 'Don't just *present* her.'

11

I paused, panting. 'I don't know what you mean.' I felt hot tears threatening to spill.

'Let her out, let her free.'

'The character?'

Ford laughed lightly. '*Yours.*'

He stepped back and gestured for Oliver to stand opposite me. 'Allow yourself to be seen.'

Oliver smiled gently and ran his eyes over my face—an action that I mirrored and found comfort in. My body became heavy, feet more firmly planted on the floor.

'Speak,' Ford encouraged, '*now.*'

The words bubbled in my gut.

'*Gallop apace, you fiery-footed steeds,*
Towards Phoebus' lodging.'

The feeling of being acutely aware of my body but slightly outside of it too. Of being unencumbered. Light and truly awake.

Present, finally.

I ran, fell, laughed and cried out. Picked up Oliver's offers and made some of my own, juxtaposing the text with my body, playing out the subliminal. The others were a circle that contracted with our movement, huddling and jogging, like a Greek chorus. Ford stayed close and whispered direction, allowing me to take full possession of the monologue.

'*So tedious is this day*
As is the night before some festival
To an impatient child that hath new robes
And may not wear them.'

Oliver lay beneath me. With my cheek against his chest, I heard the swirling of his blood, the heavy beat of his heart, and forgot that this was a test, an audition.

Ford remained still, close, until all three of us were breathing in sync.

'Thank you, Maeve,' Rhett said.

It snapped us out of the dream. I stood and just like that the cord was cut. Intimacy evaporated and we were ourselves again.

The other auditionees hovered.

'Take a seat, everyone,' Rhett said. 'Saxon, remain where you are.'

The man from the courtyard made his way to the centre of the space. *Saxon.* With the others I walked to the line of seats along the wall, shaking from the exertion of my audition.

'Which piece will you be performing?' Rhett asked.

'*Hamlet,*' Saxon said. 'Act two, scene two.'

'Very good.' Rhett leaned back in his chair and folded his hands in his lap. Ford remained standing and Oliver kneeled beside him, ready to be called into action.

Saxon stood completely still, his body straight. Almost a minute passed before he spoke. '*O, what a rogue and peasant slave am I!*'

In an instant he was charged, eyes fixed on a point above our heads. Ford flicked his hand for Oliver to move in. The men crouched low and fell forward, arching and flexing like animals.

The text came alive with the ferocity of their movement, conjuring between them a world. Saxon flickered from the man I'd met in the courtyard to the one standing before me, until both were gone and Hamlet appeared.

Oliver tripped and fell. Saxon stood over him and delivered the final lines of the monologue with visceral acuity:

'*The play's the thing*
Wherein I'll catch the conscience of the King.'

The air was fraught with tension. It broke with the crack of applause, and the room eased into an unprecedented appreciation of the work. *This is how it's supposed to be,* I thought. *Performance. Art. All of it.*

'Thank you,' Ford said.

Saxon shook Oliver's hand and came to sit with the rest of us.

Another name was called, another monologue played out. Each person strived for what Saxon had created. No one came close.

A handful of auditionees stuck around afterwards, chatting with Oliver in the foyer. I didn't want to talk about my time on the floor; I still felt raw from it. I nodded my thanks as I passed the group and stepped out into the courtyard, heading towards the street.

Saxon had resumed his perch on the edge of the garden bed. 'See you in Melbourne, Juliet.'

I held back. 'You think so?'

He regarded me thoughtfully. 'Yes.'

When, weeks later, I received the call that would alter my future indelibly, it was Saxon I thought of first.

See you in Melbourne, Juliet.

—

Now, I scanned the foyer for Saxon's face, but I couldn't see him among my peers, striking in their boiler suits and designer denim; self-appointed uniforms that made me feel self-conscious by comparison, standing alone in my black rehearsal clothes.

I looked for something to busy myself with and found a pile of A4 booklets on the reception counter. I took one and studied it. Tiny portraits of the graduating company looked up at me in various states of *openness*. Fifteen in total. The possibility that one day my face would stare back at someone on their first day of term filled me with a sense of wonder and pride.

A woman cackled loudly, startling me out of my reverie. She held the attention of a small group of rapt students, one hand on her hip, the other cutting through the air. I watched her, mesmerised.

'Careful,' a voice drawled from behind.

I spun. 'Sorry?'

A man smiled at me mischievously. 'She'll eat you alive.' He held himself with the confidence of the genetically blessed, clad in a preening blazer and button-down shirt. 'You must be Maeve.'

I gaped at him.

'Oliver told a bunch of first years about the girl who *worked* with Ford in Brisbane,' he explained. 'He gave a very accurate description. You weren't at Buddy Day.'

'No.'

'That's too bad,' the man said as he moved through the crowd, talking over his shoulder, encouraging me to follow and continue the conversation. 'We went to the Otways. Hugged some trees, smuggled some wine,' he laughed unabashedly. 'Real bonding experience.'

I'd read about the excursion in the introductory information package. Anxious about sharing an afternoon with strangers, I'd convinced myself it wouldn't matter if I wasn't there. Now I felt as though I'd missed out on something important.

'Cool,' I said.

'Yeah, cool,' he chuckled and offered me his hand, 'I'm Richard. First year.' He leaned against a shuttered-up bar and threw his arms out ceremoniously to a line of people seated along the wall in front of him. 'And these are your comrades!'

A man stood and shook my hand with both of his. 'Emmet.' He was exceptionally tall with a mop of messy, blonde hair and pockmarked skin.

15

'This is Maeve,' Richard said.

Emmet cocked his head to the side and smiled. 'Of course.'

'Of course?' A woman almost equal to Emmet in height came forward and pressed her cheek against mine in greeting. She stooped a little, presumably from years of trying to make herself seem smaller, her stature not yet weaponised on the rehearsal room floor.

'What?' Emmet replied. 'She fits the mould.'

The woman's eyes flashed. 'Really?' She shook her head and turned back to me. 'I'm Imogen.'

I liked her instantly.

Richard snapped his fingers. 'Dylan?'

A thin man with an open, youthful face and chestnut curls shut his battered copy of *Frankenstein* and saluted me with it. 'Hey!'

'I saved her from Vivien,' Richard said.

'Your first good deed of the day, sir,' Emmet responded in an RP accent.

Imogen sat down again. 'Avoid her as long as possible,' she advised me.

'She's fine,' said Dylan.

'You've got a cock,' Imogen replied. 'Maeve and I don't. That puts us directly in her firing line.'

'I auditioned with her,' Richard said. 'She did Lady Macbeth. It was terrifying.'

'Terrifying how?' I asked.

'When *she* worked with Ford'—Richard paused, looked over his shoulder and lowered his voice—'she spat in some poor girl's face mid-soliloquy.'

'Claiming she was caught in the moment,' Emmet added.

'And they accepted her?' I asked.

'She's kind of brilliant,' Dylan admitted.

'I would be too if my father was William Yates,' Imogen said depreciatingly.

'Who?'

Richard placed a hand on his chest. 'Why, Miss Queensland, I'm appalled!'

'Yates was a member of the Australian Performing Group,' Imogen explained. 'The Pram Factory?'

I nodded, making a mental note to look it up later.

'He's never stopped working,' Richard remarked.

'Did you see his Lear?' Emmet asked.

'Come on,' said Imogen. 'Was it really that impressive?'

'Yes,' Richard responded. 'It was. And, if we're honest, it's why any of us went.'

'To see his cock,' Emmet said, matter-of-fact.

'Sorry, Maeve.' Imogen grimaced. 'You must be getting a terrible first impression of us. We don't really talk about cocks all the time.'

Richard pointed at her dramatically. 'Not true!'

I knew a little about *King Lear* from watching old *Playing Shakespeare* RSC tapes in high school. I had particularly liked the scene between Lear and his daughter Cordelia, committing the *Unhappy that I am* speech to memory.

'So no matter how convincingly Yates plays Lear, we're really just waiting to see whether he'll . . . reveal himself?' I asked.

'Exactly.' Imogen stood and nodded towards the double doors at the edge of the foyer. The sign above read STUDIO ONE. Students had begun filing in, an indication that the day was officially about to begin.

Richard draped an arm across my shoulders. 'I was right!'

'About what?' Emmet asked.

'About Maeve! Steer clear of Vivien, will you?' He gave me a squeeze and let go again before pushing into the crowd.

Dylan grinned. 'Welcome.'

'I really wish I'd seen it,' I said.

'Yates's Lear or his cock?' Richard called back.

'Both,' I replied, and we all laughed.

It was a relief to be swept up in the banter, but I knew it was temporary. Conversation was one thing, the work quite another. On the floor was where I'd prove myself worthy of friendship.

II

Three storeys high and the length of two basketball courts, Studio One was the most intimidating space I'd ever been inside. Light from the street spilled in through a window above the side entrance, illuminating the dark edges of the furthest wall that the fluorescent beams on the impressive rig above struggled to reach. A demountable seating bank had been assembled by the entrance. It brimmed over with bodies. Only a handful of seats remained.

'Wow,' I breathed.

'Right?' Dylan elbowed me and leaped up the stairs.

A figure brushed past, the shape familiar.

'Maeve!' Richard called from a row near the back.

The figure looked to Richard, then to me. *Saxon.* My breath caught at the sight of him.

'Maeve!' Richard beckoned again with a wave.

I darted around Saxon and took a seat with the others. But I could sense him staring. I raised my face to meet his eyes. He jutted his chin in acknowledgement and turned away.

'Do you think it's true?' Dylan asked.

Richard crossed his legs deliberately. 'I'm doubtful.'

'What would you rather be doing,' Imogen began, 'filming in Sweden or—'

'Facilitating the growth of a new crop of artists?' Richard interrupted.

'Artists?' Emmet queried. 'Don't flatter yourself.'

Dylan was incredulous. 'Don't you care if she's here?'

'No,' Emmet replied bluntly.

'Come on!' Dylan cried. 'I want to work with her. She's a living legend!'

'Correction,' Emmet said. 'You want to *say* you've worked with her.'

Richard pulled his wallet from the pocket of his trousers. 'Fifty bucks says she doesn't show.'

'Easy win,' said Imogen. 'Her name's at stake.'

'We're talking about Quinn Medina,' Dylan explained, laughing at my bewildered expression.

'The head of school?'

Richard leaned out to face me from three seats down. 'She used to be an actor.'

'Used to be?'

'So the story goes,' Richard said.

Imogen explained: 'Apparently she lost her shit during rehearsals for *Streetcar*'—she looked to Richard—'what, twenty years ago?'

Richard threw his head back blithely. '*I don't want realism. I want magic!*'

Imogen laughed. 'And she hasn't stepped on stage since. She mostly directs now, and coaches sometimes too. Rumour has it she's been working on a film in Sweden. The lead actress—one of her protégées—has been having a hard time *getting there*.'

I nodded my understanding.

'So no one knows whether she'll be here for the start of the year,' Imogen continued. 'Her method is a little . . . curious.'

'She ruins people,' Emmet said.

Dylan scoffed. 'Bullshit.'

They were still arguing as Oliver entered, carrying a stack of black chairs.

'You on the payroll now, Ollie?' someone jeered from the crowd.

Oliver arranged the chairs in a row facing the seating bank.

'If I were,' he called back, 'you might actually have a chance of making it through third year. But your talent for blow jobs is limited . . . at best.'

The students roared.

As Oliver set the sixth and last chair in place, an ageing woman in a faded floral dress entered the room. The crowd immediately quietened.

The woman sat at the end of the row and began scribbling furiously in a notepad on her lap.

Ford entered next, head bowed towards a female colleague. The woman was strikingly beautiful; she carried herself with poise and made precise gestures as she spoke, tucking her cropped, raven hair behind her ears whenever it moved out of place. Ford indicated a vacant seat, and she sat and continued to speak, unperturbed by the sea of students watching her.

A stocky middle-aged man with a comically distinguished moustache and rimless glasses followed. He sat erect beside his colleagues and surveyed the student body with interest.

21

'Have you started?' a lithe woman called to the faculty as she entered. She wore a linen pant suit and no shoes.

The raven-haired woman beside Ford was curt. 'No.'

'The trams this morning,' the barefoot woman began, but the other woman gestured her into silence with a raised hand.

No one moved. No one breathed.

'For those of you who don't know me, I am Judith Wagner, Head of Acting.' The woman allowed for the weight of her title to land. 'Quinn's work has led her abroad.'

Richard turned to Imogen and mouthed, 'Pay up.'

'Sweden, in fact,' the stocky man added, a hand cupped around his mouth conspiratorially. 'For a film.' He emphasised the 'l' deliberately. 'Coaching Sylvie alongside one Ms Jessica Lange. Quite the Strasberg, our Quinn.'

Judith pursed her lips. 'Phillip Alcott, Head of Voice.'

There was a smattering of applause.

Richard released an audible breath. 'Huh.'

'What?' I asked, unable to contain my curiosity.

'Nothing. Just—*Sylvie.*'

Phillip made a loud humming noise, bringing the room back to quiet. He removed his glasses, rubbed his eyes, then replaced the glasses on the tip of his nose. 'I will have the pleasure of working with each of you over the course of your training. Voice is the cornerstone of an artist's practice. I'm here to assist you in finding yours. For second and third years, that is through text. First years will begin with *breath.*' Phillip crossed his legs and nodded with finality.

'A little housekeeping,' Judith said, taking charge of the introductions once again. 'Genevieve is your go-to for scheduling inquiries. Each Friday the timetable will be placed on the noticeboard inside the atrium. It is organic—meaning, subject to change. Refer to it instead of us.' Judith leaned forward to address the woman in the faded floral dress. 'Have I missed anything?'

Genevieve inhaled as though she might speak, but Judith resumed before she had the chance. 'Good. Freya, Head of Movement.'

The woman in linen waved.

'Second years can take private sessions with Freya during production week. She will sit in on rehearsals when required to. And the third years'—Freya clapped her hands excitedly, but Judith ignored her—'will take their cue from Ford.'

A murmur rippled through the seating bank.

Ford beamed with pleasure. 'As we step into *The Caucasian Chalk Circle*.'

A single voice rose from the crowd. 'Brecht?'

'The whole company?' inquired another.

Ford nodded. 'Beginning today.'

'You will be aligned to your archetype,' Judith said. 'Don't fight us on it. Risk is for second year; third year is for craft. Which brings me to the Ibsen Intensive.'

'Which play?' a student asked.

'*Hedda Gabler*,' Judith replied. 'Scene work only.'

The students cursed and groaned.

'The play in its entirety is far too advanced for a second-year company,' Judith stated calmly. 'Prove yourself with the scenes and opportunity will follow.'

The students became restless.

'First years! The company will be split in two for Voice and Movement classes. You will reconvene in the afternoons, either to participate in Improvisation with me or to be directed by Ford in Neutral Mask.' Judith raised her face to observe a group laughing at the back of the seating bank. 'As the second years can attest, Neutral Mask will strip you of learned behaviours. But once you click into an understanding of what it means to work universally—' Judith broke off abruptly, eyes darting to the entrance as an elderly woman swathed in white silk made her way towards the last remaining faculty seat.

'Fuck,' Emmet muttered.

Richard slid a gold note between Imogen's thighs. 'Fair and square.'

Imogen chuckled darkly. 'God help us.'

'Is that . . . ?' I asked quietly.

Dylan brought a finger to his lips. I took this as affirmation. *Quinn.*

At a glance she was unimposing. Her features bird-like, gait light, lipstick smeared. But she radiated a force that altered the atmosphere of the space, and we adjusted ourselves to be received by her.

Phillip rose and took her arm; she allowed it. 'Thank you, Phillip, my dear.' He hovered as she eased herself into a chair.

Judith continued. 'There will be a showing at the end of term, your version of a play to work towards—'

Quinn lay a palm on Judith's thigh and quietened her with a pat. 'Here we are, then,' said the head of school. 'Here we are.' She required no introduction, and she gave none. 'Allow me to be clear,' she said softly, peering into the faces of the students before her. 'Never assume permanence. You are privileged to be here, yes. But an artist is always in process.'

As Quinn outlined her expectations, the potential that existed within each of us rose to the surface of our consciousness. We had been chosen and we were eager to prove ourselves worthy.

'We are here to nurture your development. To encourage you in your practice. The methods we employ may be strenuous, but it is in your best interest to adhere to them.' Quinn stood, and the rest of the faculty followed suit. They filed from the room, leaving only Genevieve. She called out over the racket that had risen with Quinn's departure, 'First years, make your way to the foyer, please! The second years will be taking you on a tour of the building. Third years, remain where you are. Your introduction to Brecht begins now.'

—

'Layers,' Anya said. 'You'll need to start wearing layers.'

The tour of the drama building was as much about how to brace oneself for a Melbourne winter as it was about how to endure the course.

Anya was the second-year student assigned to me for the morning. 'It'll become second nature after a while,' she assured me.

Pairs of students milled about, walking in and out of different rooms. I wondered what they were thinking; if they were as nervous as I felt.

As if sensing my anxiety, Anya grasped my forearm. 'Ask me anything,' she said.

'Anything?'

'It's okay.' She smiled. 'I know you're the youngest in your year. I am too.'

'How old are you?'

'Twenty-two.'

Anya described leaving Adelaide at fifteen and jobbing as an actor in co-share productions across Melbourne before auditioning for drama school.

'I wanted to know it was really necessary for me.' She rubbed her shorn head; her baggy clothing hung heavily on her delicate frame. It seemed impossible that she and I were close in age; she gave the impression she'd already lived a weighty life.

As we wandered the halls, I pretended I'd be able to find my way back if I needed to. But the truth was, the drama building was a rabbit warren. Narrow corridors led to double doors which opened into performance spaces of varying lengths and sizes, lettered A to D. Their interiors were a continuation of the Scandinavian theme—bare, clean, bright. Some had windows, others curtains. The Rehearsal Room was not a performance space but the locker rooms on the first floor could be, and the black box style theatre behind the loading dock—the Warehouse— was reserved exclusively for Judith's practice. The levels were connected by the spiral staircase through the atrium at the front of the building. A service elevator at the opposite end was slow. According to Anya, most preferred to walk.

She concluded the tour and ordered me to hand over my phone. I retrieved it from my canvas bag, and Anya tapped her number into it.

'If you need anything, ring me.'

I was embarrassed she thought I might need to.

'And now, Ibsen calls.' Turning, Anya bounded down the stairs—an exit like a direction from a play.

—

I met up with Imogen again at Luncheonette, a crummy old deli by the Kings Way off ramp. Close to campus, yet far enough away to feel like a respite from it. The food was average, but the espresso was excellent, and the old Italian owner allowed us to linger well after we'd finished our meals. He liked the company, and it was good for business for patrons to be seen vying for space on his premises.

We sat at a lone picnic table in the shade of cement pillars, jostled either side by students.

'They can *cull* you?' I asked, disbelieving.

'Absolutely,' Imogen replied.

'How did I not know that?'

'Would it have prevented you from auditioning?'

'No. Well, I don't think so. It's just—'

'You told everyone you'd be gone for three years?'

I nodded and remembered the fifteen portraits in the graduation booklet where I'd expected thirty to be.

'I know someone who was culled,' Imogen said. 'It took her a while to get over it, but she's fine now.'

'Really?'

'Yeah, she works in finance.'

'Oh my god.'

Imogen laughed. 'You should see your face.'

We walked back to the drama building, picking our way through the students sitting on the steps by the glass doors.

'I told you,' a voice said by my feet.

I stopped.

Saxon squinted up at me. '*Juliet.*' He said the name slowly, deliberately, like a secret he wanted others to hear.

'You did,' I replied.

Saxon took a drag on a lit cigarette and watched the smoke curl between us. I was aware of Imogen beside me, the pressure to respond with some clever remark, but I couldn't think of one.

'See you in there.'

Saxon frowned and stubbed out the cigarette.

'Juliet?' Imogen asked as we walked towards the elevator.

'We auditioned together in Brisbane,' I said.

'And?'

The elevator doors opened; students ran from all directions and we were pressed inside.

'What's *Capote*?' I asked, to distract her.

'A film.'

'About?'

Imogen obligingly dropped the interrogation. 'An author.'

The Oscars predictions were everywhere. In the short trip to the second floor, Imogen outlined the plot of *Capote*, and in doing so revealed the fierce intelligence that bristled beneath her cool exterior. She already had a journalism degree, but she'd auditioned twice before being accepted into drama school; a small revelation that eroded my feeling that she was somehow superior. I felt safe with her, and she was kind in the way she educated me about things I should have known.

'There's a preview screening at Nova, week after next,' Imogen said. The elevator doors opened, and she walked ahead.

The hallway was crowded. Students ambled into performance spaces, and as they cleared, I saw Saxon, holding open the Rehearsal Room door. He'd taken the stairs.

'See you in there,' he said quietly.

A little game, this repetition.

I stepped inside, dropped my bag on the floor and kneeled to remove my shoes. When I looked up, there they were: my company. My mind cleared, and I was overwhelmed by the feeling of having arrived, of being a part of something bigger than I could ever have hoped.

Dressed in their black rehearsal clothes now as I was, the students were a contrast to the bright, white walls and buffed floorboards that absorbed the afternoon light shining through the windows. Cliques had formed already, drawing invisible rings around groups of three and four, setting a precedent for the year that would be difficult to break.

Richard stood in the centre of the studio with his eyes closed, his head lolling back and forth. Dylan talked at him with both hands. Emmet crouched beneath them both, rocking on his coccyx, fingers and toes interlaced. Imogen waved me over to the little group. We sat together and began to stretch.

'I'm going to audit the second-year Ibsen Intensive,' Dylan said.

'Why?' Imogen asked.

'To get a head start,' Dylan replied.

Emmet snorted. 'On what?'

'Our training,' Dylan said earnestly.

Imogen rolled backwards, brought her knees to her chest and made circular movements with her pelvis. 'It's not going to help you pass first year.'

'How do you know?' Dylan asked.

Imogen laughed.

Richard opened his eyes. 'Children, please.'

'I'm curious,' I said. 'I'll come.'

Dylan sat down on the floor, cross-legged. 'Thank you.'

Like a wave, the chatter stopped with each step Judith took into the space.

'Form a circle,' she said.

We moved quickly, quietly, adjusting the size of the sphere as each company member made a place for themselves.

'Now,' Judith began, 'these sessions are an opportunity to extend yourselves. To push the boundaries and to explore. An entry point, if you will, to the rest of your training.' Judith opened her arms to us. 'Your fellow first years. You will laugh together, cry together. Go into battle together.'

A titter swept across the group, and we glanced away from each other, self-conscious. But as Judith remained silent, we too became serious.

'Never again will you be able to make an assessment of one another without bias,' Judith said. 'Look carefully.'

Thirty people: men and women of various ages and ethnicities; archetypes specifically chosen to serve the company as a whole. The hero, the jester, the ingenue.

'We will move anticlockwise,' Judith said.

Each person said their name and where they were from, nothing more.

'My name is Maeve, and I'm from Queensland,' I said when it was my turn, then added, 'I've just graduated from high school.' Instantly I bowed my head, aware of the error I'd made in using my age as an advantage.

'Don't do that,' Judith said.

'Sorry?'

'That either.'

'Sorry. I mean, okay.'

Judith took two deliberate steps towards me. Up close, her symmetrical features were startling, like a photograph too perfect to be real. 'If you're going to make an addition, at least own it,' she said tersely. 'Especially something as impressive as being accepted at the *tender* age of seventeen. Yes?'

'Yes,' I repeated softly.

Judith gestured to Richard, and I was forgotten.

I swallowed the embarrassment and forced myself to focus on my peers as they introduced themselves in turn.

'Walk around the space,' Judith demanded when the last person had spoken.

The circle split. We walked with urgency in no particular direction, eyes narrowed as we concentrated on avoiding impact.

'Be aware of the micro, the macro.'

The sound of thudding feet on floorboards, of swishing fabric against thighs.

I was aware of being watched and of being surrounded by strangers.

'Breathe. Live in the moment.'

The smell of sweat rose off our bodies; fear evaporated in the monotony of our movement.

'Run if you feel it. Pause if you feel it.'

The afternoon slid against the back wall and turned it orange then red. It felt like minutes, but it had been hours since we'd started. People began to tire, to cough and collide.

'Stop!' Judith called.

My ears rang. Someone behind me was panting.

'Close your eyes.'

I swayed a little; white lines danced across my vision.

'When you open them, seek out whoever is in front of you.'

I blinked and there was Saxon. My heart thumped a current of electricity to my core.

'Feel out the distance between you and embrace.'

We moved slowly, cautiously.

'Do not disconnect from one another. Maintain eye contact until you absolutely cannot hold it any longer.'

Saxon's eyes burned through me. I turned away, unused to being in such close proximity to a man. He brought me back with a damp palm on my jaw. Then he dropped it to my waist; his other hand curled around the back of my neck. The gap between us closed, and I was thankful for his authority, for reminding me that this was the work.

Tentatively, I lay my hands against his rib cage, fit my fingers into the grooves between bone. Saxon tightened his hold, and I was forced to slide my arms higher, to grip him properly.

'Hold on to it,' Judith said.

Saxon's hips pressed into my pelvis, his cheek flattened against my own and we stayed like that for an immeasurable period of time.

'Release,' Judith instructed finally. 'Back to walking.'

We'd been holding one another so tightly that pulling apart felt like tearing flesh. We went about it slowly and stepped away with eyes downcast until we were pulled into the flurry of movement around us. Air cut through the places his body had fit into. I shook my limbs to accommodate the loss.

The energy became frenetic in anticipation of Judith's direction. It attuned us to our surroundings more acutely.

'Find your partner,' Judith said.

The company stopped still.

'If there is distance between you, move through it,' Judith ordered. 'If you are close, take your time coming together.'

Panic rose in my throat. I couldn't see Saxon and I wondered if I'd misunderstood the exercise. Couples formed around me. I wanted to spin, to search for him, but that seemed like breaking the rules.

Then I felt warm breath against my neck and a hand on my spine. I pivoted but knew already that Saxon had found me.

'Surrender,' Judith said.

We moved an inch at a time, eyes averted and soft. There was no question about the action, our bodies remembered and pressed harder. I slowed my breathing, aligned it to his. Our stomachs inflated and retracted, an intimacy that brought with it a wave of nausea. I tensed myself against it and we were jolted out of sync. There wasn't time to right our rhythm. It felt like failure.

Judith clapped her hands. 'Back to walking.'

I lifted my face to acknowledge Saxon as we stepped back, and I was encouraged by how open he was. Lips parted, eyes full. I needed to find the resolve to reciprocate.

The walking became meditative. Bodies seemed to float off the surface of the floor. But I felt tethered to Saxon, always aware of his position in the group.

'Stop,' Judith said. 'Find your partner.'

The floor cleared as the company split into halves. At the far end of the studio stood Saxon. There was certainty in our journey towards one another. On this third attempt I didn't shy away. I folded into him and allowed the space around me to dissolve, open to the sensation of our blood pulsing in time.

'Pull away!' Judith called.

I couldn't. It was too soon. I wanted to venture further. To *have* him, and to discover the limitless potential of performance, of all the layers that could be peeled away from oneself on the floor.

'Step back,' Judith said. 'Maintain eye contact.'

We were a lone couple with an audience. The company had formed around us and were observing our painful extraction from one another.

First my lips from his cheek, then his fingers from my hair-line. Each body part forced to succumb to gravity until we stood a foot apart: so close, though it felt like an immense distance.

'Find a natural ending,' Judith whispered.

The company seemed to lean into it, our final moment.

Saxon smiled. The casualness of it was searing, an ache that began in my chest and spread to my groin. I gasped.

'Very good,' Judith said. 'Relax.'

—

'Vivien dug her nails into my back!' Richard exclaimed as we reached the Kings Way crossing, and we all laughed at the absurdity of what we'd just worked through. 'I need a drink.'

My new friends agreed and began to walk in the direction of the Malthouse Theatre, the venue of choice for its proximity to working actors.

'You have such big hands,' Dylan said to Emmet playfully. 'Like, they really engulfed me.'

'Shut up,' Emmet muttered.

Dylan smiled broadly. 'I feel a lot closer to you now.'

Emmet clipped him behind the ear.

'Jesus!' Dylan tugged at his curls and redirected his attention. 'What was it like?'

The group stopped and waited for me to reply.

'What?' I asked.

'Your embrace with Saxon,' Dylan said.

I didn't have the words to describe the feeling of teetering between desire and loss, of knowing someone on an entirely different plane from what they presented to the world, and not being able to hold on to it. That what was revealed under the guise of the work wasn't entirely the truth, yet felt more truthful than anything I'd ever experienced.

'You don't have to answer that,' Imogen said. 'It's personal.'

'It's just . . .' I couldn't string a sentence together in my current state. 'I'm going to head home.'

'Come for one drink!' Richard urged. 'Dylan's girlfriend has extended his curfew!'

Dylan ignored him and touched my arm, concerned. 'Did I overstep?'

'No, I'd just like to get a head start on my journal. Process today before my mind turns to mush.'

'It's so fucking Orwellian,' Emmet growled. 'What could they possibly glean from our journals that they can't already see on the floor?'

'Cheer up, mate!' Richard said. 'You've got a whole term to spin those mutinous thoughts of yours into something a little more Quinn-esque.'

Imogen took my hand. 'Sure you're okay?'

I nodded as the men began to drift into the distance.

'We do it all again tomorrow,' Imogen said, and skipped backwards with a wave.

Their dark shadows lengthened against the rust-coloured shards of steel that sprang up from the sand near the Malthouse

35

Theatre. I immediately regretted not joining them, too nervous to drink in public while underage. But I longed for bed and reasoned I'd make up for it another time, not yet aware that Melbourne's best opportunities were to be had in the moment.

—

The number 1 tram delivered me to my doorstep after a twenty-minute commute through the heart of the city: past the Arts Centre, over the Yarra, along Swanston Street and into Carlton. My parents had warned me about the Carlton Crew, about Melbourne's infamous underbelly. I was under strict instructions to call my mother on the tram ride home and to stay on the phone until I reached my stop. It was always a mad rush to get off. Getting locked inside for having dallied was a rite of passage worth avoiding.

My parents had insisted that I live in student accommodation, secure with bolted doors and swipe keys. They paid the rent; I had no choice.

My studio apartment was on the twelfth floor, overlooking Melbourne General Cemetery. My mother worried that the view might be too morbid for a teenager living alone; she suggested that I avoid looking down. I had a single bed, a small television, a private bathroom, a kitchenette and a built-in desk with empty bookshelves above it. I thought myself hard done by, shut off from communal housing and impromptu dinner parties. The sprawling north beyond the cemetery, in my mind, only confirmed it. From my eyrie I watched colourful groups of dots disappear into brown buildings. Signifying everything I thought I was missing out on. But I felt frightened of the invitations I turned down.

So I went to school, I came home. I started over.

III

The timetable may have been organic, but the days passed predictably. We started at nine, finished at six. Two hours of Movement, then two hours of Voice. After lunch, the afternoon was spent with either Ford or Judith. Neutral Mask or Improvisation. Each session building on the last.

In Movement class, Feldenkrais was our focal point for first term. Freya was a student of the method. Her prime motivation was to reveal the dormant areas of our bodies that hindered our ability to move. We practised acute self-awareness, alerting Freya and ourselves to physically constricting habits. We had to learn to release them. Otherwise, according to our teacher, we were incapable of transformation.

The motions were slippery to retain and required endless repetition. The pace was slow. Whole sessions were often spent on one function alone.

Through the windows of the Rehearsal Room, I'd watch the clouds disperse behind buildings. I measured the mornings that way and would be disoriented by the time Phillip arrived. Freya's classes always ran over.

Breathing was difficult. But we were alive, weren't we? Taking breaths?

Apparently not.

The breath had to be reflexive, in support of impulse. Alignment of the spine was important as were the vibrations of sound our bodies made. We had to train ourselves to breathe properly, to take deep inhalations and exhale on a hum. To practise kinaesthetic awareness, for breath, body and thought to connect. Only then would our *authentic voices* be released, resonant and ready, and we'd be trusted with text. We spent hours standing with our feet hip-width apart, chin tilted, eyes forward, mouths open. It took effort to find the pockets of space in my pelvis, in my hips, in my sacrum to breathe into. All that oxygen made me light-headed.

By lunchtime I was exhausted, and I'd have to leap over mental hurdles—*I don't feel it, I'm doing it wrong*—to make it to the afternoon.

Ford was a man I desperately wanted to impress. After what I'd experienced in my audition, I wanted to draw the same kind of fervour from him. But Neutral Mask demanded skills I didn't yet possess, and I faltered beneath the weight of my own expectation.

The world of Neutral Mask was one of poetry. Ford directed us to walk, to watch, to wave. And to surrender. To don the mask and transform ourselves into the elements—fire, rain, earth—without idiosyncrasy and still maintain our humanity. If we were brave enough to leave our egos at the door, he said, Neutral Mask could redirect us to our most intuitive selves. It was a goal without an end point. We were learning that 'the self' was forever shifting.

Improvisation classes with Judith, on the other hand, were terrifying in that they followed no particular course. Walking, running and falling were always the entry point, then we would be directed in pairs, in groups or, most frighteningly, alone.

Create the seven stages of laughing.

Create the seven stages of crying.

Build a monologue from the word 'lover'.

Form a dialogue from the phrase 'I like to eat ice cream'.

There was never time to prepare; we had to find it on the floor in the moment. The personal at the forefront always. Risk meant revelation. Vulnerability was used and praised.

By the end of each day, I was bruised from the inside out.

—

The company sat on chairs arranged in a circle. I stood alone in the centre of Performance Space A. I let my arms hang, tucked my pelvis under and tried to recreate what I'd observed in others.

'Be present, Maeve,' Phillip said.

I pushed all the air out of my lungs through my mouth as a sign I understood. Bright spots speckled my vision.

Phillip placed his hands on my lower back. 'Inhale!'

I inflated my rib cage.

'Touch on sound,' Phillip commanded.

One deep, breathy note moved up from my stomach and out of my mouth. 'Ha.'

'There she is!' Phillip said.

The class nodded in agreement. It felt like a betrayal.

'Release your jaw. Good. Again.'

'Ha.'

Phillip smiled. 'Much better, Maeve. Take a seat.'

'Is that how I'm supposed to sound all the time?' I asked.

Phillip laughed. 'Dear girl. Yes!'

'But it doesn't feel like my voice.'

Phillip considered me. 'It's about being in your body,' he said. 'We need to access your breath in order to make use of your imagination. Make sense?'

I nodded, completely confused.

—

'A child is not self-conscious,' Judith said as she walked between us. 'A child is not private.'

Stop thinking, stop thinking, stop thinking.

It was as though I were floating along the ceiling of the studio, watching a miniature version of myself pretending to be a child, instead of inhabiting the life of one.

'Let's pause for a moment,' Judith said. 'Dylan, you may continue.'

Relieved, I abandoned the exercise of enacting how a toddler might play. My thoughts were working against me, locking me off from my body. There was no reason for it. I'd simply held on to the tension of the morning and let it filter into my work.

The company formed a circle around Dylan and lowered to the floor.

Dylan sat twisted, his stomach exposed, preoccupied with the label on the inner seam of his t-shirt.

'Expand on the action,' Judith directed.

Dylan trailed the seam to his big toe then sprang up from the floor and ran. The group splayed at the surprise and laughed when Dylan stopped to flick a switch in the far corner of the studio. He flicked it on, then off, and went back to running.

'And . . . rest. Thank you.'

Dylan broke character and rejoined the group.

'Working with abandon takes courage,' Judith said. 'Well done.'

Dylan brought his palms together as if in prayer. 'Thank you.'

I felt discouraged. To be singled out meant Dylan was capable of something the rest of us weren't—at least, not on that particular day. Exhaustion and inhibition altered our ability. Often there was nothing to distinguish between the performance and ourselves. Sometimes they were one and the same.

—

Ford centred his afternoons around one exercise only.

Neutral man takes a journey.

Neutral man is lightning.

Neutral man walks into a forest and finds that it is on fire.

It was expected that you stand, choose a mask and begin.

If you were stopped part way through, there was no reprieve. You were to start over immediately. If you heard the phrase, 'It's a bit confused, no?' after making it to the end of your piece, you'd failed. Miserably.

Ford sat back in his chair and observed me expressionlessly.

I held my chosen mask, the ridges of it light against my open palms. I knew from how long I'd worn it that my face was red from the pressure of the wood: a physical reminder that the mask owned you. *Do not disrespect it.*

'Thoughts?' Ford asked the company ranged on either side of him.

I could sense their trepidation. To comment without any indication from Ford as to whether or not the work was strong might inadvertently reveal their own ignorance.

Ford repeated the title of the exercise slowly. '*Neutral woman wakes up on a beach, finds a rock and throws it into the ocean.*'

The company seemed to drift inside the statement.

'I enjoyed her stillness,' Dylan offered finally.

Ford inhaled. 'As did I.'

The company relaxed.

'When she picked up the rock, it wasn't a question,' Imogen said. 'There was purpose—'

'The wake-up was illustrative,' Vivien interrupted.

Imogen shook her head. 'I disagree.'

'Does it matter?'

Imogen leaned out to face Vivien further along the line. 'Sorry?'

'It's subjective, but I think Maeve tends to err on the side of caution. I want to see'—Vivien paused—'less perfection.'

'You're talking about risk?' Ford asked.

'Yes,' Vivien replied.

'I'd say getting up first is quite a risk,' Saxon said.

'First doesn't mean best,' Vivien countered.

'We're in process,' Saxon said.

'Then she can afford to go harder.'

The company nodded; some took notes.

'Easy to say from the sidelines,' Imogen muttered.

'I don't see you up there,' Vivien said. 'This is a safe space, right? We're encouraged to give our opinion. I don't appreciate being attacked.'

The company held its collective breath.

Ford raised a palm. 'Okay, folks, let's move on. Maeve, take a seat.'

I left the floor and placed my mask beside the others on a fold-out table at the edge of the space. The masks looked up at

42

me with the same vacant expression I felt my own face had taken on after Vivien's criticism.

I returned to my spot on the floor beside Imogen. She placed her hand over mine, eyes forward.

'Who's next?' Ford asked.

Imogen stood quickly and selected a mask. The only thing worse than negative feedback was the defeat of not getting up at all.

—

The bench outside the Rehearsal Room rocked beneath me as I bent to tie the laces of my Cons. As I sat up, Saxon passed me on the way to the staircase at the far end of the hall. It was well past six o'clock. Few students remained.

'Thanks for the back-up today,' I called impulsively.

He turned. 'It takes guts to get up first.'

I felt heat rise from my chest and curl around my throat. There had been few opportunities like this for private conversation. We moved in different circles, were in opposing morning classes.

'We haven't debriefed since our first session with Judith,' I said, unsure how to talk to him outside of the work.

'True.'

'Is that what we're aiming for?' I asked. 'That level of commitment?'

'The embrace?'

I nodded.

'I think so. It doesn't happen often. When it does, I try to savour it.'

'Sound advice,' I replied, trembling beneath the intensity of his gaze.

'You need a ride home? I'm in Fitzroy. You're northside, right?'

'Carlton.'

'So it's on my way.'

The offer hung between us.

'Saxon?' Judith appeared at the top of the stairs. 'A moment.'

Saxon kept his eyes on mine. 'Sure.' Then he turned slowly and walked towards our teacher.

Without acknowledging my presence, Judith placed a hand on Saxon's shoulder and ushered him down the stairs, disrupting our exchange and whatever had occurred within it.

—

The days blurred.

I *participated*, got up first, threw myself around the Rehearsal Room. I tripped, I cursed, I bled. Skin off my ankles, a red lump on my elbow. Proof, I thought, of my hard work.

I tried to breathe.

I called home and lied to my mother about how well I was doing in class.

I contradicted myself, tried to laugh it off, felt chagrin at the pit of my stomach. I read and read and read, mispronounced Antonin Artaud's name.

I tried to forget about the exasperation in my father's voice when I first declared that I wanted to be an actor. Thought about Saxon instead, about Neutral Mask and Improvisation. Felt the pressure, all the time, to *pass*.

'Everything okay at home?' a woman asked me outside Flinders Street Station, pointing to the plum-sized bruise behind my ear.

'I'm a drama student,' I replied proudly, as though that explained it.

I stared out my window at the graveyard until the light changed, until the sun slipped away, wondering about tomorrow.

We're in process, I'd tell my empty apartment.

We're in process, the city would reply.

—

Economy of movement. That was the phrase. Be economical physically. Allow the rhythm of an idea to take over, find the freedom in it.

I couldn't.

'Surrender!' Ford called.

I had no way of interpreting the word, of measuring its importance as I worked on the floor alone: *Neutral woman is escaping.*

'Breath is essential! As are the eyes!'

I held too much emotion, couldn't rid myself of it.

'Stop!' Ford would command, and I'd obey. 'Turn to the back wall. Begin again.'

And I'd repeat it. *Neutral woman is escaping.*

Tension spread through the space and extended to my peers. I was wet beneath my armpits, across my back, behind my knees. I began to slip on the moisture left by my own footprints.

'Stop! Again.'

Ford was pushing me, hard. The humiliation of it; the *shame*. I was inefficient. Everybody could see that.

After the fifth or sixth interruption, he let me continue. I climbed an imaginary wall, scaled it and leaped to the ground below. I tried for a natural ending, turned to the back of the room and removed my mask.

Ford looked pained. My classmates concerned.

I breathed through my nose, tried to contain my panic.

'You do not perform Neutral Mask, Maeve. You *become* Neutral Mask.'

The exercise became a point of discussion. I remained on the floor, allowed the feedback to hit me.

'It was excruciating to watch.'

'Too much tension.'

'Too much restraint!'

And from Vivien: 'Appallingly demonstrative.'

Ford didn't comment; he let each student speak until the room fell silent. Then he said, 'Tomorrow we explore the man-made: rubber, steel.' And he left, feet light on the floorboards, hands behind his back, head down. The students followed.

I fell to the floor. My limbs shook, my chest heaved.

'I stood in the wings once, at the ballet,' Richard said above me, solid. 'The dancers were poised until they came off stage. Then they'd fall, just like that.' He pointed at me. 'Expired.'

'Jesus, Richard. Expired?'

A new flock of students entered the space, flooding it with their exuberance.

Richard kneeled, took my hand. 'Only momentarily,' he said. 'Get up darling, come on.' He pulled me to standing.

—

Voice class exposed you.

Breath is imagination.

Breath is imagination.

Breath is imagination.

Breath is imagination.

Breath is imagination.

Breath is imagination.

I had it written all over my journal. On the inside cover. In capital letters. In red pen. Over and over. A mantra I didn't quite understand.

I thought the cumulative effect of going to class each day would make my voice stronger, but it wasn't the case. I had to undo, let go of and reset before claiming whatever voice was buried beneath layers of affectation. The men in our class were able to access it quicker. The women had more to peel back, having settled into voices that were smaller and breathier. Voices that took up less space.

A good voice could be felt—*good* being subjective, of course. It came from confidence, a kind of *I don't give a fuck* energy that Phillip picked up on and commended you for. If there was a question in your voice, he found it. If you didn't believe what you were saying, he knew.

Phillip would slap his stomach. 'From here!' Also his chest. 'Not here!' Then he'd rough you up a bit by stepping into your personal space to watch you inhale. There was always the expectation that you had to do something with it, the breath, carry it over some invisible line and turn it into truth.

'Speak from where you draw the breath,' Phillip said.

But sometimes I couldn't locate it. Part of it might be in my throat, a portion of it in my diaphragm. Disconnected. Not enough to make a sustained *ha* sound, let alone an entire sentence.

'Increase your awareness,' he'd hiss, and tears would fall as your breath undid you. By that stage it didn't matter. It was a breakthrough. You'd bring it back, that feeling, that understanding, to the next class and imitate yourself. Only that wasn't what he was after either.

I found out today, I wrote in my journal, *that I tend to work through my nose and speak from my throat. I need to be mindful to release and let go of the energy of the thought before the next. Speaking quickly is a manifestation of something else. Make the decision to be seen and heard!*

There was a psychology to it, the work not entirely physical. Phillip's methods were often paradoxical, not properly explained, but we had to show him we understood, that we were trying to swallow our perceived versions of ourselves and take on the one he saw for each of us.

—

Sylvie.

The more conscious I became of my own failings, the more my envy of her reputation grew. The students spoke her name like a prayer: softly, reverently. Her interpretation of Nina in *The Seagull* the year before had been so moving that she'd been approached by a European director to star in a film adaptation of the same play. She was allowed leave from her training on one condition: that Quinn coach her through rehearsals and get her settled on set.

Without a face to put to her name, I conjured images of an English rose type. Pale-skinned, buxom, with a wispy, apologetic voice.

Richard laughed when I prodded him for information. He'd sat in on rehearsals for a play she was working on once, during a tour of the drama school when she was still a second year. 'You'll see,' he said and explained that there was no accurate way to describe her. It was a distinctiveness she had that others tried to emulate.

Sylvie. The actress.

Omnipresent. Like a threat.

IV

Initiation was a point of contention; a welcome that over the years had grown into something a little more sinister. There were half-hearted calls for it to be cancelled—a party was enough, surely. But a handful of fervent second and third years could not be dissuaded. They wanted retribution for what they'd endured when they were the newcomers.

'A few drinks, a few whacks,' Richard said as we climbed the stairs to the second floor.

I stopped. 'Are you serious?'

A pair of second years bumped into me and cursed. I apologised.

'Think of it as foreplay,' Anya said, and pulled me to the railing to avoid further collisions.

'What?'

Anya suppressed a smile. 'Ophelia.'

'Desdemona,' Richard murmured suggestively. 'You've got the chops, save it for second year.'

'But seriously, you can't pike. Initiation is non-negotiable,' Anya said. 'We'll pick you up and we can go together. Keep you out of harm's way.'

'There'll be an open bar,' Richard added.

It was bait. He knew my parents gave me a small weekly allowance to cover groceries and tram fares. 'Poor little rich girl,' he'd said when he found out. I was mortified, never mentioned it again.

'Fine,' I said.

Richard cheered, and I was filled with dread.

Anya took the steps two at a time and swung back to face us on the landing. 'Text me your address,' she called, and disappeared.

—

A bottle of champagne sat precariously beside Anya's handbag on the passenger seat of her beaten-up Holden Commodore.

'Careful!' Anya said as I got in. 'It's open.' She leaned over the handbrake and kissed me on the cheek. 'Celebratory roadie.'

'What are we celebrating exactly?' I asked.

'Your initiation!' she cried.

I picked up the warm bottle and took a pull. The bubbles burst against my fatigue, and I thought, *Initiation has already happened.* My body felt it through the work. The party was a ruse.

'Good girl,' Richard said from the back seat. 'May I?'

I handed him the bottle. He threw his head back and took not one gulp but four.

Anya pulled out from the kerb sharply. 'Seatbelts!'

I was thrown against the door and Richard across the back seat.

'You're a maniac, you know that?' he yelled.

'Oh, shut up!' Anya replied. 'At least I have a licence.'

'What do I need one for? I've got *you*, don't I?'

'Spoilt!' Anya reached an arm around her seat and slapped him. Richard recoiled and squealed like a child.

'Am I an idiot?' I asked. 'Are you guys together?'

'God, no!' Anya said. 'We're old friends from Adelaide. Richard moved here a few years after I did. We were roommates for a while.'

'Remember that place? The first one?' Richard bent forward so that his head was in line with Anya's and my own. 'Basically a crack den. You're a lucky girl, Maeve. Set-up like that.' He cocked his head in the direction of my building.

'I'd like to move out eventually,' I said, embarrassed.

'Don't!' Richard replied. 'Stay put, enjoy it. Privacy. My god, what I'd give for that.' He lowered his voice. 'Now tell me: what did you get up to this afternoon? Spend it with anyone in particular?'

'Richard, please,' Anya chided.

Richard ignored her. 'Maeve, darling, there's a little rumour going around that you're *involved* with someone from our company.'

I shifted in my seat. 'Who?'

'Saxon.'

'Well . . .' I hesitated. 'I'm not.'

Richard collapsed into peals of laughter.

'I'm not involved with him!'

'But you'd like to be!' Richard declared.

'I was alone this afternoon,' I replied.

Richard clicked his tongue. 'Shame.'

'You should have called me!' Anya flicked her face in my direction. 'I know what it's like to find yourself in a new city where you don't know a *soul*.'

'Well, *I* found a beautiful little bar on Gertrude Street with a very impressive wine list. Pity about the clientele.' Richard took another swig from the champagne bottle and handed it back to me. 'Next time, you're coming with me, Maeve. You'd lift the calibre of the place simply by walking through the door.'

'He wants free drinks,' Anya said.

'True,' Richard began, 'but it's suddenly become apparent to me that I've been neglecting my civic duty.'

'Which is?' Anya asked.

'Maeve's education!'

I lifted the bottle. 'Starting with this?'

'Exactly,' Richard said earnestly. 'This is your time! You're young, you're gorgeous and you have a bottle of champagne between your legs! What more could you possibly want?' He flung himself back against the seat.

'I want to be taken seriously,' I said, surprising myself.

'Then don't play to your stereotype.' Anya turned the wheel, slammed into a car space and faced me. 'Prove to the rumour-starting cunts that there's more to you than that beautiful face of yours.' She pinched my cheek. 'Now, give that to me before Richard guzzles it all.'

I handed her the bottle. She sculled the rest.

'God, you're a savage,' Richard said.

'Shall we?' Anya was already halfway out of the car. She met me on the footpath and slipped her arm through mine. 'Listen, a party like this is the perfect equaliser.' She turned to me and said sagely, 'Just don't go and fuck a third year.'

'Let her live, for god's sake!' Richard jeered from inside the car. 'Life's too short!'

I followed Anya down a deserted side street. The smell was rancid. I held my breath. Behind us, Richard hummed to himself as he leaped over piles of rubbish.

There was no sign. Just a door without a handle, speckled blue. Anya pushed against it and leaned into a cacophony of sound. Bass, glasses clattering, slapping flesh and laughter. She turned back to me and grinned. It was exactly the kind of doorway my father had warned me never to venture through.

I stepped inside.

Anya took my hand and led me down a concrete stairwell. 'A friend of a friend,' she yelled back, before throwing ironic air kisses to those seated on the stairs.

In the basement we were immobilised by the press of damp bodies pulsing in time to the music. Anya stood on tiptoe to survey the crowd: three companies of drama students, no civilians.

'Ready?' she asked and nodded in the direction of a mirrored wall across the room with liquor bottles looped in fairy lights. The crowd created a dark tableau that undulated like the ocean whenever the tiny bulbs flared.

Anya gripped my hand tighter and thrust forward. In the bursts of light, I swivelled my head and saw burgundy walls, cracked vinyl booths and framed portraits of scantily clad women. In the dimness, I stumbled against wooden furniture and tripped over faux Persian rugs. The venue looked like an antique store overrun with irreverent children.

'THANK FUCK!' Anya screamed as we came up for air against the scratched surface of the bar. She placed her chin on my shoulder and sang along to 'Love Will Tear Us Apart'.

'Vodka doubles!' Richard announced from behind us and elbowed his way to stand beside Anya. 'Naughty girl! You told the owners Vince Colosimo was coming, didn't you?'

Anya shrugged cheekily. 'Free venue? You're welcome.'

Richard took her face in his hands. 'Proper con artist, this one!'

Three glasses appeared before us, shimmering wet.

'Chin-chin!' Anya cried and clinked her tumbler against mine. I took a sip and winced.

'Go on, then,' Richard urged. 'Get on with it!'

Anya rolled her eyes and climbed onto the bar. 'Hear ye! Hear ye!'

Voices remained raised, the music continued to blare.

The barman presented Anya with a thick, wooden paddle. She curtsied and swung it close above the heads of those below her, eliciting a burst of profanities.

'HEAR-FUCKING-YE!' she bellowed.

A male voice whooped, and cheers broke out. Someone turned down the music.

'Darling first years,' Anya said in a mocking tone, 'to ascertain whether you are worthy of your position, we must test the strength of your character. Tell us a story!' Anya jumped off the bar and pushed her way into the centre of the room. 'No accolades, nothing dignified.' She spun, creating a sphere of empty space around her. 'We want . . .'

'Filth!' voices called.

'We want . . .' Anya's eyebrows lifted in anticipation.

'Muck!'

'Precisely.'

A bottle of vodka was produced by a bodiless hand. Anya swigged from it and grimaced. The students cheered.

'When we are sufficiently satisfied, you will be rewarded,' she said. 'Don't tempt me with the alternative!' She laughed, placed the bottle by her feet and raised the paddle above her head. 'We simply wish to get to know you better!'

A woman in a sequined jumpsuit pulled me away from the bar, 'Let's go, pet,' she purred. She prodded my arse with the pointed tip of her boot. I staggered forward. My drink sloshed against the back of a broad man in leather. He turned and caught me around the middle as I slipped on the wet concrete.

'Careful, darlin',' he said into my hair.

I rested against him for a moment, winded.

'Thanks, mate,' a female voice said, and I was yanked away from the man. 'You good?' Imogen looked me over.

I was flooded with warmth at the sight of her. 'Yes.'

She thrust a pint into my hand. 'Go on, neck it,' she said and from the crook of her elbow she pulled another, three-quarters full.

I laughed. 'Double-parked?'

'Got to think ahead,' she replied and planted a kiss on the corner of my mouth.

I drank the warm beer and held on to her as we were jostled by students either side of us. When we were finally contained, a tight huddle of first years, the second and third years ceased their jeering and positioned themselves on top of the furniture.

Imogen eyed them with wry suspicion. 'Is this really necessary? It's all very American.'

I chuckled into my glass, giddy with nerves.

'Shall we?' Anya yelled and hoisted herself onto the back of a velvet couch. 'Dylan!'

The room began to chant his name.

I let go of Imogen and twisted around in search of our classmate. A path was cleared and Dylan was nudged forward to stand before Anya.

She crossed her arms and looked down at him, smiling. 'Do you denounce all ties to Stella Adler?'

Dylan straightened himself at the mention of the legendary acting teacher. 'I do.'

'Meisner?'

'Of course.'

'And vow to honour Quinn Medina for as long as you practise your art?'

'Yes.'

'You have the room, sir.'

Dylan cleared his throat. 'I was dux of my high school.'

'Say again?'

'I was dux of my high school.'

'And?'

It was an accomplishment that carried no weight. Anya threatened him with the paddle and, encouraged by the horde, coaxed an anecdote from Dylan that set the tone for the evening.

'Fucked your cousin?' Anya repeated.

'Second cousin,' Dylan corrected, brow furrowed, smile creeping.

Imogen spluttered her drink into the hair of the woman in front. 'Well, fuck me!'

'Can't be true,' I said.

'Doesn't matter,' Imogen replied.

Anya gestured for Dylan to kneel. He obliged and tilted his head back, mouth open to receive the bottle.

'Dylan, of first year!' Anya hollered as she poured the vodka down Dylan's throat.

He swallowed and shook his damp curls like the fur of a beast.

One by one my company were called upon to deliver their story. 'Emmet!' 'Vivien!' 'Imogen!' The ability to hold court was considered an indication of talent; those who roused the loudest response were rewarded with instant notoriety.

Vivien described being made to recite a monologue from *Abortive* at a bar in the Czech Republic at the age of twelve, by her father. Now, she swayed to the music with her arms loose beside her, the surrounding women imitating her self-possession. When we locked eyes, she snarled.

Feet stomped the concrete, voices boomed. Richard received his standing ovation and came to stand beside me.

'That didn't happen!' I shouted at him. 'You never lived on the street!'

'No?'

'Definitely not!'

'Can't let the truth get in the way of a good story.'

The anecdotes became bolder. Perfect performances about adventure, about sex, about loss. And they compounded, each student picking up the unspoken challenge of bettering the story that came before theirs.

I drank from whichever glass hovered in front of me, dreading the moment my name would be called, the alcohol erasing any belief that I was interesting enough to hold the attention of a crowd.

Emmet took on an Irish accent, began to heckle a student as they told their story.

'*Howie the* fucking *Rookie*,' a voice yelled, congratulatory, and Emmet was rewarded with a bottle of dark spirits from behind the bar. He continued with the character, and the student was dismissed.

'He's brilliant,' Richard uttered in amazement as Emmet began to punch himself in the eye. 'A shapeshifter!'

'I can't do that,' I said to Imogen despairingly, and she laughed.

'No one can.'

Emmet took an enormous gulp from the bottle and sprayed it from his mouth. The students became fevered.

'It's sordid,' I said in shock.

'It's art!' Richard cried.

The music rose, everybody screamed to be heard above it. A joint was passed around. I allowed myself to be held by a stranger, to be pulled closer from behind. A palm against my stomach, directing me to move. I closed my eyes, pretended not to care, tried to dance without inhibition.

Then I heard my name: 'Maeve!'

Imogen grabbed my face, kissed my forehead reassuringly. 'Piece of piss.'

I wasn't ready.

'Do you denounce all ties to Stella Adler?' Anya called.

Over the heads of the students, I answered: 'Yes!' And I was ushered into the empty crescent of space before Anya, the prick of the crowd's interest like needles on my skin.

'Meisner?'

The routine had been repeated so many times that I knew when I was supposed to speak. But before my peers I was mute. Anya continued anyway and I wished that I was on stage, blinded by light, unable to see the pity in the eyes of my audience.

'Maeve?'

'Virgin!' a voice shrieked.

'Damsel!' bawled another.

I swallowed. 'Misogynists!'

The room cheered at that, and I laughed uncertainly, desperate for it to be over.

Anya gave me an apologetic look. 'Make something up,' she mouthed.

But I had nothing, no memory to use as a beginning. There was only Queensland, my parents, the ocean. And Saxon.

I searched for his face and found him waiting. Encouraged by the smallest of impulses, I stepped towards him, drained his pint and threw it to the floor. With the sound of cracking glass came exclamations of assent. I could go further, extend the rules of the game and overcome my failure to participate properly.

I couldn't look at him directly. I went straight to the physical and placed my hands on his chest. He brought me close, slid his mouth over mine.

My eyes were still closed when he stepped away and I realised how vulnerable I'd made myself. An immense volume of voices rose to greet my embarrassment, but Saxon saved me from it, kissing me again.

I heard gasps, a loud smack. Pain bloomed across my backside.

'Sorry,' Anya said, 'rules are rules. No story, no vodka.'

The room was a warm swell of movement. I focused on Saxon. He held me inside an understanding: everything had changed.

The students encircled us, called out, and I did what they wanted. I hauled myself onto him, wrapped my legs around his waist, laughed into his mouth.

'The ingenue has been broken in!'

'Get a bloody look at her!'

'It's mimesis!'

My body roiled under the immense weight of the moment, but Saxon held me together. The embrace once again, only more animal. I willed him to devour me. And with everyone watching, he did.

—

I rolled over and groaned. Faraway light cut a shard against my bedroom wall. I slid to the floor and peered through the blinds at the bustling world below.

I wasn't sure how I'd made it home. *Romeo, Romeo.* The name brought with it a lightning rod of remembrance. A dark cab, foreign limbs, the bright white of reception.

Saxon.

I whipped around in panic then saw that my single bed was empty. My body relaxed. I was alone.

I crawled to the bathroom, dragged myself to standing, and saw a greasy-haired, dark-eyed version of myself in the vanity mirror.

Juliet.

I smiled at her.

We'd given it a nudge and I'd survived. Pressed up against him, moving in sync. Hair stuck against my forehead. Sweat. Drinks. More drinks.

I lay against the bathroom tiles; their cool pressure dulled the heat in my bones.

Monday tomorrow. The certainty of seeing him would carry me through the day and out of my hangover to the work. I'd be in front of him and he in front of me. A form of intimacy I was beginning to appreciate, understood only by people like ourselves.

—

'What the fuck,' Imogen said. 'Where did that come from?' We were walking towards campus in the drizzling rain.

'Smashing the glass?' I asked, knowing that wasn't what she meant.

'No, the fucking rom-com movie moment.' Imogen stopped, placed a hand on my arm and bent forward to look me in the eye. 'Literally everyone kissed their embrace partner, but that . . .'

I felt stupid for using it, the embrace. It undermined my feelings for Saxon but put a spotlight on them as well.

'Not everyone,' I said and turned away.

'Dylan and Emmet do not count!' Imogen called.

'You didn't hook up with your partner.'

'Don't change the subject.'

'I can't explain it. I'm . . .' I could see the drama building ahead, our friends waiting on the steps.

'You're what?'

'Drawn to him.' As soon as the words were out of my mouth I realised how immature I sounded.

'Be careful.'

'What's that supposed to mean?'

'Nothing. Just . . . it was an exercise.'

I rolled my eyes.

'It isn't real,' she reminded me. 'We're only halfway through first term.'

'And?'

'Be smart,' she said. 'Don't get distracted.'

The warning sent a flurry of warmth to my throat.

Imogen nudged me. 'Speaking of which, I'm never drinking vodka again.' She launched into a detailed account of her hangover. I wanted to circle back, desperate to relive my time with Saxon at Initiation. But as we got closer to the drama building, Imogen's warning began to resonate, and I remained silent, concerned that my carefully controlled narrative was about to slip out of my hands and into those of my peers, to do with as they wished.

—

Studio One was dimly lit. Four students dressed in nineteenth-century period costumes roamed the space, seemingly unaware of each other, yet connected, as though tethered by an invisible string. If one crumpled to the floor, the others gathered around the fallen. If one ran, the others followed. Strewn across the space were random objects, set pieces that had no proper position but aided the actors in their play. An element of Quinn's process: Introspection. I was naive enough to believe that the practice was entirely her own. I'd soon learn that Introspection was made up of various acting techniques, altered often to procure what she wanted from her actors.

Text was spoken in extended time. Meaning had to be wrung out of every word. The actors could move on only when instructed to do so by Quinn. She sat in front of the seating bank behind a desk, her presence like a velvet blanket that enveloped the room. You breathed her in as you entered.

'Quick!' Dylan whispered and beckoned me to the centre of a row. We sat alone, the second years dotted around us, waiting patiently for their turn to experience the world of the play. They would conjure it, recall personal memories and flesh out the possibilities of the text, so that when they spoke it at speed during the next phase of the process, they would have a personal relationship to the story, as though they'd actually lived it. It was dream-like, imaginative work.

'This is—' I began.

'I know,' Dylan said, transfixed.

A slender woman with long, blonde hair had taken a sheaf of fabric and was trailing it behind her as she ran around the room. She jumped over objects and darted past her scene partners. They chased her down in barrelling laughter.

'I want for once in my life to have power to mould a human destiny.'

'Pause,' Quinn said. 'Repeat: *life*.'

The blonde woman inhaled. She picked up a copper pot that sat at her feet and began to stroke it. Tears streamed down her face. After a prolonged silence, she spoke again. '*Life*.'

'Yes,' Quinn said. 'Continue.'

Entranced, I watched as each actor spoke, using an object or physical activity to enhance their connection to a word, connect it to a phrase. You could hear it in their voices when they found it.

It took my eyes time to adjust to the light after the hours we'd spent inside the cocoon of Studio One. Dylan and I walked through the glass doors to the steps outside, dazed and exhausted.

'I want to do that,' Dylan said.

'Me too.'

'I'm tired of all the physical work.'

I turned to him, frowning. 'I thought you loved it.'

'I love language more.'

I elbowed him affectionately. 'You're pathetic.'

In the short time we'd been in training, a quiet familiarity had grown between us. Physical contact and hours of sustained eye contact had forged something. I hadn't the faintest idea when Dylan's birthday was, but I knew exactly how he'd stand before tumbling into a spinal roll.

I nodded towards the foyer. 'In order to do *that*, we need to do Neutral Mask and Feldenkrais first, right?'

'Apparently,' Dylan replied.

63

I slung an arm around his thin shoulders. 'Say it! If *you* start to question the process, what hope do the rest of us have?'

Dylan laughed. 'Okay, okay.'

'Go on!'

'In order to do that—'

'Thank you, that's all I needed to hear,' I teased.

A scream halted our conversation. Vivien tore past us towards the street. Richard grabbed her by the arm and pulled her out of the path of a passing cyclist.

'Don't fucking *touch* me!' Vivien screeched.

'For god's sake, Viv!'

She responded by hitting him in the chest with closed fists. Richard recoiled. He rose his arms to shield his face as the onslaught continued, grimacing and calling her name in defeat. Students filed out of the drama building to watch.

'What's going on?' I asked Dylan.

'Vivien stumbled upon Richard and Oliver at Initiation.'

I turned to him. 'So?'

Dylan shook his head. 'Even I know about this. Pay attention, Maeve.'

The penny dropped. 'Richard and Vivien?'

'Are fucking. And Vivien is . . .' He raised his eyebrows to indicate the scene playing out in front of us.

'Territorial,' I suggested.

'Bingo.'

As Vivien shouted profanities and Richard pleaded with her, I wondered about their reputations, about their ability to retain the confidence of the faculty. I felt embarrassed for them. And betrayed by Richard too. He had urged me to avoid Vivien, and yet here he was, deeply involved, despite her belittlement of me.

Judith cut a path between the students and clapped her hands like she did at the end of an exercise. 'Back inside, everyone!' she called, and took Richard roughly by the elbow. He looked at her, perplexed. Vivien seized the opportunity to slap his face with an open palm.

Richard winced in pain. 'Christ!'

Vivien threw her head back and laughed callously.

Ignoring her, Judith spoke directly to Richard. 'A word.'

The crowd dispersed. Judith shoved Richard forward into the foyer. Vivien took her time as she followed them, defiant.

Eventually, Dylan and I were alone again, shocked into silence.

Pay attention, Maeve.

'What?' I asked.

'I didn't say anything,' Dylan replied. 'I'm going to get a coffee. You want anything?'

'No, thanks.'

Dylan patted my arm and left me alone on the steps, looking out into nothingness.

Saxon sat down beside me. 'Hey.' A cigarette paper hung from his lower lip. He leaned close and pulled a tobacco pouch from the back pocket of his jeans. 'Where you been?'

'Auditing Ibsen.'

'That so?' Saxon took the paper and began to sprinkle tobacco into it. 'I could use an outside eye.'

'For?'

'The god self-devised.'

Neutral Mask. We'd been set the task of creating a two-minute piece based on an ancient Greek god for assessment at the end of term.

'Okay.'

Saxon raised the cigarette to his mouth. He flicked the lighter once, twice and cupped the flame. When he inhaled, I felt as though I were witnessing something private. He looked at the sky, then at me, like an invitation.

'Get anything out of it?'

'*Hedda Gabler?*' I asked. I thought about the room, the text, the magic of it. 'Yes.' The word was resonant, full.

Saxon stood. 'Good.' He took his cigarette and walked in the direction of Luncheonette, smiling back at me as he crossed the street. '*I want for once in my life to have power to mould a human destiny.*' He'd been auditing too.

I'd imagined a conversation, something coy before class as our first interaction after Initiation. But this served us better. I went with it.

'Repeat *life!*' I called back.

'*Life!*'

I clapped. 'Better!'

Saxon bowed and turned away.

We would never address Initiation. It wasn't the beginning of things, anyway. It was a comma, a pause before going deeper.

—

There weren't any performances at the Malthouse on Monday evenings. We sat in the dugout of the deserted courtyard nursing tallies, shivering a little, the sun having set hours ago.

'Should we call it?' Imogen asked.

'One more drink,' Richard said.

Emmet peered into his backpack. 'We're out.'

'The Railway?' Richard looked between us, desperate.

'I'm cooked,' I said.

We stood together and began the short walk to St Kilda Road to catch our trams home. The number 8, the number 1, the 67.

'She's going to make my life a living hell, isn't she?' Richard asked.

None of us responded.

'We weren't . . .'

'Exclusive?' I offered.

Richard groaned. 'Such a dirty word.'

'Vivien's ego's been bruised,' Imogen said. 'Just pray to God or—'

'Or Quinn Medina,' Emmet interjected with a wry smile.

'Or Quinn Medina that you don't get paired with her in class.' Imogen cupped a hand under Richard's chin. 'You're a stupid, stupid man.'

'Yes,' Richard muttered. 'It's been said before.'

V

I had a morning routine, carved out by repetition. Something to hold on to when the day started to slip. I'd rise early. Wash my face and put on a version of what I'd worn the day before. Fruit, toast, ten minutes of the morning news, then onto the street for my commute through the city. On the tram, I'd find a seat by the window and take out a book. *Sophie's World*, *Nineteen Eighty-Four*, *Anna Karenina*. Novels I'd not heard of until my training, stories that seemed to mean something to my peers. I wanted to add to their conversations. I wanted to know what they meant and stop merely pretending I did.

Dylan would meet me on the steps outside the drama building, a book of his own in his lap. We'd go inside and warm up together in silence before the others arrived.

Each student would announce themselves as they entered the space—a heavy sigh, an anecdote from the weekend. Richard was the loudest. Blazer draped over his shoulders, newspaper in hand, he and Emmet would debate the news of the day and I'd be drawn to their chatter, pulled out of my morning practice. How smart they were, to be able to riff like that at eight thirty in the morning.

I hated the weekends; they dragged without classes to shape them. I didn't know yet how to take myself to the cinema or read a book in a crowded cafe alone. So I wandered the streets, earbuds in, trying to acquaint myself with a city I felt on the outskirts of, not realising that simply being there was enough.

—

A vintage dress seemed to me like a badge of belonging. All the female students wore them to class, slipping out of them to reveal their rehearsal clothes beneath; a little routine I admired and wanted to partake in.

I'd overheard two second years talking about stalls at the weekly flea market in Camberwell. 'Go early,' one had said to the other, 'before all the good stuff goes.'

One Sunday morning I took the number 72 tram from Melbourne University to Camberwell. Fog obscured the tracks, the sun shone far off and bright. I wore jeans, paired with my Cons and a light pullover. I was cold. I entered a cafe on Camberwell Road and ordered a chai latte, holding it close to my chest, too proud to ask for directions.

The streets were near deserted. I walked slowly, as though window shopping, until I saw a group of women turn a corner beside an expensive-looking homewares store and disappear down an alleyway. I followed them and found myself in an open-air car park, swarming with people.

Cars lined the lot, boots open, full of goods. Second-hand jewellery, shoes, boxes of scarves. There was an urgency to the way people scanned the rails and rummaged through crates. I mimicked their rhythm, flicked through flowery skirts and searched for the size on the bottom of worn shoes. I wrapped belts around my waist hurriedly, not discarding a thing until I'd made my choice.

An hour later I caught the tram home, a full plastic bag beside me. The morning had been a wash of pastel pinafores and brown corduroy, of women dressed as if they belonged, as if they didn't care what people thought.

I pulled the bag onto my lap, feeling a sense of accomplishment. Inside was a pair of cowboy boots, a red dress with white hearts and a brown leather belt. I'd spent thirty-four dollars.

Gazing out the window, I watched the city pass, moving through it like I knew where I was going. Imitating insouciance.

—

I was walking along Spring Street the following Saturday afternoon when the invitation came. I stopped still and stared at the text message, then up at the brooding sky. The hours no longer felt like mine alone to kill. And I knew I was ready to say yes.

'We ordered for you!' Richard called over the heads of Emmet and Imogen at the counter of Cookie.

Imogen cleared her handbag from the stool beside her. 'Best fucking spread in town.'

'So I've heard,' I replied.

'This isn't your first time?' Emmet asked, shoving a betel leaf into his mouth.

'Afraid so.'

Richard poured me a glass of white from a bottle on the counter. 'To new beginnings.'

I listened more than I spoke until the wine ran out and Richard ordered more. In their company, there seemed nothing wrong with drinking through the afternoon. I thought of *The Moving Body* sitting on my bedside table. I decided, with the rationale of a drunk, that I'd make up my allotted reading another time.

We chose to walk. La Mama wasn't far.

The initial shock of the city had been blunted by the hours I'd spent walking through it. My eyes skimmed over the homeless men by Parliament Station, the graffiti tags and rubbish scattered along the kerb. I saw only the turning leaves of the Carlton Gardens beyond.

La Mama looked more like a house than a theatre. The foyer floor was sticky beneath my feet, the brick walls cold. But the place had a reputation, one to be revered, and you felt it as soon as you stepped inside. Imogen had bought tickets in advance—a remount of a Berkoff that Ford had directed three years earlier with five second-year drama students, now graduated, with a working company of their own.

Late, we shuffled along the narrow row of seats, brushing against the knees of middle-aged patrons, all red lipstick and untamed hair.

The stage was small and bare in front of a black curtain. The theatre became dark, the outline of five figures visible as our eyes adjusted. Then a snap of light. One woman. Four men.

The language was brash and offensive; it was the sole means by which the actors could transport us, convince us that what we were witnessing was real. They succeeded. I couldn't move. Not to sip my wine or to uncross my legs or to blink or to breathe. I felt changed by each word, by the enormous pressure to one day arrive at the place the actors before me had already reached.

We floated out of the theatre and onto the street. A hot cheek against mine, a slap on the arm. Rushed *goodbyes* and *see you on Mondays*.

I looked out at the darkness and felt the afternoon settle inside me. I smiled to myself, reassured, no longer on the outskirts.

—

Neutral man is the colour orange.
Neutral man is air.
Neutral man is ice.
Neutral man is the moon.
Neutral man is a mountain range, moving over time.

VI

Then just like that, he asked me.

'Free tonight?'

'As in now?'

'Yeah.'

It was late. There'd been no lead-up, no warning. I shut my journal and walked barefoot from the corridor outside the Rehearsal Room to Performance Space C.

The studio was long, fifty metres of polished floorboards leading to wide windows that overlooked the city. By the entrance was a ladder that led to a small platform with a tech desk. Along each wall black curtains hung, ready to be drawn for performance.

'A little excessive, don't you think?' I asked, placing my things by the door.

'All I could find.'

Saxon moved to the centre of the floor. He circled his head from shoulder to shoulder. 'I don't have a mask. Bear with me.'

'Where should I sit?'

Saxon nodded to the base of the ladder. I walked there quietly, sat down and waited for him to come to neutral standing. It was a performance in itself, how patiently he brought himself to readiness, and I realised that I always rushed this moment, believing that my preparation would bore an audience. Saxon illustrated otherwise.

He bolted suddenly, then eased his pace, and I was brought back to the present. He ran in a wide circle, a repetitive motion made compelling by the precision of his intent. With each step he gathered momentum towards an imaginary world, and I was reminded of his audition piece. The power of it. The force.

He stopped abruptly, widened his stance, and slung an imaginary spear. After firing, his rigid limbs became soft and undulating. The movement brought him to the floor, and the god became a man: propped up on his elbows, pelvis grinding into the wood.

As if caught, he stood and sprinted towards the city, stopping precariously close to the glass. He swivelled to face me, shoulders heaving from exertion, the vigour of his work fully felt.

Saxon's breathing evened, then he was still. He lowered his head, shook it and came to sit beside me, heat emanating from his muscular frame.

'Ares,' I said.

God of war, seducer of Aphrodite.

Saxon wiped sweat from his forehead with the back of his hand and looked out across the floor. 'Well?'

I couldn't think of a single note. The work was faultless. 'It's a bit confused, no?' I joked, imitating Ford. Saxon laughed but said nothing.

I turned to face him. 'The work is . . . you know what the work is. I'm not sure why you asked me here.' A lie. I knew. I waited for him to respond.

Nothing.

I stood and walked towards the exit. I didn't hear his footsteps and gasped when he spun me to face him. He gently pressed me against the door, allowed his lips to brush mine. The handle jerked, the door opened, then slammed closed again with our weight.

'Excuse me!' called a muffled voice.

'How long did you book the space for?' I asked.

'I didn't,' Saxon replied casually.

We moved aside and Genevieve entered, unsmiling. 'Locking up.'

Saxon attempted to smooth things over, but Genevieve seemed unimpressed. I collected my things and slid around them to the elevator. I pressed the call button once, twice, then again.

Saxon came to stand beside me. 'Sorry about the interruption.'

'Me too,' I whispered back.

Genevieve walked behind us along the passage. When she was gone, Saxon moved closer and interlaced our fingers, dissolving my thoughts of what happens to an actor when their relationship is put on display.

I couldn't sustain the moment. The elevator doors opened and I stepped inside.

'Juliet,' Saxon said.

I turned to face him and saw Ares challenging me to stay. But the doors closed before I could decide.

—

Richard held his head in his hands. 'I don't know what she wants.'

We were at Degraves Espresso during a rare free period, debating the destination of passers-by. But our game was soured by Richard's mood. Vivien would not relent in her criticism of his work during class.

75

'Rave?' I suggested, nodding at a man in an oversized tie-dyed t-shirt that fell to his knees. He wore expensive Ray-Bans and clean Doc Martens.

'Stop it!' Richard said. 'I can't focus, it's no fun.'

'Sorry.'

'But no. That young man runs a clothing store on Flinders Lane.' Richard winked at me and sat back in his chair. 'You know, when I told my best friend from home about you, he couldn't believe it.'

'Believe what?'

'That I call a seventeen-year-old girl from *Queensland* a dear friend.'

'Fuck off,' I said, a little awkwardly; I was making a conscious effort to pepper my vocabulary with profanities like my friends. I raised my coffee and looked out at the crowd to hide my discomfort. 'I know exactly what Vivien wants.'

'Yes?'

'To humiliate you. Either make it up with her or admit defeat.'

'Perhaps you should think about taking your own advice.'

'She'll eat me alive, remember?'

'Ah yes, survival of the fittest.'

'I choose avoidance.' I leaned close. 'But you . . . I suggest the straight and narrow.'

Richard pouted. 'Where's the fun in that?'

We finished our coffees, and Richard proffered an arm. Together we moved through the bustle of Degraves and up Flinders Street to catch a tram back to campus.

'You're a darling,' Richard said when we arrived, then he left me by the steps with the smokers to find Vivien. His swift departure a blow that brought back his words: *a seventeen-year-old girl from Queensland.*

'Maeve!'

I was startled by the sound of Ford's voice. It sounded so much broader outside the Rehearsal Room, like one of the characters in the Berkoff play he'd remounted at La Mama. It was endearing. As was the sight of him with shoes on, jogging towards me outside the drama building, leather satchel slung across his chest.

'Don't fear it,' he said. 'Use the physicality to free you.' He didn't touch me, just squared himself so that our stances were mirrored. It made him seem less of a deity of the place, more like a contemporary, which I presumed was his intention.

'Like Juliet,' I said, surprised by my own assertiveness.

'Yes, exactly,' Ford replied with a grin. 'Like Juliet.' And he walked off, saluting students as he went. I watched his figure disappear inside the foyer, reeling with appreciation at being told exactly what I needed to hear.

VII

First years were expected to tend the bar and work as ushers for the third-year performance season during the last two weeks of term. Opening nights were especially important. There was the potential to be noticed, to be drawn into conversation by the theatre elite. Imogen and I were nervous. Emmet was indifferent.

I looked up from the glass I was cleaning at the sound of raucous applause. 'Shit. Here they come.'

Imogen began to line up full glasses of red and white wine on the bar in preparation for what we'd been warned would be an onslaught.

Emmet swung open the double doors of Studio One and stood aside as the audience spilled out. They moved towards Imogen and me at speed, intent on the complimentary drinks.

Emmet let himself into the bar through the back and drained a glass of red. 'Incredible what a couple of days can do to a production.'

'I'm jealous,' I said.

'You should be,' he replied.

The first and second years had been given access to the first full dress run the week before. There had been large pauses. Lines lost, cues missed. But the third years continued unperturbed, buoyed by a collective confidence in the story they'd woven into themselves. With time left to solidify their choices, *The Caucasian Chalk Circle* had the potential to become the kind of production future companies would strive to recreate. And Emmet had been in the audience as an usher on opening night.

Imogen held a heavy tray of glasses and indicated for Emmet to take them. 'Do the rounds.'

Emmet shook his head. 'I'm off the clock.'

My awe of the third years made them appear luminous. I watched them disperse through the foyer, no trace of character remaining. If I were close enough to them, I could learn something.

'Emmet?' Imogen called, but he was already out the door.

'I'll do it,' I said.

Imogen handed me the tray. 'Angel!'

The air was thick with the warmth of too many closely confined, inebriated bodies. I squeezed between them. The tray emptied.

'Where's the champagne?' A demanding voice, a firm grip on my forearm.

I twisted and found myself held by the head of school. 'I didn't realise we had any,' I said.

'Get some,' Quinn ordered. The foyer swirled around us as she surveyed me coolly. I felt the importance of the moment, the pressure to say something impressive, but before I could, her attention was abruptly withdrawn.

'Oliver, my dear,' she said, releasing me. 'A triumph!' Quinn stepped forward and opened her arms in a gesture that attracted the attention of the room.

My chest tightened in disappointment at the lost opportunity. I got back to work.

'Do we have champagne?' I shouted at Imogen across the bar.

'Fuck.'

'I guess not.'

'Fuck, *fuck*!' Imogen reached into the back pocket of her dress pants. 'Take these.' She threw a set of keys at my chest. 'There should be a box in Genevieve's office.'

'It'll be warm,' I said.

Imogen sucked in her cheeks and looked at the crowd. 'I don't think it'll matter,' she said, and went back to refilling the glasses of reaching hands.

She was right. The din had risen, the lines had blurred. Faculty members mingled with third years, industry with patrons. The energy of the opening had unified everyone. *The Caucasian Chalk Circle* was a success.

I pushed through the foyer to reception. The counter was closed, the window shuttered, but behind it I could make out the faint glow of lamplight. I slipped the key into the side door and opened it. 'Hello?' Loose pages strewn across work stations, dark monitors calling to be awoken. The inner workings of the school within reach.

A male voice. 'In here!'

Leaving the door open, I walked towards the light. In Genevieve's office Saxon was kneeling over a cardboard box.

'I was supposed to stock the fridge,' he said.

'I didn't realise you were on tonight.'

Saxon swivelled on his knees to face me, a bottle of champagne in his hands. 'I'm not really.'

'What are you doing?'

Saxon twisted the metallic tab, pulled at it with his teeth and popped the cork. It shot past me into the darkness.

'We were interrupted the other night,' he said and handed me the bottle.

Bubbles foamed out of the opening; I licked them away. 'We were.'

'We'll have to pick up from where we left off.'

I considered him, unsure whether his interest in me was a transference of lust from Ares or just residue from our time working together in Judith's class, as Imogen had insisted. Or neither. Or both. The work had obscured my view of things.

I handed him the bottle. 'Rehearsals? Sure.'

Saxon cocked an eyebrow. 'If that's how you like it. Starting now?'

I faltered.

'Juliet.' Saxon reached for my hand. 'What are you afraid of?' Then his eyes flickered towards something over my shoulder.

'Quinn's waiting,' Judith said from the doorway.

I jerked my hand from Saxon's and turned to face her. 'We were just unpacking the champagne.'

Judith laughed. 'No harm, no foul.'

I brushed past her as I hurried through the door.

'Don't forget what you came for.' Judith nodded at the box of champagne on the floor.

I went back and picked it up awkwardly.

I carried the box out into the reception area, where I paused to steady it against the wall. Hearing playful banter, I looked back into Genevieve's office, expecting to find myself the butt of some kind of joke. But my presence had been forgotten. Judith had one hand clasped on Saxon's upper arm, the other around the neck of the champagne bottle. He spoke to her emphatically as she tipped her head back and drank. Then she bent forward, obscuring my view of him.

Staggering under the weight of the box, I returned to the party.

Imogen and I quickly uncorked the champagne and filled glasses, but the urgency for it had been lost. Quinn was speaking. She stood on a chair beside the door of Studio One with a full tumbler of red. The crowd looked up at her adoringly.

'To create work of this standard takes courage,' she declared. 'Without being on the floor, there is no way to understand how deeply one must venture in order to procure it.'

Imogen and I leaned against the bar and passed an open bottle back and forth as Quinn spoke. The atmosphere was weighted with our reverence for her art. But when Saxon entered the foyer, I felt the impact of his presence and knew that to be a player in this world was as important to me as becoming one in his.

There was a coffee cart inside the entrance of the Australian Centre for Contemporary Art that gave drama students a discount. We hurried there after the *Hedda Gabler* showing in an effort to warm ourselves against the chill that had set in across the city. Even with a clear sky, the sun waned, the wind was fierce. Melbourne could be cruel.

'It was their first attempt,' Imogen said.

'Doesn't matter!' Dylan argued. 'I sat in on rehearsals. I saw what they put themselves through to get to that point.'

We turned into the alcove that led to the glass doors of the venue. The shelter gave warm relief from the elements.

'It was a *showing*,' Richard said.

'And what? Preparation doesn't count?' Dylan asked. 'It's still a performance. Where were the stakes?'

Richard gripped Dylan's shoulders. 'The stakes were there—'

Dylan spoke over him. 'The dialogue lacked rhythm! Their choices were inconsistent!'

'In Quinn critiquing their work,' Richard continued. 'In a cohort waiting for them to fuck up.'

'Fear is fatal,' Imogen agreed.

Dylan turned to her, agitated. 'What?'

Emmet ruffled Dylan's curls. 'You'll get your turn, mate.'

'Don't patronise me,' Dylan replied and shook away from them.

Richard turned to the guy behind the coffee cart. 'Three flat whites, a chai latte and'—Richard looked back at Dylan—'a babycino for you?'

Dylan scowled. 'Get fucked.'

Richard chuckled and continued with the order.

'I liked it,' I said.

'But you're taking the process into account!' Dylan exclaimed. 'The showing should stand alone.'

'Sure, if you're working for the MTC,' I said. 'But we're not. We're in training. The second years are *in training*.'

Oliver strode in behind us. 'And the third years?'

Richard didn't miss a beat. 'Are on their way out!'

'So we're basically fucked.' Oliver was serious. 'This god-awful industry. From Brecht to obscurity! Make the most of it, kids.'

Richard looked over his shoulder at him. 'Who, may I ask, is hosting the end-of-term party?'

'Celeste!' Oliver announced. 'Her place is heaven. Like a private gallery with an open bar. Courtesy of her mummy and daddy, of course.

'Southside?' Richard whined.

'Don't glower, doll,' Oliver tutted. 'It's unbecoming.'

Their attraction to one another was palpable. If Vivien were present, she would have been incensed by this flirtation. Oliver knew that Richard was only permitted to maintain their friendship at a distance.

'Be there!' Oliver warned and leaned over the coffee cart to place his order with the barista. Richard nudged him with his hip and handed us our drinks. We walked back into the wind.

'Quinn's method isn't for everyone,' Emmet said contemptuously, picking up the conversation about the showing where we'd left off. I felt a prickling of apprehension; Emmet was a wild card and his temper flared often. But he was talented, could take on a persona with a playful, child-like ease. And he was smart, a compulsive student, with a slew of degrees behind him. Integrating his intelligence into the curriculum, however, was a challenge, no matter how well he recited the *Iliad* or philosophised about humanity by way of Russian literature. We tiptoed around his temperament and understood that someone always had to pay his share. Emmet was practically penniless.

'Do you know how many people would die to be in your position?' Dylan asked, exasperated. 'Like, *literally* die. Imagine if they'd harnessed their fear instead of letting themselves be led by it.'

Dylan was Emmet's antithesis. Eager and earnest, his feelings plastered to his face. Emmet was scornful of his wealth, his pedigree, the mansion he lived in with his parents in Malvern, as though these things made Dylan the enemy of all artists.

Emmet stopped. Richard looked at him then back at Dylan, concerned. 'Drop it.'

'Where was the fight?' Dylan asked. 'We're here to take risks!'

Emmet crossed the distance he'd put between himself and the group. 'You don't get to decide where the fight is!' he shouted, prodding Dylan in the chest.

Dylan stepped away, visibly afraid. 'Steady on!'

'The actors have to feel that themselves,' Emmet barked, 'in the lines, in the movement!'

'Very true,' Richard agreed.

Dylan became querulous. 'Don't take his side! You saw what that showing was: a bloody mess!'

'Your understanding of the work is myopic, *boy*,' Emmet said, disgusted. He turned back and paused by the entrance to the arts space. Shoulders hunched, neck protruding; a pained, haunted figure.

Dylan turned to us, wide-eyed. 'What the fuck?'

'Is he okay?' I asked.

'Not sure,' Richard replied.

Emmet lifted his face to the sky in contemplation. When Richard approached, he slipped inside the building.

Dylan began muttering to himself, pushing the hair off his face in a nervous, repetitive gesture.

'We should check on him,' I said.

Imogen reached for me. 'Definitely not.'

I sensed something larger at play. 'But—'

'Maeve, trust me,' Imogen said wearily.

Embarrassed, I didn't prod further. Instead, I watched helplessly as the shadow of our friend disappeared.

'Let's go,' Imogen urged, and we wandered back to campus in silence.

—

The entire student body, including the faculty, were in attendance for the Greek god Neutral Mask showing on the last day of term. They were a blurring, dark mass against the back wall that I tried desperately to ignore. But I could feel their anticipation, the vibration of their bodies; still but not entirely silent.

Only three gods had been selected: mine, Vivien's and Saxon's. The other pieces had been chosen from group-devised work. Remembered, altered and rehearsed for the showing.

The Greek god I'd chosen was Poseidon, lord of the ocean, of storms and earthquakes. A masculine, ill-tempered god who took his revenge on those who disobeyed him. After what Saxon had shown me of Ares, I knew that I had to strive for more, to subvert my archetype.

'It was exciting, no?' Ford had said two days earlier during assessment, as I stood alone on the floor, mask in hand.

'I wonder if she could have used the space more broadly,' Vivien queried.

'It was a choice,' Ford said. 'Am I wrong?'

The company waited.

'No—I mean, yes,' I replied, taken aback at being allowed to comment on my own work. 'It was a choice.'

'It showed restraint,' Imogen contributed.

'I agree.' Ford leaned forward to look at her. 'Maeve was engaged. Open.'

'And specific with her movement,' Dylan added.

'Not at all illustrative,' Saxon said.

Ford smiled. 'Or perfect.'

It was a breakthrough, and I had been rewarded with the opportunity to showcase my work.

Now, as I ran, I wondered which expression might be cast upon Ford's face. I hoped that he would be open-mouthed, an indication to the audience that my work still surprised him. The exercise may have been set, but there needed to be a little spontaneity too, energy in the form of risk.

Live in the moment. Judith's command shot through my mind. I found it useful not only in her class but Ford's also, and in life. The phrase helped me to weigh an experience or a session against the opposite—a pedestrian choice.

Live in the moment.

The mask pressed against my nose; I controlled my breathing, careful not to expel too much air through the mouthpiece and distract the audience or bring them out of the exercise. There could be freedom in movement and freedom in breath. I had to trust the work and myself.

I crouched low, mask forward, then propelled my body up towards the ceiling. I reached with my fingertips in a straight line above my head. I crouched again and repeated the movement three times, then rested there. I counted five beats, uncurled and came to standing, vertebra by vertebra. I tilted my chin, pulled my shoulders back and released my fingers from my palms. I focused my attention on the blank wall above the heads of my peers and allowed myself to be seen. Then I turned and removed the mask.

There was a knowingness in the way the students applauded. I turned back to them and stilled, open to their acclamation.

In the centre of the audience, Ford sat silent, open-mouthed. I flushed with relief and placed my mask on the fold-out table for the final time. It marked the passing of something. I'd never embody the ocean again or throw an imaginary rock. Never shift my energy to evoke the colour red, the colour yellow, the colour blue.

I found a place for myself among the cohort. Received back slaps and congratulations. Neutral Mask, the real unifier. True Initiation.

—

I know nothing, I thought as I looked out over the cemetery.

First term was over. There was a party to attend. But the epiphany had me immobilised.

I'd become meticulous about my practice, warming up as instructed, touching on sound and manipulating my body when ordered to do so. I participated more than most, but I knew less about how to breathe than I had a few months earlier and was unsure how to utilise Neutral Mask in the scheme of my training.

I *had* managed to fill my bookshelf with a handful of paperbacks, to swallow coffee and to tolerate red wine. Did that count? It was a kind of training.

I laughed at myself.

I know nothing. An acknowledgement; a small relief.

It looked cold outside. I pulled my desk chair into the ensuite-sized bathroom and stood on it to view my reflection in the square mirror above the sink. I wore the vintage dress from Camberwell market and a new brown cardigan draped over my shoulders; expensive enough to prevent me from doing a proper grocery shop that week. Worth it, I thought, for the effect. I looked like a second year, almost.

When I stepped outside it was as cold as it looked, and the cardigan did little to shield me from the wind. I wrapped it around myself and shivered as I walked towards Melbourne University for a tram that would take me south of the river.

Lygon Street teemed with people awash in the glow of restaurants and boutiques trading late over the weekend. Elderly women eating gelato, children hanging from the limbs of their young parents. Outside Tiamo, a snaking line of students with books and bottles in hand began to shout the chorus of 'Reckless' above the clamour. I sang along.

'Juliet!'

His face was shadowed by the interior of a Corolla; it took a moment for me to place him, out of context.

Saxon extended his arm through the back seat window. 'Coming?'

The door swung open, and I slid in beside him. The possibilities of the night, near. My heart pounded against my rib cage.

'Thank god!' Richard turned to face me from the front seat. 'These fools won't partake!' He passed me an open bottle of sparkling wine.

I turned it in my hands. 'French?'

'Don't get too excited,' Vivien said from the driver's seat. 'It was seventeen dollars.'

Richard waved a hand dismissively. 'Details, details.'

'Not really my thing, champagne,' Vivien said and moved suddenly out into the traffic.

The movement jolted me against Saxon. I acted like it was nothing.

'But it isn't,' I said, trying to bridge the gap between Vivien and me. 'It can't be called champagne outside the region.'

Richard looked back at me and kissed the tips of his fingers. 'Sweet fruits of my labour!'

'Spare us the histrionics, Richard,' Vivien teased.

I laughed shyly. 'Sparkling still does the trick, though.'

'It does the trick, all right!' Richard concurred.

It was a collision of worlds that I attempted to subdue with the wine, taking longer swigs each time the bottle was offered. Saxon cradled a beer between his legs and blew smoke out the window, commenting every so often as Richard steered the conversation. Vivien said very little.

I was astonished by the change I saw in the city as we crossed the river into Toorak; at the houses suddenly larger and box-like; at the luxury cars conspicuously dotted through the traffic.

On a wide, leafy street by Kooyong Road, Vivien found a spot to park and told us to get out.

'Thanks for the lift,' I said.

Vivien removed a flask from her handbag and waved it in the air without turning back: *you're welcome*.

I pinched Richard's thigh. 'Officially schooled in monogamy, are we?'

'*O, teach me how I should forget to think!*' he responded theatrically

Saxon passed us, carrying a carton of beer on his shoulder.

'*Romeo, Romeo*,' Richard cooed, looping an arm through mine.

I protested. He ran and I was flung towards the party.

Bodies lounged on the front lawn, out of place in the shadow of Celeste's home: a Federation-style bungalow, lovingly restored.

'Oliver wasn't kidding,' I said as we stepped inside—polished floorboards, ornate light fixtures and cream walls plastered with Bromley nudes.

At the end of the hallway, past the staircase that led to the second-storey extension, a drum fire-pit lit up a large courtyard.

Students crowded around it, rolling cigarettes, smoking joints. The smell of it made me heady.

Celeste stood by a vintage trolley cart in the kitchen pouring Veuve Clicquot into champagne flutes. She was tall, with a neat bob; not particularly beautiful, but she held herself in a way that made you believe she was. Richard placed his hands on her thin waist and kissed her lightly on each cheek. 'Celeste. I mean . . .' He looked around the dining room with exaggerated awe. Celeste rubbed her nose against his. I was surprised by their familiarity. Richard's lack of reverence for the third years made me timorous by comparison.

He introduced us. 'You know Maeve?'

'I've *heard* of Maeve.'

I reddened. 'Really?'

'Of course!'

Celeste led me to the courtyard. I expected Richard to follow but he moved off down the hallway. 'We're bored with one another,' Celeste said. 'You're fresh meat.'

Beside her, I realised what an enviable position I was in. The courtyard filled and the newcomers hovered behind those seated by the fire. I was flattered to be included, but the swiftness with which the talk about art turned to failure made me melancholic. I wanted to ride the high of the showing, enjoy the beautiful chaos of my surroundings and ignore the probable need for a back-up plan after drama school. So I excused myself, refilled my glass in the kitchen from a warm bottle on the benchtop and wandered with it down the hallway in search of something to attach myself to.

Richard lay on the staircase, a cluster of people sprawled around him: Imogen, Dylan and a couple of second years I didn't know particularly well. I leaned against the banister, sipping my drink, unable to lock into what they were talking about. After a few minutes I continued towards the front of the house. A gust of air hit me as more students entered, exclaiming in wonder at the home they'd stepped into. I smiled and pressed myself against the wall to allow them to pass.

People swayed to music and smoked on the front lawn, their bodies lit by the house behind them. I inhaled, closed my eyes and lifted my arms above my head, the culmination of a term's work pulsing out to the ether.

I knew that he was watching. It was an ability I'd retained from class. *Be aware of the micro, the macro.* I stayed with the movement, felt out the music, until I could no longer deny myself his reaction. I opened my eyes. Saxon stood by the road between a pair of second-year students. They spoke at him animatedly while he smoked. He was facing me, but his features were obscured in the dim light. *Move*, I thought. *Come closer.*

As if reading my thoughts, Saxon flicked the butt of his cigarette away and crossed the short distance between us without excusing himself from the conversation. 'Come on,' he whispered and continued walking.

I followed him down the narrow path beside the house. Midway along, he stopped and leaned against the brick wall. I focused on his lips, watched them part with the outward breath, overwhelmed with desire. I eased my pelvis against his groin and brought my face close to his.

A woman cleared her throat. 'Maeve?'

'Fuck,' Saxon muttered.

I pushed off him and turned towards the voice. Imogen was glowering at me.

'Two minutes,' I said to Saxon and moved along the path to the courtyard.

I found Celeste. 'I'm off.'

She turned to face me. 'No!'

'Early flight back to the Sunshine State,' I replied.

'That so?' Imogen asked from behind.

I ignored her.

Celeste planted a wet kiss on my temple and sauntered away.

'Stay,' Imogen said.

I looked at the floor, at the pavers, at the tiny green sprouts in between.

'Maeve.'

'Keep this between us?' I asked, looking up at her finally. 'I need to find out for myself.'

Imogen sighed and wrapped her arms around me. I breathed in her familiar scent and felt a burst of affection for her. I would never heed her advice. She knew that and gave it anyway.

Imogen pulled away. 'Go on, then.'

'Thank you.'

I went along the hallway and past the stairs, where Richard was pressed beneath Vivien's body. I took their lust as permission.

Saxon was waiting for me on the pavement. Behind us, the lawn seethed with students. Dancing, smoking. Watching. If this were to be mine, it had to be private.

'I don't want anyone to know,' I said, thinking of reputation, of failure.

He studied me. 'All right.'

I walked ahead of him and hailed a passing cab.

'Lygon Street, corner of Princes, please,' I said to the driver.

In the back seat of the taxi, Saxon drew circles on the inside of my wrist with his fingers. I looked out of the window, at the speeding cars, at the trees lining the street, concentrating on the blur of the buildings, practising restraint.

We pulled up by the entrance to my building. As Saxon paid the driver I stepped out of the cab and walked towards reception, certain he'd follow. I heard a car door slam, tyres squeal, and felt faint with what I thought it meant.

'Goodnight, Juliet,' Saxon called.

I pivoted and he moved closer, each step a dare, until his lips were on mine.

'Come inside,' I heard myself say.

But he was already pulling back. Rolling a cigarette. Lighting it up.

'Agony,' I breathed.

He swept a strand of hair behind my ear and whispered, 'Repeat.'

My solar plexus felt the definition of the word and summoned it again. 'Agony.'

Saxon nodded. Then a cloud of smoke. And he was gone.

TERM TWO

TEAM TWO

I

I was hit by a wall of cold, autumnal air as I stepped off the plane in Melbourne. It wasn't what I'd been expecting, the reality of it far worse than the weatherman had warned.

The bus ride into town was bleak. Paddocks and grey partitions divided the landscape. But after twenty minutes the bus rose along the red rib cage of the CityLink Gateway to be met by the city itself, immoveable and waiting. It galvanised me against my own fear somehow, and the guilt I felt at having squandered my holiday didn't seem to matter in the long shadows of those buildings.

I'd felt displaced in Queensland. The sun I'd been craving seemed to sting, the humid air felt too thick to breathe and everything looked smaller than I remembered. Even the house had a different smell. I had new thoughts, new opinions to share, but there didn't seem to be space for it. My family were used to a former version of myself, the one who hadn't yet been cracked open by drama school.

'Stop bunging it on,' my father had said at the dinner table on my first night home. 'You're talking like you're having tea with the bloody queen.'

I tried to explain Neutral Mask and how freeing it had been to train under Ford.

'I did drama in high school,' my aunt said in response. 'We never did *that*.'

My grandmother wrinkled her nose. 'Why didn't you go to NIDA?' she asked. 'Mel Gibson went there. None of that "be the colour pink" business. Plain old Shakespeare.'

I didn't dare contradict her. How many taxi drivers, sales assistants, baristas had I explained it to already?

'NIDA has a great reputation, but it isn't my choice,' I said. Not that being accepted into the drama school had been my choice at all. It was a knowing, a hope. But how to explain that without sounding petulant and disrespectful?

'Think you're better than Gibson, do you?' my grandmother scolded.

The family laughed and moved on. My mother took my hand beneath the table and held it reassuringly. I wanted to lie under the sheets of my childhood bed and return to Melbourne simultaneously.

Now that I was back, I realised how naive I'd been to think that my time at home could have reversed something in myself; that all I'd learned might be lost. Seven days was not long. But I'd felt the pressure to return to the work while also defending it to the people I loved. Only my peers could understand what that felt like.

We hadn't seen the full scope of talent yet. There was potential for surprise, for someone who might have been hopeless at

Neutral Mask to reveal themselves to be a master of Collective work, and I wondered whether I might fall behind those I had already secretly surpassed in my mind. I evaluated myself against each company member. Vivien and Saxon were surely at the top. I didn't think I was too far behind. But a new curriculum could reset the hierarchy. It was one thing to make it through first term, quite another to make it through the year.

My phone vibrated in my pocket as the bus coasted into the terminus of Southern Cross Station.

Meet me before school. Saxon.

I wondered who he'd got my number from.

Where?

His reply was immediate: *State Library. 8 am.*

The weight I'd been carrying dissipated and was replaced with an eagerness for the day to pass. The memory of his hands, his mouth, were something to distract myself with. The figure he cut against the stark white walls of the Rehearsal Room even more so.

I got off the bus and floated towards the tram stop, dragging my suitcase behind me.

—

Saxon leaned against the sandstone walls of the State Library on the corner of La Trobe and Swanston streets, beguiling in dark denim and leather.

His smile drew me to him, and I found myself gently pressing the outer corner of his eye to watch the flicker of gold that spun from each pupil. A small revelation in the daylight.

Saxon twisted my palm from his face to kiss it. 'Hi.'

Hi.

He ordered long blacks from the barista at the cafe inside the library. The bitter taste was an assault. I endured it as I did the fear we might be recognised.

I don't want anyone to know, I'd said. How you behaved outside of class shaped the opinion of your peers. I wanted my work to stand alone, to be taken seriously.

As we continued south along Swanston, Saxon pointed out his favourite restaurants from the many trips he'd taken to the city over the years. In between his anecdotes, we fell comfortably into the pockets of silence that spread between us, and I forgot my anxiety about being seen together.

At the National Gallery of Victoria, Saxon pulled me into an alcove by the entrance. The iconic Waterwall sent mist into the air. Tiny droplets collected on my cheeks.

Saxon brushed them away with his fingertips. 'Saturday?'

I nodded.

Then he kissed me. Cigarettes and coffee. I wondered what he could taste in return.

'I'll go first,' he said, and left me there pressed against the wall of the building. He'd taken it seriously, my condition for our assignation.

I listened to the sound of dinging trams, of leaves scratching against cement and the heavy slosh of falling water. I counted to sixty, then emerged from the alcove, turned the corner and crossed the street as Saxon boarded the number 1 tram.

—

Sylvie returned.

When she walked by me on the steps outside the drama building on the first day of term, I immediately recognised her otherness. She wore a 1950s vintage dress with red lipstick, her long hair floating behind her like a veil.

I was immediately infatuated.

Sylvie's time on *The Seagull* had come to an early, dramatic close. Rumours about her exit from the film alluded to her Method-like process of embedding herself in the persona of each character she played.

'Quinn had her discharged from a psychiatric facility,' Richard whispered once Sylvie had passed us.

Imogen slapped his arm. 'Who told you that?'

'Upon release she was found wandering Carlton Gardens in the middle of the night,' Dylan added.

Richard gasped. 'How Victorian!'

'Stop!' Imogen stood up from the steps and walked into the foyer. I watched her go but didn't follow.

'Are you serious?' I asked, once Imogen was out of view.

Richard shrugged. 'Summoned to finish third year, apparently.'

Emmet, who had been silent up until now, grunted. ''Course she bloody was.'

A steady flow of students began to move through the glass doors. We only had a minute or two before assembly started.

'What do you mean?' I asked.

'There's a celebrity director in the mix for the Shakespeares,' Dylan said.

'Oh, the possibilities!' Richard mocked.

'Hang on,' I said. 'What happened to her?'

'Sylvie?' Richard looked at me, confused.

'Yes. Sylvie.' Saying her name felt deeply personal and I realised, ashamed, how desperately I wanted to know.

'It's not really any of your business,' Emmet said. 'Or any of ours.' He left Dylan, Richard and me on the steps.

Dylan whistled. 'Yikes.'

'What's going on with him?' I looked to the others. 'He wasn't at the end-of-term party. He's been kind of . . .'

'Taciturn,' Dylan supplied.

Richard laughed. 'How long have you been waiting to use that word in a sentence?'

'Piss off!' Dylan replied, half smiling.

Richard nudged him then came back to my question. 'He won't say.'

'Really?'

Richard stood. 'Really.'

I didn't believe him.

———

We'd missed the introductions.

Dylan, Richard and I squeezed onto the narrow landing of the seating bank in Studio One and sat with our knees hugged to our chests like children. The staff were positioned as they had been on the first day of the year, an imposing row of six.

'May I remind you,' Genevieve said, 'you *must* book a space with me in advance. If I don't approve it, it doesn't happen.'

'There will be a shortage,' Quinn interrupted. 'Second years have priority, with not one but two scene studies this term: a contemporary and a Shakespeare. Rhett will return to direct half of the cohort in *Much Ado About Nothing*, and the other half'—Quinn paused, and the students seemed to hold their collective breath—'will be led by William Yates in *Twelfth Night*.'

I snapped my head towards Richard. 'Holy shit. Vivien's dad?'

He raised his eyebrows but didn't respond.

'I knew it!' Dylan cried.

Quinn cleared her throat. 'Third years will be working with me on *Victory*, a fabulous play, rarely performed.'

'Jesus,' Dylan whispered. 'Tough going.'

'It'll be sink or swim,' Richard agreed.

I knew nothing about *Victory*, only that it had been written by Howard Barker, the most difficult playwright I'd ever read.

'Which brings me to our first years, who will continue their vocal training with Phillip, begin animal work with Freya, and spend the afternoons in the Warehouse with Judith for Collective.' Quinn leaned forward in her chair deliberately. 'Be kind to yourselves and to one another. The work requires stamina.' Quinn opened her palms to indicate the staff beside her. 'We are here, of course, to guide you, but ultimately, only you can steer the course of your training.'

I thought of Sylvie and shivered.

Quinn nodded ceremoniously. 'Thank you.'

The students rose from their seats. The staff exited without interruption.

'Couldn't they have eased us into it?' Emmet asked as we made our way out of the space. 'Classes, right off the bat.'

'What, you want another tour of the building?' Dylan dared.

'Yeah, actually,' Emmet replied. 'I have no idea where the Warehouse is.'

Imogen fell into step beside me. 'How about Yates, eh?' She turned to Richard. 'You knew, didn't you?'

Richard smirked. ''Course I bloody knew.'

We gathered by the elevator.

'How long?' Imogen asked.

'Most of last term,' Richard replied.

'Just when you think you know someone,' I teased.

Richard patted my cheek. 'Don't be jealous, darling.'

I backed away, realising as I did that he was right: I was jealous. Vivien now preceded me as his confidante.

'I'm taking the stairs.' I spun on my heel and walked towards the atrium, ignoring the sound of Richard's laughter.

'Are you sure you're okay to be here?' I heard a woman whisper beneath the stairwell.

'Of course,' another answered.

I froze.

'No one would blame you for taking a little more time.'

'It's my third year and Quinn said—'

I took one tentative step closer. My Cons squeaked on the polished cement, causing the two women to glance in my direction. 'Sorry,' I said. 'I wasn't eavesdropping. I just—'

'Oh, Maeve!' Anya reached for me. 'Sorry, we were . . .' Anya turned to Sylvie and abandoned the explanation. 'Maeve is in first year.'

Sylvie had clear blue eyes that fell on me without focusing on any one point. 'Hi,' she said. 'Welcome.'

'Thanks,' I replied, self-conscious suddenly. A moment passed, then another. The women waited, one a friend, the other a vision, not entirely real.

'I'm going to head up,' I said.

'Of course,' Anya responded, clearly relieved. 'Let's get a drink soon!'

'Definitely,' I answered and turned towards the stairs.

The pair picked up their conversation again in hurried whispers.

I ran all the way to the Rehearsal Room, dropped my bag, shucked off my shoes and found a place in the centre of the floor, aware of Saxon against the furthest wall, mid-practice.

'Are you okay?' Imogen asked. 'You look like you've seen a ghost.'

'I'm fine.'

'Not convinced,' she said, and left me alone to warm up.

I blinked and closed myself off from the room. Sylvie's ethereal figure appeared before me. I couldn't help but wonder what she'd seen, what she'd experienced.

Quinn had her discharged from a psychiatric facility.

I pushed the image from my mind and came to readiness.

—

'Coyote,' Freya called.

There were forty-five species to work through that morning. We would return to each animal over the course of the term, to build on and perfect, as an entry point to character. So far, however, the work made little sense.

On hands and knees, I curved my spine and looked for someone to imitate. I had no idea what a coyote was. Beside me, Dylan snarled at the wall and tore his nails along the floorboards. Moments like this took me completely out of the task, and I'd wonder, *What does any of this have to do with becoming an actor?*

'Chicken.'

I wriggled into a squat and tucked my wrists under my armpits. I knew what a chicken was.

'Stop,' Freya said. 'Saxon, continue.'

We dropped our movement and followed Freya to where Saxon was crouched in the corner of the room with his face close to the floorboards. He raised his head, then his right foot and scratched at the floor repetitively.

'Observe,' Freya said softly, 'how Saxon has *embodied* the chicken.'

My peers nodded silently. I bit my lip to stop myself from laughing.

'Brilliant,' Freya said to herself. 'Simply brilliant.'

Absorbed, she held one hand against her throat, the other in the air beside her, flinching with each movement Saxon made.

'Yes,' Freya gasped, 'go, follow it!'

Saxon swivelled sharply and ran on the balls of his feet after a tiny, imaginary creature. He pounced, pecked and used his toes to place the invisible thing in his mouth.

Freya was delighted. 'Good,' she said, then, 'onwards.'

The company spread themselves around the studio.

'Neutral standing and . . . Maltese Shih Tzu.'

—

'No, my fair cousin,
If we are marked to die, we are enough
To do our country loss; and if to live,
The fewer men, the greater share of honour.'

The weight of his name was enough to pull an audience. Every student was in attendance. *Yates on Shakespeare.* An hour-long lecture in Studio One.

He was handsome, roguish, of an indeterminate age. He stood behind a black chair and leaned on it every so often for emphasis, his face upturned, his eyes blazing.

'By Jove, I am not covetous for gold,
Nor care I who doth feed upon my cost;

It ernes me not if men my garments wear;
Such outward things dwell not in my desires.
But if it be a sin to covet honour
I am the most offending soul alive.'

It was as though Yates had chosen the St Crispin's Day speech specifically to rile us up, to align us with himself. A fellow artist, one who was working. *You can do this*, he seemed to say. It was like being let in on a secret. I wanted to write everything down, though there was nothing to record. Just a feeling that would diminish once plastered to the page.

'He that shall see this day and live t'old age
Will yearly on the vigil feast his neighbours
And say, "To-morrow is Saint Crispian."
Then will he strip his sleeve and show his scars
And say, "These wounds I had on Crispin's day."'

He delivered the speech with calm authority. Each word measured, no trace of strain. I wondered how many years he'd spent drilling the text into himself so that he could release it with such ease. Though somehow I knew it wasn't technique alone. It was *him*.

'But we in it shall be rememberèd,
We few, we happy few, we band of brothers.
For he today that sheds his blood with me
Shall be my brother; be he ne'er so vile,
This day shall gentle his condition.
And gentlemen in England now abed
Shall think themselves accursed they were not here,
And hold their manhoods cheap whiles any speaks
That fought with us upon Saint Crispin's day.'

The audience roared with emotion. Yates was serene. He didn't swat away the praise. He embraced it and waited for calm.

Then he spoke about truth, how iambic pentameter was a code to unlocking it, that we shouldn't be frightened or intimidated by it. He answered our questions, laughed at the insistence on his genius, and brushed off the suggestion that fame led to longevity.

'Few of you will make it,' he said sombrely, as the session drew to a close.

Genevieve rounded us up and we left the theatre with those words ringing in our ears, contemplating who might fail, who might get a little work and who might be the Yates of each company.

—

There were mornings during the first week of term when Phillip left us mid-practice. We'd stand there obediently and wait for his return. *Breathing.* Spread around the room like discarded mannequins. He might be five minutes or an hour. If we moved, he'd notice. My knees would ache, the white walls would begin to morph into strange, amphibious creatures, my eyesight faltering.

It was mortifying to be caught out. Phillip would fling the Rehearsal Room door open, and after so much silence we'd flinch. He'd inspect us like a drill sergeant.

'*Get out!*' he'd scream if we looked him in the eye. His red cheeks puffed out, moustache twitching.

The first time it happened to me, I apologised, forgetting Judith's warning in our first class together. *Don't do that.*

'Dear girl, you can't recover from this. Go and contemplate your impatience!'

In the passageway I'd hear his voice, full of blistering authority, and think of my father in his office, my mother swimming in the sea. How difficult it would be for them to understand that it was all necessary. That the spark of desire to work was too hot to be extinguished. The other students felt it too. Their creativity aired like a sigh, like a relief. A home for it at last.

II

Saturday.

I met him on the corner of Brunswick and Gertrude streets, as instructed, and felt it immediately—the current of creativity that ran beneath the road. It spread from the street corners into vintage stores and restaurants, into pubs and warehouse spaces available for hire. This part of town; a wash of artists and ageing lefties who'd made good on their property investments long ago. Couples brushed past us. Yellow berets, flannel coats. There was a self-assurance to how they dressed, how they walked, how they spoke to one another.

Saxon didn't take my hand or wait for me to fall into step beside him. Instead, he crossed the road to a bar with a wide glass window that overlooked Gertrude Street. He held the door open for me.

'Carlton?' he asked as he made his way to the bar. He rested against it, looking on as I removed my cardigan and sat down by the picture window. He laughed with the barman and returned with two pints. We drank them quickly.

'Another?'

Yes.

We'd already felt out the shape of one another; the work wasn't why we were here. To mention it now would have been reductive. Saxon was allowing space for something else. I complied by leaving drama school out of the conversation.

'It's not a love story,' he said.

'No?'

'Definitely not.'

Saxon knew all about *Wuthering Heights*. He stroked my thigh and fleshed out his argument. We switched to red wine in scratched glasses.

'It's obsession,' he said.

'Borderline toxic,' I replied, drawing on second-hand information.

'One interpretation, sure.'

'Yours?'

Saxon kissed my neck lightly. 'No.'

I promised to read it, comfortable enough with him to reveal that I never had.

'I have a copy at home,' he said.

''Course you do.'

'No, really.'

It felt grown-up to discuss literature with a man in a bar, as though the perimeters of my world were expanding.

'You'd let me borrow it?' I asked.

'If you promise to return it.'

We stepped out onto the street. I swayed a little, the diminishing sunlight having brought on a drunkenness I hadn't felt indoors.

I reached for his arm. He tucked me inside his jacket, shielding us both from the wind.

He lived in a share house, a single-fronted terrace on a wide street. His housemates, two women and one man, all in their twenties, lazed on the median strip, rugged up against the weather. Saxon ran over to them. I opened the rusty gate and waited by the front door. I heard promises of *next weekend* and *dinner*. Then his palm was on my spine, his breath in my ear.

'It's all ours,' Saxon said, turning his key in the lock.

I stepped into the first room off a narrow corridor. The smell of him came from within it. The floorboards were worn, the paint peeling. There was a fireplace, a stack of books atop the brickwork. A double bed, neatly made, between mismatched side tables, a dish with keys on one of them, a battered Moleskine journal and a framed photograph on the other. The photo was of a woman with a young boy in her arms, both smiling at the lens.

'Your mother?' I asked. 'There's a likeness.'

Saxon stared at the frame. 'Everyone says so.'

He looked as he did the first day I'd met him: closed off, some kind of darkness brewing within. *Hamlet.*

Embarrassed, I changed the subject in a bid to bring him back. 'It's freezing in here.'

'The fireplace doesn't work.'

'Aesthetic purposes only?'

Saxon took a step towards me. 'Exactly.' He took his time removing my cardigan, then my dress. 'All right?'

'Yes,' I whispered back.

He kneeled and pulled off my cowboy boots, peeled down my stockings and ran his tongue along the length of my thigh.

I dissolved to the floor. Then he was above me. I raised my hips to his and matched his breathing, the boards burning against my back.

I'd never been given the permission to look, to really feel it. There had been darkened rooms, swift movements. Not this. His hand behind my neck, the intimacy of *time*. I absorbed it, absorbed him, and felt true release when it was over.

We lay silently, uncovered, as footsteps moved along the corridor. I could have stayed. He would have let me. But sharing his bed, rising for breakfast, felt far too personal.

I'm not ready, I thought. 'I'd better go,' I said.

'I'll walk you,' he replied and handed me his copy of *Wuthering Heights*.

I'd imagined a book with scrawlings in the margins, dog-eared pages, a coffee-stained cover. That's exactly what he presented me with. It was reassuring to be right.

He was gentlemanly. I teased him about it as he walked along the kerb. Saxon laughed and slipped his arm around my waist. With each car that passed he drew me closer.

From then on Saturdays were ours. I'd receive a text with a location and directions. We'd explore the city together, two Queenslanders attempting to make a home for themselves. His bed was a magnet. The walk back to my place a full stop.

—

Saturdays felt like a distant dream when each Monday I was thrust back into the work.

Led by Judith, Collective progressed at a rapid pace. It took every ounce of strength to keep up, to stay motivated over each four-hour session.

We began class with a bastardised version of kundalini yoga that we relied on as an entry point to the work. Meditative trance music played through the Warehouse, and we'd shake every inch of our bodies to it, sometimes for ten minutes, other times an hour, to pull our minds out of ourselves and into the room. Then the music would stop and we'd peel away from the floor and wait along the fuzzy edge of golden light from the rig above that divided the space.

Collective was an extension of improvisation; a process of development that evolved with each new company. It was an approach to theatre-making I'd never encountered before: a collaborative, intuitive process amalgamated from the methods of the many forefathers of performance.

We were instructed to rise in groups of five and *work from impulse*. We'd walk, run or find stillness until someone made an offer, an action to mark the beginning of the improvisation. It had to be bold. A sprint. A fall. Something to juxtapose against what was happening around you. It needed to climax and sprawl and come to a natural ending without knowing the plot beforehand.

Once we were familiar with the structure, Judith introduced other elements. Music, gesture, repetition and voice. We'd feel it out for a week before adding another layer. It was messy but there were moments of brilliance, of utter clarity. We felt it when we saw it and were encouraged to continue.

One afternoon I lay pinned beneath Emmet, smothered by his enormous frame.

'What does it need?' Judith yelled from the darkness of the audience.

There were two other men behind me somewhere with Imogen.

I waited for Emmet to move. He kneeled back and released me. His initial offer had been violent. We'd been running, all five of us, when he clipped me by mistake. Instinctively, I turned to him. Then he wrestled me to the floor. The other men continued running while Imogen watched. Once Emmet released me the others stopped running, and I walked the length of the space alone.

We repeated it. Now, there had to be a third.

What does it need?

When Emmet found me again, I didn't fall. I took his hand, pressed my stomach against his and slowed my breathing. Emmet took the offer. I rested my face on his chest, and we slow-danced. The men stopped running and watched. Imogen ran until the light from the rig faded, and all that could be heard was the sound of her breath, caught somewhere between her chest and her throat.

'Rest,' Judith called.

It could have been a love story or an escape or an affair. There'd been no decision made by the players, only offers picked up on the floor. The audience filled in the gaps, fleshed out a through line from what they'd witnessed.

Sometimes there were sessions when you couldn't lose yourself in the preparation of kundalini, no matter how hard you shook, and you didn't have the right to enter the work. You'd sit sidelined. Those days were crippling. As an artist. As a person.

Then there were sessions like this one, when inhibition left you. You could respond, make offers, take risks. Like magic, the work came from you. And everyone scrambled to meet it. Your place within the company secure and rising.

—

We sat straight-backed on chairs that scratched through our clothing, facing one another in a circle. My bare feet were numb. The heaters weren't working and there was no way of warming ourselves.

A large, rectangular window looked out from Performance Space A onto Clarendon Street, its corners misted with ice. Dylan's head obscured my view. I leaned slightly to the right to see if the buildings had brightened with the rising sun. They hadn't. I groaned inwardly. We still had an hour or more left of class.

'Stop with the singsong storytelling,' Phillip interrupted.

Imogen paused.

There had been no salutation that morning. Phillip's mood gave a clear indication of how class would pan out: slowly, mercilessly.

We each had a sheet of A4 paper in our laps. The same text, used for sight reading. Imogen had drawn the short straw and been ordered to go first.

She cleared her throat.

'Don't,' Phillip scolded. 'That's a habit. A bad one.'

Imogen nodded. The sheet of paper quivered in her hands. Before she spoke again, Imogen edged forward and tucked her tailbone beneath her pelvis. She looked to Phillip for reassurance. He gave none.

'*All were weary,*' Imogen said, as though she were trying to pull the meaning out of each syllable, '*all but the sun. He seemed to glory in his power—*'

Phillip raised a palm to stop her. 'Again.'

Imogen took a clipped breath. '*All were weary, all but the sun.*'

'You're reporting it,' Phillip said. He rose and came to stand behind Imogen's chair. 'Breath is . . .'

'Imagination.'

Phillip laughed and placed his hands on her lower back. 'Indeed. Now, relax your jaw. Breathe into my hands and speak from here.'

'All were—'

'Breathe!' Phillip interrupted.

'All were weary—'

'You're not listening. *Breathe!*'

'All—'

Phillip stepped away from her and bent at the waist with long, limp arms, dehumanising her with his imitation. Imogen's chest trembled with barely contained anger.

'All were weary,' Phillip snivelled.

Imogen dropped the page and stood, looking Phillip directly in the eye. '*All were weary, all but the sun. He seemed to glory in his power, relentless and untiring, as he swung boldly in the sky, triumphantly leering down upon his helpless victims.*'

The irony wasn't lost on any of us.

Phillip pointed at her. 'Now, *that's* how you create a world.'

Imogen stalked towards the door. She let it slam behind her. No one followed.

'Begin,' Phillip said to Vivien, seated beside Imogen's empty chair.

When class was over, I went looking for my friend.

'You don't smoke,' I said, approaching Imogen outside Luncheonette. She was shivering.

She looked at the cigarette in her fingers. 'No.'

'He's a bully,' I said.

'The piece required anger. Phillip can say he pushed me to find it. Not that I'd report him. We just have to take it. All of it.'

'But that isn't fair.'

'I don't want to fail.'

117

I tried to make light of it. 'It's just sight reading.'

'Is it?'

I hesitated. 'Yes.'

'We both know that isn't true.'

Leaves swirled around our feet, collected in the gutter.

'How does it come together?' I asked.

'What?'

'Neutral Mask, sight reading. Animal work.'

'It doesn't.'

'Right. *Autonomy*.'

'Autonomy,' Imogen echoed.

'It's fucking hard.'

Imogen laughed; a croak, all resonance gone. 'It is.'

I slipped my hand into hers and led her back to the drama building.

—

At night, I lay awake and thought about Saxon, awed and delighted to be chosen by him. How my body responded when he touched me, how I lit up and burned. And I wanted to. All the time.

He underpinned everything, became my benchmark both on and off the floor. His offhandedness and yet total commitment to our training was simultaneously alluring and baffling. How gently he held it; how firmly too.

I was motivated by the private world we'd created within the parentheses of the school. I dreamed about *Romeo and Juliet*, thought myself clever to have both: Saxon and the work, my character still intact.

On Saturdays he asked me questions, remembered the answers. I didn't know what ceviche was, had never tried pappardelle. He took me to restaurants and watched me eat, asked about my family. And I'd unravel, tell him about the road trips and campfires and afternoons by the sea after school. The simple ease of being with my parents. He'd tell me I was lucky, and I'd underplay it, wishing I had something darker to dredge up. Something more interesting.

In Port Melbourne we'd sit by the fire at old pubs by the bay. I learned to chat with the locals, hook into a conversation about the footy. I'd only ever known surf clubs, knew a separate set of rules. But I stood with the rest of them when the opposing team scored, shouting at the television above the bar. Saxon ribbed me, but he listened, would trail me to the water. Flat and iridescent at night, like an oil slick. From behind he'd hold me against his chest, mollifying my homesickness. The bay was nothing like the ocean.

He made me CDs with the track titles written in blue marker around the rim. The songs he selected were tender, a window into the softest part of him that I willingly fell through. We'd listen to them at his place, and he'd appraise me like a painting while I undressed. I loved it, played to it. Felt achingly *seen*.

Sometimes I'd look at the photograph of his mother and feel a stab of concern, her absence an essence that filtered through his room. But I never brought her up, dared not disrupt the equilibrium of our time together. Though the question was always at the forefront of my mind: *Where is she?*

III

Graduation was an opportunity to get boozed, the ceremony a pretence. We knew a Bachelor of Dramatic Arts degree meant nothing. The real achievement was making it to the end of your third year. Though that didn't guarantee you a career.

'Two hours?' Richard lamented on our way to the Arts Centre, where proceedings were to take place. It was obligatory for all drama students to attend; to formally farewell the previous third-year company.

'Then drinks and canapés,' Anya replied.

Richard pulled a mini bottle of Yellow from the front pocket of his suit pants and dropped it into my canvas bag. 'Party pies don't count,' he said with a snort.

Quinn gave a rousing introduction. Images of past productions shimmered against the wall behind her as the graduating company filed past, tears falling, to accept their piece of paper, their token of acknowledgement for all they'd endured. It allowed the parents in attendance to pretend for a moment that their children were pursuing a career in accounting or law.

The remaining companies applauded from the dress circle and shouted lines from their favourite plays, in-jokes that made the first years feel inferior. But it was a short scene from *A Glass Menagerie*, performed by two members of the graduating company, that made the biggest impression. The work was strong, transformational. It was all anyone could talk about in the foyer afterwards.

We took drinks two at a time from a white-clothed fold-out table. Red, white, sparkling. Whatever was left. The only thing that mattered was getting our fill before the tab ran out. We were raucous and aware of being so, uncaring. These weren't our parents. We didn't know the graduating company beyond their mini black-and-white portraits. We were safe—for the rest of the year, at least.

'Let's get out of here,' Richard said.

He took my hand and led me along the plush carpet to the stairwell. I looked back over the thinning crowd, at the parties of two and three. The graduates. They'd survived it. Their collective experience was almost tangible. I wanted to bottle it, gulp it down.

I pulled at my cardigan as we stepped onto the pavement. 'Fuck me!'

It was a still evening but the icy air was a shock. It left you breathless, shrivelling your lungs with each inhalation.

Richard pulled me into a hug. 'Toughen up, darling.'

'Where are the others?'

Richard nodded ahead of me.

Judith, Vivien, Imogen and Anya stood together in a tight group, smoking a joint. Richard drifted over and took it from Anya's fingers.

Anya pushed him. 'Greedy!'

'Making up for lost time,' Richard replied.

'Terrible manners.' Judith reached for the joint. 'Can't you do something about him?'

'I've tried,' Vivien said.

Richard buried his head in her neck. 'And failed!'

Vivien squealed.

I stood slightly outside the group, unsure how to involve myself, wondering how and when my friends had crossed the invisible line that divided staff from students. Smoking a cigarette together was one thing, a joint quite another. Perhaps the line didn't exist for them at all. They were adults. I still felt like a child.

'Let it pass through you,' Judith said.

Richard held the joint between them pointedly and grinned.

'The *work*. Whatever sticks is useful to you personally. What doesn't . . .' Judith shrugged and shook her raven hair from her face.

'And the curriculum?' Imogen asked.

'Ah, yes,' said Judith. '*That*.'

Richard gestured to the building. 'It doesn't matter, beyond here.'

'But we still need to pass,' Imogen said.

'Do you?' Judith asked rhetorically.

I frowned. 'Aren't our options limited otherwise?'

Judith offered me the joint.

'No, thank you,' I said.

'*Virtue itself turns vice, being misapplied,*' Richard quoted affectedly.

Vivien snickered and answered, '*And vice sometime's by action dignified.*'

'Fine,' I said, chastened. I took the joint and inhaled, the paper wet between my lips.

'Good girl,' said Judith, taking it back. She flicked her eyes in Anya's direction. 'Anya can tell you all about the curriculum. She knows it well.'

I glanced at Anya. 'Because she's a second year?'

Judith had a toke. 'Of sorts.'

'Well,' Imogen said, 'the more you know, the better prepared.'

'Care to comment, Anya?' Judith asked.

'No,' Anya muttered.

Vivien lay her head on Judith's shoulder. 'Come for one more.'

'Past my bedtime.' Judith kissed Vivien's cheek and gave Richard the joint. She strolled back inside the Arts Centre without another word.

'Shall we?' Richard turned and jogged towards the Yarra.

Vivien ran after him and jumped on his back.

Anya pulled a crumpled cigarette packet from her coat pocket and pointed it at Vivien and Richard. 'I didn't see *that* coming.'

'That's Richard, though, isn't it?' Imogen quipped.

'That's Richard, all right,' Anya replied.

We followed our friends towards the city.

'I should have left,' Anya said.

There were few exceptions to the rules. Anya, however, was one of them—a second-year repeater. Some treated her with caution, as though they might be tainted by association. Others followed her, as if she held the secret to their own passing.

'They wouldn't cull you now, after making you repeat,' I said. It felt like a betrayal to acknowledge it so openly.

Anya stopped and lit a cigarette. 'I had an opportunity to leave. I didn't take it.'

We clumped together on the Princes Bridge, people darting around us, gruff and accusing.

'Why would you want to?' I asked.

'They can't stop you from being an artist,' Imogen said.

'Exactly. It was weak of me to stay.'

'No.' Imogen wrapped an arm around Anya. 'Quite the opposite.'

Heads close, they walked in step and shared the cigarette. Two women, united by circumstance, with a drive to become better versions of themselves. I could learn from them. I was trying to.

From the street, the bar looked inviting. Not because of the expensive decor or the glossy marble floors, but because of the people inside it. You wanted to know them. To be their friends. The drama kids, in pre-loved outfits, overtly affectionate with one another. Even the suits, holding their champagne flutes by the stem, were woven into the scene, amused. The bartenders wore crisp, white collared shirts with bow ties. All men. Their perfectly parted hair a sure sign I couldn't afford the drinks. I wondered who'd chosen the venue.

Anya pushed open the glass door; music and voices of varying pitch like a slap in the face as we entered.

'Vodka?' Anya asked.

'What?' I yelled. 'No!'

'We're doing it,' she said, already on her way to the bar with Imogen in tow.

A deep voice, close to my ear. 'You must be a first year.'

I tensed, but when I saw who it was I relaxed, proud to be singled out by him. 'I am.'

'Youngest in your class?' William Yates asked.

I nodded.

'Twenty? Twenty-one?'

'Seventeen.'

Yates clapped softly against the solid glass in his hands. 'Brava.' He stood back and appraised me. 'You know, you'd make a fabulous Miss Julie.'

'Really?' I asked. Had he seen me in class? In Collective? I tried to recall a time when he'd audited our work. I couldn't.

'Definitely.' He stepped closer and lowered his voice. '*I think I could drink out of your skull, and bathe my feet in your open breast, and eat your heart from the spit!*' His eyes darted across my face. The words made me blush. 'You know it? Surely.'

I did, though I couldn't continue the monologue. But I understood: *Miss Julie* was *flattery*. The play was well known, well loved. A classic. The central character was a woman of privilege, cruel and self-sabotaging. Masculine in energy, exploited to the point of madness by her lover, her valet. By the end of the play, Miss Julie teeters into hysteria, becomes wild and lascivious. It was an absolute gift of a role.

'I'd love the opportunity to play her,' I said, as if it were an audition.

Yates laughed. 'One day.' He took a sip of his drink. 'Here with anyone?'

'Friends.'

'Yes'—he slowed his speech—'but are you here with anyone in particular?'

It made my stomach sink, the obviousness of it. I fumbled for a response.

Yates grazed my chin with his forefinger playfully. 'Let's get you a drink.'

'I'm fine, thank you.'

'Try this then,' he said and offered me his glass. 'Go on.'

I took it but the smell of the liquor made my eyes water.

Yates curled his fingers around my wrist. 'Top shelf, I assure you.'

I shook him away. The glass hit the floor and shattered. The room turned towards us.

Yates looked about him in mock horror. 'Christ!'

I kneeled to collect the shards of glass and heard applause, some scattered laughter. A bartender appeared beside me with a dustpan. 'I'm so sorry, it was an accident,' I whimpered.

Yates grabbed my upper arm and pulled me to my feet. 'No need to make a scene,' he said through gritted teeth.

Anya appeared beside me. 'I leave you alone for one minute.' She turned to Yates, and recognition dawned on her face. 'Mr Yates, lovely to see you. Vivien's at the bar.' Anya turned and pointed to where Vivien, Richard and Imogen stood.

Yates's expression was blank. 'Thank you, Anya,' he said. He let go of my arm, took a step towards his daughter, then turned back. 'Well done this week, Anya. *Very* convincing work.' Then he slid into the crowd.

'Drink that,' Anya said, handing me a new glass.

I shook my head.

'Do it.' I obeyed and gulped down the liquid. 'It's up to you,' Anya said, taking my hands, making a point of holding on to them, 'but I think we should get you home.'

I nodded.

She didn't ask me about it. We didn't pick up our conversation from earlier either. It was as though drama school didn't exist. She tried to distract me with talk of Adelaide, of the theatre scene there. It only made me feel worse. But I laughed as she ran along the carriage of the tram, shouting my name like a character in a foreign film. She was trying. I owed her for that.

126

Saxon was sitting on the steps of my building. 'Rough night?'
I couldn't respond.

He pulled me onto his lap. 'Anya called me.'

It felt like my fault—the glass shattering and *Miss Julie* before it. But Saxon's presence reminded me that wasn't true. He came up and waited for me to shower. When I stepped out of the bathroom, my hair wet, my face scrubbed clean, he was peering at the wall above the television, where I'd blu-tacked photographs of my family.

'This isn't how I imagined you'd see my place for the first time,' I said.

'I like it,' Saxon replied. 'Your home. You.'

I saw my reflection and his in the darkened windows that overlooked the cemetery. I looked small beside him, wrapped in a towel, his figure bundled in a well-worn flannel coat.

'Get in,' he said, nodding at the partition that divided the living room and my single bed. I pulled a set of pyjamas from beneath my pillow. He watched me put them on, and when I got under the covers he lay on top of them beside me.

'*Miss Julie*, huh? The man's a genius, but still.'

'He quoted it.'

Saxon sat up. 'Which bit?'

'*I think I could drink out of your skull . . .*'

'Jesus.'

'I know.'

'*And bathe my feet in your open breast—*' Saxon said.

'Don't!' I squealed, embarrassed.

'Stop thinking about it,' he said softly and kissed me.

We lay together quietly, and when his breathing slowed, I gave myself permission to rest.

—

'Need a drink?' Richard asked me after a particularly draining Collective session the following week.

'Desperately,' I replied.

We went to the Malthouse and sat among the patrons in the dugout of the courtyard and drank our wine like water beneath portable heaters. It gave me a headache. Dehydration and alcohol were a terrible, maudlin mix.

Theoretically, I understood what *working from impulse* meant. But it was elusive some days and I'd berate myself for not being able to find it. Hours were spent searching for the story, for my place within it. It took stamina to make it through the afternoon and sometimes you just didn't have it in you.

'It's witchcraft,' I said.

'It isn't,' Richard replied.

'It absolutely is!' I wanted him to agree with me. 'And it's infiltrating every aspect of my life.'

Richard laughed good-naturedly. 'This *is* your life.'

'Sure.' I took a sip and looked out into the darkness. 'But—'

'But nothing. You aren't the work, and the work isn't you.'

'It's one and the same.'

'No.' Richard leaned forward, close enough that I could feel his breath on my face. 'Just because you had a quiet afternoon in Collective doesn't mean you're a terrible actress.'

'What about Dylan?' I asked.

Earlier, Judith had introduced music and, with it, Dylan brought emotion, a soliloquy about his father that the remaining players became the chorus for. I hadn't offered anything and couldn't help comparing Dylan's experience in Collective to my

128

own, deeming his superior. When Judith asked him what he'd felt, he told her that the music freed him physically, that it gave his work texture.

'You're learning to layer,' Judith said, congratulatory.

Dylan wiped his nose with his sleeve. 'I think so, yes.'

I'd wanted to reach across the circle during debrief and hit him.

'He had a breakthrough, that's all,' Richard said now.

'A very public breakthrough,' I replied.

'What are you saying?'

'I'm saying,' I began, trying to untangle my thoughts, 'I want to do that.'

'Then try again tomorrow.'

'Come on. You don't think he had that ready to go?'

'You think the tears were premeditated?'

I shrugged.

'I highly doubt it,' Richard said. 'He's too precious.'

I felt petty, pulling apart Dylan's work to justify what was lacking in my own. 'You're right.'

Richard embraced me. 'But okay, yes. The work's a headfuck.'

'Thank you,' I said, vindicated.

'Richard!' a voice boomed from behind us.

Richard turned, jolting my head from his chest. 'Yates? You didn't?'

'I'm afraid I couldn't wait,' Yates replied.

Richard stood and shook his hand. 'As good as they say?'

'Even better.' The men laughed together. 'Vivien will kill me, of course.'

Richard turned to me. 'I'm sure I can find someone to take the spare ticket.'

My heart raced. 'But I don't know what it's for.'

'Hazard a guess,' Richard offered.

I surrendered. '*The Importance of Being Earnest.*'

'Talk of the town!' Richard exclaimed.

Yates's face spread into a smile. 'With good reason. Take the spare. I'll join you. Worth a second look.'

'I couldn't,' I said.

Yates opened his arms to me. 'Ah, but you must!'

A sudden silence spread between us.

'You two know one another, yes?' Richard asked.

'I don't believe we do,' said Yates.

'Maeve,' I said and offered my hand, pretending like we hadn't already met.

'Pleasure.' Yates kissed my cheek instead. 'Is Vivien with you?'

Richard hesitated. 'No.'

Yates looked at me, his face a question, then he slapped Richard on the back. 'Fair play. Tell her I'll speak to her tomorrow, will you?'

Richard sucked his teeth. 'I will.'

Yates strode towards the theatre and swung open the wooden doors. 'Good man!' he called and stepped inside.

I tilted my empty glass in the direction of the foyer. 'Another?'

'Let's call it a night.'

I laughed uncertainly. 'Unlike you.'

'I'm meeting Viv.'

'So?'

Richard kicked the gravel beneath his feet. 'She can't understand it.'

'What?' I asked tentatively.

Richard sighed. 'Us.'

'There *is* no us,' I scoffed.

'I know that.'

'Everyone knows that.'

Richard considered me. 'Do they?'

I shoved his shoulder, a little too hard, hoping our usual play might break the tension. It didn't.

'She's jealous,' Richard said.

'Really?'

'Don't gloat.'

'I'm not!'

'You are.'

'What? We can't hang out anymore?'

Richard remained silent.

'Bullshit.'

'It's my fault,' he said.

I panicked. 'Has it got something to do with . . .' I couldn't find the words. 'Her father? The other night?'

Richard seemed genuinely confused. 'What?'

'Nothing,' I said quickly. 'Nothing.' I paused. 'Are you scared of . . .'

Richard looked at me pointedly. 'Of?'

I stumbled. It was too honest, cut too close to the bone. 'Failing.'

'What are you insinuating?'

I searched for an answer in the dark. 'Sometimes it's a matter of knowing the right people.'

'Oh, Maeve, come on!'

'It's true—'

'Don't—'

'Richard.' I said his name meekly, not wanting to lose him. Knowing I would. I felt helpless, small, with nothing to offer. No famous father, no pedigree. Just connection. Friendship.

'Yes?' His breathing was shallow. I knew from class that it meant he was trying to contain something: a thought, a feeling.

'I just want to understand things better,' I tried. 'It's like there's a whole language beneath the words everyone says that I can't hear.'

His features softened. 'Darling, look . . .' He took my hand and swayed our linked arms back and forth between us like a rope. 'It's simpler than you think.' His tone was affected, his vowels more rounded, like he was trying to explain something to a very small child. 'Not everything is a double entendre.' He wrapped me in his arms, rested his chin on the top of my head. 'Vivien simply won't have it, and I want to see where things lead. From the outside,' he said gently, 'you and I make no sense as friends. An ingenue and—'

I fell back into banter to save face: 'An outrageously handsome, intellectually elite *artiste*.'

We pulled apart. 'Man,' he said unhappily.

Appearances mattered.

'Let's go.'

The conversation was over; he'd lightened his load and burdened me with it.

We left our empty glasses on the gravel and walked towards the National Gallery of Victoria. Before crossing the road for a tram, Richard stopped. 'We good?'

"Course,' I replied. But something had shifted. Neither of us wanted the other, but enough people thought we did. Now it hung between us threateningly. 'See you in the morning.'

'Maeve?'

'Yeah?'

Richard paused before circling back. 'I'm sorry.'

IV

Collective seemed to exist outside of time. A haze of movement and sound. *Running, walking, stillness.* The black floor. The golden light. Five students working in the space. Afterwards, I could never recall what I'd done; was never sure whether I'd participated enough.

The day didn't end when I left the building. It followed me onto the tram, through my front door. It danced on the dinner plate in front of me and infiltrated my sleep. I never felt rested. I was bruised along my spine, across both shins and on each knee. I didn't feel it until I stopped moving, until I lay still in bed.

Even then I could defend it. The work.

—

Friday night was our time to report back to one another. To check in and measure the success of our afternoons spent within the dark walls of the Warehouse.

133

Drinks at the Malthouse now extended to dinner. We'd pick up a bottle each and a six pack for good measure from the Vintage Cellars on Little Bourke and bend our knees against the incline to a pink-walled dumpling bar up the road that had three separate levels. We'd stuff ourselves with pork wontons and shallot pancakes and air our grievances, toast our wins and pick apart the inner lives of our peers. Always just the four of us. Richard, Imogen, Emmet and me.

Those Friday nights were an essential part of my first semester, an era we'd reflect on later like the *good old days*. Though they were short-lived. Richard was the first to break it. Vivien started to join us. Then Saxon. Then whoever else felt like taking Richard up on his widely extended invitation. Our table of four sometimes grew to an entire floor. We toned ourselves down for our peers, our guests, aware that if we didn't, we'd expose ourselves as they were doing.

I started leaving early. Sometimes I'd slip out with a kiss to Imogen's cheek before it all got too rowdy, before someone spilled a bottle of wine, or fell asleep on the floor.

I was loose with our secret on evenings like those. Saxon and I would drift down the stairs, out of the restaurant and into the night together. To his bed. To our Saturdays.

—

The dissension connected to *Victory* spread through the drama building. It was an ensemble piece but, even so, sixteen actors split between a handful of hefty roles meant cast members had to double up; chorus work was introduced. There was a feeling that floated between companies that Quinn's direction hindered the third years—except for a select few—from showcasing their talent.

134

A talent which, beyond the walls of the drama building, would be judged solely on the work of the individual. An audience didn't see the decisions made by a director or the time a cast spent trying to adhere to them. It was the performance of each actor that lingered or didn't.

There was resentment between the second years, a rivalry between Shakespeare casts that grew steadily. Those who were working with Yates used his name as evidence of their own superiority; Rhett's name, too, carried enormous weight, but every second year was already under his advisory for the scene studies. Only half could say they'd been *chosen* to work with Yates.

The scene studies were a random selection, made by the students, recast multiple times. The way company members imagined themselves was often at odds with their archetype. There were two options, a contemporary and a Shakespeare, and some students were willing to fight to prove a point, to take the stronger scenes for themselves. They didn't mind hurting one another for the sake of the cause. The cause being one scene, from one play, performed *once*.

Our struggles in Collective seemed small beside those of the companies above us. We first years kept quiet, suspended in a process that muddied our perception of what we were reaching for. An elusive, final product that potentially didn't exist.

—

'Be bold!' Judith called.

Five bodies walked through the space then stopped simultaneously. After a beat, Vivien began to laugh. The light of Yates spread through our rehearsal room in the guise of his daughter; we all felt it. I avoided working with her where possible, loyal to

Richard, but Judith encouraged us to work together, our opposing energies being advantageous to the work.

Judith clapped her hands together. 'Go further, Vivien!'

I felt her behind me and started to run. A kids' game of chase. The other actors remained still. Eventually Vivien slowed her pace and settled again with the others. I took my cue from her and did the same.

'Good. Repeat it!' Judith yelled.

It became a motif.

Vivien increased her pace and darted around the actors to catch me. Her laugh became a growl, the game of chase, a hunt.

The push didn't hurt as much as the thud implied. I brought my hands to the back of my ribs and pressed them there, waiting for an ache that didn't come. Adrenaline coursed through me.

'You think I cannot stand the sight of blood,' Vivien began.

'You think I am as weak as that,' we said together.

She knew. It was an acknowledgement of the conversation between her father and me.

Everything was worthy of being used on the floor. I couldn't afford to be precious about it. As Vivien looked at me, her chest rising and falling as she sucked at the air, I wondered what had taken place on this floor in the years before I arrived. How many secrets did it hold? How many first years had buried their frustration here, only for it to rise again in twelve months' time in another form, in a play? Rivalries persisted. The process compounded.

'More,' Judith ordered. '*More.*'

Vivien smiled. Another push, a little harder this time. When she came at me again, I lifted my elbow instinctively to protect myself and clipped her jaw with it. She looked at me, disbelieving, launched herself at my head.

'*You think I am weak,*' Vivien growled, taking a fistful of my hair. '*You think I love you because the fruit of my womb was yearning for your seed.*'

I tried desperately to take hold of Vivien's wrists to relieve the pressure on my burning scalp. She began to walk, slowly at first, then quicker until I was sliding along the floorboards behind her, shrieking in pain.

The other actors remained still. No direction from Judith, no intervention from my peers. Only the sound of Vivien's voice. I gave into it then, aware that from an audience's perspective this was performance. I tried to pre-empt the monologue, to find a modicum of meaning to cling to. *What does it need?* I conjured a place for myself in the piece, echoing the text after Vivien had spoken it, like the ghostly embodiment of Miss Julie's rejected and repressed desires.

As though she could sense my consent, Vivien ended it: '*—but the lackey's line goes on in the orphan asylum—wins laurels in the gutter and ends in jail,*' she said icily.

And finally, I fell.

'Rest,' Judith said.

Vivien smiled beatifically and came to stand beside me. 'Did I hurt you?' she asked and proffered a hand to help me up.

I shook my head: *no.* It was a gift, an anecdote, an *experience.* Only we would ever know that her aggression came from anything other than what was found on the floor; that it was retaliation for my friendship with Richard and for being the recipient of her father's attention.

'Note how Vivien raised the stakes,' Judith said, 'and how Maeve chose to meet them.'

The remaining players joined the circle; Vivien sat down beside Richard.

I shuffled towards Imogen and eased myself to the floor. 'You're bleeding,' she whispered.

On the tram home I stood in the aisle and called my mother. I cried unashamedly, alluding to homesickness, too afraid to tell her the truth about the work. How I wanted it, how it hurt. I ignored the pitying looks from the other passengers and listened to my mother's voice. I closed my eyes, felt the jolting motion of the tram and imagined myself beneath the ocean of my home state, tussled by the tide.

—

We ate lunch together sometimes, hidden in the alcove of the Rehearsal Room. I always brought mine from home, a habit from high school, but I ended up eating half of Saxon's, takeaway bought from Luncheonette.

'Do you ever feel outside yourself?' I asked.

'On the floor?'

'Anywhere.'

Saxon took a moment to respond. 'Rarely.'

'Not even when you're being a chicken for Freya?' I teased.

Saxon laughed. 'Especially not then.'

It felt good to make him laugh.

'I just get up and do it.'

The simplicity of his response struck me. I inched closer and kissed him, breaking my own rule. School was out of bounds.

When I pulled away, Saxon looked at me suspiciously. 'Dangerous.'

I liked the word. I felt as though I were acting in a play of my own creation. 'Very.' I lay back against the cold floor, my arms above my head. Saxon bent forward and kissed the exposed skin between my pants and my shirt.

'Close your eyes,' he said.

I obeyed and raised my hips off the floor. Saxon slid my pants along my thighs, past my knees and made the cotton of my underwear wet with his tongue. 'We don't have long,' he said. An instruction. *Concentrate*. Even so, he took his time and I allowed myself to get lost in it. To abandon thought as I strived to do in Collective.

—

Fifteen minutes on all fours, flexing like a cat. Half an hour chewing imaginary leaves. An orangutan. A giraffe. What was the difference? The placement of the tongue apparently, the placement of the jaw.

Freya's frustration with us was palpable most days. She'd demonstrate what we were incapable of doing ourselves. Her specificity of movement, the culmination of years spent observing people, animals, inanimate objects, was a fascinating glimpse into the kind of artist she was outside of the drama building.

'A puppetry ensemble?' I asked quietly as we watched Freya enact the life of a gorilla.

'Apparently,' said Richard.

Freya's classes, though exhausting, were a kind of reprieve from Collective and Voice. She asked little of us by comparison, the stakes were low, animal work seemed unimportant. As a company, we'd become complacent.

'Richard,' Freya said, still now in the centre of the floor. 'A chimpanzee, please.'

Richard's knees cracked as he stood. 'Fuck.'

He made wide, lazy gestures.

Freya followed him, staying close. 'Detail!'

Richard's movements became smaller as he scratched himself, removed a crumb of food from the fibre of his t-shirt and ate it.

'More,' Freya said.

Richard stopped and looked to our teacher. 'More what?'

'Don't break it!'

Richard blinked at her. Freya exhaled and morphed into a chimpanzee herself. After a moment, Richard joined her.

'The nerve,' Imogen said, smiling. 'Only Richard.'

Students had collected by the Rehearsal Room windows in the hallway and were peering in to watch Freya and Richard work, an indicator that class had yet again run over. For once it didn't matter; we were enthralled.

With Freya to mirror, Richard's rendition of the primate became clearer. He pulled insects from her imaginary fur and they groomed one another as I'd seen animals do at the zoo. Then their physicality shifted. Freya took Richard's hand, transitioned from a squat to a kneel, and began to paint his fingernails from a tiny, invisible pot of polish.

'I like this colour,' Freya said in a small, bright voice.

Richard cottoned on immediately. 'Me too.'

They were children now, in play.

'Oh my god,' I breathed.

Freya had been withholding how to transition from animal to character until we were ready.

'You see?' Freya asked and stood.

Richard, still on the floor, nodded.

'Do better,' she said sternly to the company and walked out.

The new class filed into the studio. Richard didn't move. I collected his things and dropped them by his feet.

'I need a minute,' he said, removing his journal from his satchel.

Imogen and I left him and made our way to the next session.

'Who would have thought?' Imogen exclaimed.

'What?'

'That Richard's breakthrough would happen in Movement.'

I took my position on the floor of Performance Space A, distracted by what I saw behind closed lids: Freya the artist, puppet in hand, beneath a cone of light.

—

One rare, golden Sunday Richard invited us over. We drank white wine from the bottle and ate a simply prepared bowl of gnocchi in the courtyard of his Carlton home. He was a great cook, a great host.

'Has it not crossed your mind?' Imogen asked.

'Put your claws away,' Richard scolded.

Imogen persisted. 'Why attend drama school at all?'

'Maybe she has something to prove,' Richard suggested.

'To whom?' I asked.

'To *Papa*,' Imogen said.

'To herself,' Richard replied firmly.

I picked up the wine bottle and drank. 'She's difficult to work with.'

'Sadistic,' Imogen agreed.

I turned to Richard. 'You like it rough, though.'

Richard laughed. 'You know me too well.'

'And isn't that the problem?' I responded.

'Careful,' Imogen warned.

I pointed the bottle in her direction. 'You agree, though, don't you?'

Imogen took the wine from me. 'Vivien is his choice.'

'Erase me from the selection!' I cried.

'You're an egotist,' Emmet said.

We all turned to him.

I felt affronted. 'No, I'm not.'

'Their relationship isn't about you,' Emmet said.

'She brought me into it.'

'She's not here!' Emmet exclaimed.

'Exactly! And why is that?' I asked.

My friends were silent.

I turned to Richard. 'Did you invite her?'

Richard opened another bottle of wine. 'Of course I did.' He handed it to me and watched as I took a mouthful. 'Have you and Saxon ever done it alfresco?'

I choked on the wine.

Richard smiled. 'Don't play coy, darling.'

'Don't change the subject!'

'You two are fucking, aren't you?' Richard asked.

It was becoming more difficult to deny. Saxon and I worked together in Collective often. Our chemistry was undeniable.

'Yes.'

Richard pointed at me. 'More than fucking, I think.'

I conceded with a smile. The conversation about Vivien melted away and nothing more was said about Saxon. But I knew the parameters had changed. My admission, my slip, had rendered me vulnerable. I was property of the school and the students who occupied it; my life to be drawn from and used.

—

It was draining to constantly find the will to rise to the floor, to take risks, to throw yourself into the unknown day after day after day. Towards the middle of term, I was finding it increasingly hard to let go. I couldn't get up; I couldn't join the others in Collective. My peers were unconcerned; my failure to participate created space for someone else.

By the third day of this paralysis, I was listless. A knot had formed in my stomach—a physical manifestation of anxiety that prevented me from eating. I needed to explain myself or ask for help. I approached Judith at the end of the session, and she told me to meet her in her office in half an hour.

It was a small, carpeted room on the first floor. A single, freestanding lamp cast imposing shapes across the wall above her desk. Beside it rested a framed poster. A woman kneeled on a stage, her face lifted to the light. The title across the top read *Medea*.

'I was young,' Judith said, following my gaze. 'Older than you, but still . . .'

I saw it then, the resemblance. Her features were softer, but the angst was there behind the eyes. I stared at Judith's younger self and drummed up the courage to speak. 'I'm having trouble offering anything,' I said.

'Today?'

'And yesterday. The day before that as well.'

Judith crossed her arms and waited for me to continue.

'There doesn't seem to be room for me up there.'

'You can pick the players,' Judith replied.

'I've forgotten how.'

'The nature of the work is organic.'

'I know, I just . . .' I dug my fingernails into my palms to stop myself from crying.

'It's not about you,' Judith said. 'And it is.'

I swallowed. 'Okay.'

Judith leaned back against the desk. I stood before her awkwardly, conscious of her appraisal. We'd never been alone before. It felt like a mistake suddenly, to be here. I shrank beneath her energy, so much stronger than my own.

'You lack confidence,' she observed. 'Maybe you lack it out there as well.'

'Out there?'

'In life.'

I stepped back. 'You can't know that.'

Judith raised an eyebrow. 'I can, actually. It's a deeply personal experience, training to become an actor. We reveal more about ourselves on the floor than we realise. I didn't have the opportunity to study like you. I learned through working—a different kind of education. My teachers . . . they weren't as generous.' Judith looked into my eyes without blinking and took my chin between her thumb and forefinger. 'You need to dig deeper.'

'I'm trying.'

'Try harder,' she said and released me.

I wanted Judith to tell me what to do. I wanted guidelines, principles, rules to follow. But nothing like that existed in Collective.

With Neutral Mask there had been a structure. In Voice and Movement classes, there were steps to take. Collective challenged me to think differently about everything I'd ever been taught, and Judith knew it, though there'd be no concessions.

'Can you tell me how?' I asked softly.

'Do you want to be an artist, or do you want to be right?'

I felt the skin of my palm puncture from the pressure of my nails as I squeezed. The pain gave me a moment to breathe.

'It always needs something,' Judith said. She turned to her bookshelf, selected a slight book and placed it in my hands. *The Empty Space* by the British director Peter Brook. 'Find it.'

Judith opened the door to her office. I nodded and walked out.

Self-loathing engulfed me. In the bathroom on the lower ground, I retched up clear liquid. Judith's insight felt too personal, piercing the parts of myself that I tried to conceal. It was as though she knew exactly where I bruised, as if she'd once endured the same.

I called Saxon. On his doorstep, our bodies fused, and we tumbled into his bed soon after. The comfort of him brought me back.

I pulled the book from my bag and read beside him beneath crumpled sheets.

'Did Judith give that to you?' Saxon asked, rolling towards me. 'She gave it to me once too.' Before I could ask when they'd had a private tutorial of their own, he pulled me to him, took the book from my hands and began to read aloud. After a while, the words lost all sense and were replaced completely with the heaviness of sleep. *It always needs something*: my last thought before drifting into nothingness.

—

Under Yates's direction, the Viola in *Twelfth Night* rose to the challenge of the role and fell from it just as rapidly. The second year—Scarlett—was a woman I'd never spoken to but admired from afar. Her auburn hair was always curled, her shoulder-padded dresses distinctive. She had a whiff of Sylvie about her, only she seemed sturdier, less transcendent. Within four weeks of rehearsals, she vanished from the school, leaving only a note taped to the noticeboard in the atrium. On the morning of her departure, students hovered around it.

'Had it coming.'

'Psychotic bitch.'

'Glutton for punishment.'

I felt vaguely disgusted, exceedingly interested. I pushed to the front and read the note: '*I was sleeping with Yates—*'

A hand in front of my face, the note torn apart.

'Back to class!' Genevieve growled. 'Go on, shoo!'

'Lucky you're in first year,' Emmet said beside me.

I turned to him sharply. 'Assuming I'd bite.'

He gave me a derisive smile. 'Whatever helps you sleep at night, princess.'

I didn't know yet how to deal with him, how to meet his acid asides with a similarly biting retort. I waited until he was out of sight before heading up the stairs for Movement class.

Scarlett was not reinstated as Viola. She was recast as Maria the maid. I chose not to delve into the implicit warning.

V

The entire afternoon had been set aside for the second-year contemporary scene studies. Mostly, the students had rehearsed alone, making use of their training, an opportunity to prove they were capable of working autonomously.

Dylan was beside himself with excitement. He and I stayed close, weaving through the cohort between performances, between spaces, holding a crumpled sheet of A4 paper—our map.

Quinn walked among us with a regal, caustic air, dressed, as always, in white. Students parted for her like the sea, our Messiah.

Every so often I got a glimpse of Sylvie. She walked alone or beside Quinn, rarely interacting with her peers. I never saw her at the Malthouse. But then again, I rarely saw third years there anymore, not even the ones who'd seemed keen in the beginning to impart their wisdom. When I did encounter them, they looked tired. Worn out.

'How's *Victory* going?' I heard someone ask as we moved through the door of a storage room on the ground floor.

'I don't know, mate,' came the reply. 'I don't know.'

Dylan gripped my hand and tugged me to the ground. We sat cross-legged on cold cement. Dylan spread the sheet of paper out on his knee and pointed.

Anya and Blake / storeroom / *Blasted* by Sarah Kane

The light swelled as people entered. There was nothing in the space except for an old, stained mattress. A stereo played atmospheric sound—dripping water, the humming of a ventilator. It was disconcerting. A day ago, the storage area had been a colourful junkyard of abandoned props and set pieces; now it had been configured as a barren hotel room.

The door shut, and for a moment we sat in complete darkness. The exuberant chatter of the students was doused with the light. We'd been briefed prior: *Respect the actors.* We were in their space, witnessing their work as the artists they saw themselves as, for the first time.

The door opened again. Anya walked through us and stepped over a tripod that lay on the floor: a flimsy partition between her and the audience. Anya's scene partner, Blake, was a short but sturdy man with a bald head and thin-rimmed glasses. He cut an imposing figure as he followed behind her. The pair stood opposite one another as the door shut again. An orange glow filled the room as a second-year student manipulated the light from a freestanding lamp so that shadows were cast on the actors' faces. The effect was foreboding, adding to the tension that spread between them. When they spoke, it was as if they'd been standing there forever, living and breathing in a world separate from ours.

Suddenly I saw Anya beyond how I knew her. She was transformed. The weight of her work was present, but not forced or too deeply felt. She sat comfortably inside the dialogue, as if the words were truly hers, spoken for the first time. I understood as I watched her how difficult it was to gain the trust of an audience, to suspend their disbelief. It was a gift for us, to be transported like that from one world to another over the course of an afternoon. I felt Dylan beside me, breathless, and I knew he felt the same thing, that we'd talk about it, pull it apart, try to implement our new understanding into the work we were doing with Judith. Reinspired.

A collection of companies sat on the steps by the building's entrance at the end of the afternoon with bottles of cheap red pilfered from the bar by a second year who had a key.

I leaned back on my elbows and looked up at the grey sky, my legs stretched in front of me. The alcohol wiping away any threat of tomorrow, any doubt.

Dylan never came for drinks anymore. He usually left early, always opting to drive. But tonight, he drank with me. Stayed with the pack. His girlfriend must have given him a leave pass. I rested my head on his shoulder and felt anger towards this phantom woman. *She's suffocating him*, I thought; Dylan's youth wiped away by his girlfriend's inability to understand the path he'd chosen. She was studying to be an engineer.

Eventually we peeled away from the steps and moved en masse towards the city, leaning into one another, holding hands, it didn't matter whose.

We climbed the narrow stairs between a chemist and a kebab shop on Swanston to a dive bar that smelled of cigarettes and stale beer; the kind of place they took a hose to at the end of the night.

It was early, happy hour extended until eight, and the place was busy because of it. Saxon placed a bottle of beer in my hand

and watched me pull from it. Bodies pressed into us from either side. I reached around his neck, brought him close and kissed him hungrily.

The bathrooms were along a short corridor past the bar. I tugged at his belt and led him to the ladies room. I pushed the door open with an elbow and stopped still at the sight of her. Sylvie raised her head from the sink and scrunched up her nose.

'Sorry,' I said, as though it weren't a public place.

Sylvie looked between Saxon and me slowly. 'This is the ladies.' She extended her arm, a rolled-up twenty between her thumb and forefinger. Saxon stepped past me and took it. He said something in a low voice that I couldn't hear. Sylvie laughed. He bent to the basin and snorted.

'Thanks,' Saxon said when he was done.

'It's Maeve, isn't it?' Sylvie asked and offered me another note.

'I'm fine.'

Sylvie shrugged. 'Long day, no?'

I realised her version of the afternoon was very different from my own. She'd been bored by it.

'Good, right?' Sylvie said to Saxon.

'You got a number?' he asked.

Sylvie retrieved her phone from the snakeskin purse that hung over her shoulder. 'Guard it with your life.'

I stood there mute, watching them transfer the number from her phone to his, heads bent close, talking low. It dawned on me that they knew each other. Dylan's words floated back to me. *Pay attention, Maeve.*

I retreated from the bathroom. Saxon called my name, but I wanted to leave before he found me, before my hurt faded.

'Barker. I mean, how do you even begin to pull that apart?'

Dylan was drunk, I could tell by the way he moved his hands to his flushed face as he spoke. The second year he stood with looked past him, past me, for an exit, and I felt embarrassed for us both. Kids, whose world was so small all they had to talk about was the work.

'I'm gonna go,' I said into the space between them. Dylan kept talking, didn't draw breath. I left him there.

The street was cold. I ducked around bodies moving hurriedly in both directions and darted around trams, ignoring the ding-dinging of angry drivers. I jumped on the number 1 just as the doors were closing.

'Careful there,' a man said and offered me his hand.

I took it. 'Thanks.'

He pulled me up the stairs and onto a seat. 'Are you all right?' Only then did I realise I was crying. I left my hand in his. He was well dressed. Handsome. Familiar somehow, this total stranger. Generic. 'You shouldn't be alone,' he told me, and suggested a drink. I agreed, ignoring the buzz of my phone.

We got off the tram and walked along Elgin Street to a pool bar on Brunswick. I knew it; I'd been there with Saxon.

I listened to the man talk. His world was so very different from my own. There was comfort in it. A nine-to-five job, his own car. A starter home around the corner. Would I like to see it?

Sure.

The man looked at my wineglass. I'd emptied it quickly. 'One for the road?'

It broke the spell, the reality of what another drink might lead to. When his back was turned, I ran. Out of the bar, along residential streets and past suits on their way home from work.

The cold air slapped my face, but I felt warm in my joints, the drink like armour against the night.

Back in my apartment, I sat on the floor of my shower and let the hot water scald my back, unable to make sense of my anger. There'd been no fight, no accusations and yet something in me felt crushed under the weight of a new understanding. There were questions I'd not asked, not known I *should* ask. Drama school, Melbourne, the world—so much bigger than I'd realised.

—

Nick Cave played through the stereo. It was the last exercise of the day.

Five of us stood in a straight line, looking out over the rest of the company. Heaving and keeling over, repeating the movement out of sync. Over time, the sequence built and burst into a run. Like animals let loose we charged at the walls, at one another, waiting for someone to make an offer. And it was me.

'By Gis, and by Saint Charity,
Alack, and fie for shame!
Young men will do't if they come to't,
By Cock, they are to blame.
Quoth she, "Before you tumbled me,
You promised me to wed."
So would I ha' done, by yonder sun,
An thou hadst not come to my bed.'

The buried text came from nowhere. I played with it. Repeated it. Danced to it, a melody of its own.

Saxon punctuated the verse with a grunt. Then another. He fell to the floor and curled himself into a ball as though attacked by an invisible assailant. Vivien stopped running. She walked in front of me, caught my eye, reached forward and pinched my cheek, hard. The pain was excruciating; I elongated Ophelia's words to bear it, determined not to show any weakness.

'*Alack, and fie for shame!*' Vivien said belligerently, and released her hold on my cheek when I repeated the line. Then she took up the role of aggressor from the opposite side of the space and began to simulate a beating of Saxon. Breath engulfed my brain with the relief of being set free, and I spoke the text with maniacal elation.

The rest picked up the sequence again. Heaving and keeling over, to the sound of Vivien's laboured breathing and Saxon's body as it slapped against the floorboards.

There was a silent acknowledgement between us as we stepped out of the light. Satisfaction in our exhaustion. We'd been listening.

Imogen leaned towards me while the others debriefed.

'Where'd that come from?' she asked.

'I don't know,' I replied. Though some part of me felt it, the culmination of days, a readiness I wasn't sure I'd arrive at.

'And Vivien?' Imogen whispered.

'Out of nowhere,' I said in disbelief.

I'd taken the lead and, with the concession of my pain, Vivien had let me.

—

'Is he smart enough for you?' Richard asked then placed a dumpling in his mouth.

It was a small gathering, ten in total. We sat close around a circular table by the kitchen in the ground-floor dining room of the pink-walled dumpling house on Little Bourke Street.

'Fuck you,' I replied.

'Fuck *you*, darling.'

Everyone wanted to work with Saxon. He moved instinctively on the floor, leading when the story called for it or pulling back to allow others to find their place. Richard knew this. Intelligence could be measured in more ways than one.

Everyone wanted to work with Saxon. He moved instinctively on the floor, leading when the story called for it or pulling back to allow others to find their place. Richard knew this. Intelligence could be measured in more ways than one.

'Is this retaliation?'

Richard smiled at me as he chewed. 'For what?'

'Seriously?' I scoffed.

'I just wonder whether you're stimulated.'

'Want to join us sometime? Find out for yourself?'

Richard took my hand. The game was up. 'I'm happy for you.'

I turned to Saxon. He was looking at the floor, nodding as Emmet spoke at him with both hands. We hadn't discussed my abrupt departure a few nights earlier. I was both relieved and annoyed; part of me was spoiling for a fight, wanting to call him out for something I didn't quite understand.

'And you?' I asked, turning back to Richard. 'Did you give her a commitment ring or something? She's sharing the limelight.'

Richard, caught mid-sip, spat wine across his plate. I laughed as he gasped for air.

'Touché,' he said.

We understood one another.

Vivien surrendering on the floor during Collective wasn't what Judith had called growth, or a leap in our development as artists. Rather, Vivien saw me as less of a threat because of my failure to participate in the weeks leading up to that session. And, as per her stipulation, Richard and I no longer spent time together alone, a sign that he valued his relationship with her more than his friendship with me.

'That's bullshit,' Emmet said loudly, slamming his fist on the table, gaining the attention of the room.

'Come on, mate,' Saxon said.

Emmet thrust a finger in his face.

'What's going on?' I asked quietly.

Richard stood and at the same time so did Emmet, pushing his chair back into a passing waiter. Dishes cracked against the floor. Emmet didn't stop to apologise; he fled. Richard ran after him.

Vivien rushed to the door and looked out. 'They're gone,' she said.

She returned to the table and retrieved her phone. She keyed in a number then pressed the phone to her ear as she paced.

Imogen took napkins from the table and spread them along the lino beneath it, apologising to the waiter as she mopped up noodles. Saxon kneeled to help her, and I did too.

'What happened?' I asked.

Saxon kept his eyes on the floor. 'Not sure.'

Imogen smiled at the waiter. 'Thank you. Sorry.'

'He just flipped,' Saxon said.

Imogen redirected her attention. 'He's been doing that lately.'

'Really?' I felt out of the loop.

Imogen flicked her eyes towards mine but dropped them again quickly and spoke to the waiter. 'We'll pay for'—she gestured to the mess of noodles on the floor—'all of this.'

'He was talking about a play he'd seen once that Quinn had directed,' Saxon said.

Imogen groaned. 'Fuck.'

'I said, "That must have been something." Then he—'

'Went off on a rant,' Imogen said. It was a statement, not a question.

'Yeah,' Saxon replied.

'They're at Meyers Place Bar,' Vivien said, finishing her call.

155

The others were working their way through the dishes left on the table as Imogen, Saxon, Vivien and I threw notes down and left.

We found Richard and Emmet at the back of the bar. A bottle of red, already half drunk, sat atop a small table between them. Richard had his back to us as we approached. Emmet was despondent, his head bent low, legs crossed at the knees, spine curled.

Vivien leaned over and kissed Richard on the ear, then she rubbed Emmet's back and took a seat beside him. I'd never seen her be that solicitous with anyone.

Emmet lifted his head but didn't raise his eyes as we joined them. 'Sorry about all that,' he muttered.

We were quick to reassure him. *Forget about it. No problem. It happens.* We left it there, ordering more wine and getting drunker than we expected to.

It was two am when we stumbled out onto Bourke Street.

Saxon ran his palm from my tailbone to the nape of my neck and held it there. 'I'm going to get this one to bed,' he said, nodding at Emmet, who was slumped against a lamp-post.

'I'll help you,' I said.

'Nah,' Saxon said. 'Best you don't.'

'Are we good?' I asked.

Saxon looked troubled. 'He's been sleeping in his car. Couldn't make rent.'

I was too selfishly preoccupied with what Saxon might be thinking about us to summon up much empathy. 'Oh.'

'We're taking him to Richard's.' Saxon kissed me on the forehead and turned away.

I reached for his fingers and tugged at them. 'I'll see you tomorrow?' *Saturday.* I moved closer and brushed my nose against his cheek in a bid for intimacy.

"Course, Juliet.'

He got into the back of a cab with Richard and Vivien. Emmet was in the front seat, his head propped against the window.

I watched as they drove away.

Imogen pulled an open bottle of white wine from her handbag and gave it to me. 'Nightcap?'

I sloshed the liquid against my lips.

'*Why, sir, for my part I say the gentleman had drunk himself out of his five sentences,*' Imogen slurred.

'Hypocrite.'

Imogen laughed. 'Come on.' She held my hand and walked me to the corner of Lygon and Grattan. 'Text me,' she said: our shorthand for the promise of announcing ourselves home safe.

'Always,' I replied.

Imogen stumbled into the darkness, jumped lightly and clicked her heels together. A gesture for me alone. I applauded.

VI

'You're late.'

I looked at my wrist, at an imaginary watch. 'Am I?'

The tech ushered me out of the doorway. 'Lizzy.'

I extended my hand. 'Maeve.'

Lizzy didn't take it; she waved for me to follow her instead. She had short, curly hair, a round face and broad shoulders. Like me, she was dressed in black, our uniform for the evening.

Production students from our sister school were assigned plays like we were assigned scripts. Lizzy would be assessed on her skills as a production manager, her chosen field of study. The stakes were just as high for her as for the second years who'd be performing *Much Ado About Nothing* to a paying audience for the first time.

I was taken aback by the transformation of Performance Space B, though there was little visually to be impressed by. It was more the feeling of stepping into a sacred space. The energy was different from what flowed through the halls outside of it.

'So'—Lizzy threw an arm out—'the set.'

Two demountable seating banks had been assembled in an L-shape to create a square performance space. From behind, it looked like a mistake. The budget for set design was minimal in second year; the effect of light and sound was the only real way to elevate the story beyond performance.

The floorboards had been kept bare, and the only set piece was a platform painted to resemble marble steps. Half-a-dozen students were warming up on it. Rhett walked between them, reading glasses perched at the end of his nose. He held a small notebook in his hands and referred to it as he spoke to the cast. Lizzy walked with purpose, weaving through bodies in motion while I tried to avoid being hit in the face by a flying forearm.

'Backstage.' Lizzy flung back the edge of a heavy curtain to reveal a narrow area, dim apart from a blue light that shone beneath a row of chairs against the wall. Above them, a window overlooked the street, a reminder of where we were. A clashing of real and imaginary worlds.

I caught a glimpse of the labelled costumes hanging from a steel rail before stepping out into the bright light again at the opposite end of backstage.

'That's it. If you need me, I'll be here.' Lizzy took a seat behind the lighting desk. There was a collection of empty Diet Coke cans and loose paper strewn across it. She lifted a headset to her ear and propped it there. 'Questions?'

'Where do I sit?'

Lizzy pointed to the seating bank and looked down at the lighting desk. My cue to get going.

'Thanks.'

'Wait until quarter to seven then head downstairs,' Lizzy said without raising her head. 'Call out: "*Much Ado*". Hold the lift, get the patrons up here. Check their tickets. Do it once more, then give me the all-clear. No latecomers. You good?'

I nodded.

Usher had been printed on an A4 sheet of paper and stuck to the fabric of the last chair of the first row, a torch beneath it. I sat and watched the actors warm up. There was a certainty to how they moved, to how they prepared themselves; not one version resembled what I was currently learning. They'd cobbled together a warm-up that worked for them and appeared unperturbed by the presence of Rhett as he observed and gave notes for the impending performance.

'Maeve!' Rhett called from across the room.

The last time we'd seen each other was in Brisbane at my audition. I had an answer prepared, in case he asked me how I was, how I was finding drama school. *It is more than anything I could ever have expected.*

I sat up a little straighter and waved. 'Hi!'

Rhett nodded, then turned back to his cast.

You're an egotist, Emmet had said. I watched Rhett with his actors and was reminded of my place: a first year, an usher.

I hadn't been particularly excited about sitting through two and a half hours of Shakespeare. Not that I had anything to compare it to other than the second-year scene studies the week before. I'd never seen a Shakespearean play performed live in its entirety. I had a vague feeling that it would be laboured, that the text would be an encumbrance to the story. But Rhett's direction allowed for the actors' choices to flourish, and I lost myself in the connections made between them. The plot was clear, the dialogue rich. I noted my naivety; I'd absorbed the opinions of the general public. Skill was what set a strong production apart from a poor one, and audiences had endured too many of the latter.

Time passed quickly and I was surprised when the house lights rose.

I guided the patrons to the exit and waved at Lizzy when the last one left. Fluorescent lights flickered above the rig, and students appeared from behind the black curtain in various stages of undress. They hugged one another and pulled at their costumes, talking over the fading exit music.

'You're relieved of your duties,' Lizzy said to me, peeling her headset away from her ears.

'Thank you,' I said and snuck another look at the actors.

They had formed a circle on the floor. Rhett dragged over a chair to join them. They held notebooks at the ready and laughed together at a private joke.

Rhett clapped his hands and said, 'Congratulations.'

—

Emmet moved in with Richard permanently. He slept on the couch and kept his possessions tucked away in a small cardboard box beside it, a duvet cover folded neatly on top. No one mentioned it. No one even sat on the couch when they visited, opting for the floor instead—a gesture made for his sake. We tiptoed around the gloom that had engulfed him, careful not to appear too upbeat, masking our own feelings in case they offended his.

Emmet had a tendency towards cruelty. He'd call us self-indulgent when we spoke about class, or judgemental when we picked apart the work of a company member.

'We're actors, for god's sake,' Richard said one evening as Imogen, Vivien, Saxon and I sat around his living room floor eating slow-cooked lamb ragu.

'Not yet,' Emmet replied, then fell silent.

We tried to coax him back into the conversation, but he lay his head on a pillow and closed his eyes.

We stopped visiting for a while after that.

—

The third years were exhausted well before opening night and seemed indifferent to the success of *Victory*, though they were vocal about their collective wish to never have to perform it again. There was a physical and mental cost for what Quinn had extracted from them through her process, and they could no longer view what they'd achieved objectively. *Victory* was a work of ingenuity, Quinn's and theirs both. But it was a production that required something of an audience too—not participation exactly, but a willingness to be pushed. A rave review in *The Age* did little to boost ticket sales. The play was violent and confronting— and it was long. Only the truly dedicated remained for curtain call. It was salt in the wound for the third years that the company below them had managed to sell out both Shakespeare seasons with the name of Yates and the reputation of Rhett Lambert tied to each.

I volunteered to usher *Victory* three times. I was fascinated by the play and by Sylvie too. Something within her shone. It was as if she dipped into a deep well of knowledge, of life, in order to play her character, Devonshire, and it heightened the work of those on stage with her.

The last time I ushered for it, I stayed on past my duties to help with closing the bar. It was almost eleven when the cast of *Victory* emerged from the dressing rooms, the patrons having already made a run for it. I stole a glance at Sylvie, curled up beside Quinn on a couch in the foyer. They passed a glass of red between them and whispered like conspiring teenagers as the remaining cast filtered out.

'Juliet,' Sylvie called.

My heart thrummed. 'Sorry?'

Sylvie turned to Quinn. 'Perfect, no?'

'Indeed,' Quinn agreed. 'But we must keep this to ourselves.' She beckoned me over. 'Bring the wine!' she said as an after-thought, and I grabbed a bottle of red.

Sylvie presented me with an empty glass. 'Does it matter?'

'I can't be seen to be playing favourites,' Quinn replied, 'and your Juliet is still too fresh in the minds of those who saw it last year.'

I relaxed; Juliet was a reference to the work.

'Regine then, for the Ibsen Intensive,' Sylvie offered.

Quinn considered me. 'Come here.'

I took a step towards her.

'Lower.'

I kneeled. Up close, her lips were stained with wine, the whites of her eyes had a yellowish tint. I looked into them, unblinking.

'She needs a little more . . . life,' Quinn said. 'But *Ghosts* is certainly a possibility.'

Sylvie took a sip of her wine. 'So much can happen in a year.'

'As we well know,' Quinn replied.

Sylvie reached for me. 'Join us,' she suggested.

But I pleaded exhaustion. Theirs was a conversation locked off to me by my inhibition, a fear that their perception of me might diminish if I spoke. *They're just people*, I reminded myself, *no more worthy of reverence than anyone else*, but I didn't really believe it.

'Give us a little Juliet then, before you go,' Quinn said.

Sylvie inspected her glass, ran her thumb around the rim.

'I—I haven't warmed up,' I replied clumsily.

'Act three, scene two: that was your audition piece, was it not?'

'Yes.'

'Well, you couldn't possibly have known how to warm up properly back then.'

The wine bottle was heavy in my hands. I stood and placed it on the ground beside me. But I couldn't summon the words.

'*Gallop apace*,' Sylvie offered.

'Yes, thank you.'

Their stillness brought back the humiliation of the audition room. How bare I felt, how *exposed*. Then, as if breaking point were the true and only place I could begin from, the words came. Not confidently, though; not enough to hold their attention. Quinn relaxed into the back of the sofa and began speaking to Sylvie again. I looked above Sylvie's beautiful head, noted the tension in her neck: a small concession; she couldn't ignore me completely.

'Closing up!' a security guard called out.

'Jacob, my dear, we won't be a moment,' Quinn responded, charm personified.

The man melted in her presence, nodded. 'Sure Ms Medina, I'll wait outside.'

Once he was gone, Quinn turned to me. 'Never speak unless true impulse propels you to.'

Fear slithered up my spine. 'I didn't want to keep you waiting—'

Quinn closed her eyes, impatient. 'Never.'

'Yes,' I replied, submissive.

'You have an energy'—Quinn stood and prodded my chest with her fingers, caging my heart—'here. With discipline you could refine it.' She nodded slowly. 'The Collective showing will be very revealing.' She took the wineglass from Sylvie and sipped from it. 'Now, finish up.'

'*Lovers can see to do*—'

'Not the bloody *monologue*,' Quinn hissed. 'Your duties. *The bar.*'

I worked quickly.

Sylvie looked ahead blankly as Quinn called commands.

There's a smear. Use a cloth. Cork the wine.

When I'd shuttered the bar, I addressed her with as much self-possession as I could muster. 'Goodnight.'

Quinn eyed me. 'Yes, goodnight,' she said and resumed her conversation with Sylvie.

I hurried away, the hushed voices of the women fading as I slipped through the exit.

I took even, measured steps until I made it across Kings Way, then I ran, fleeing the shame of Quinn's contempt, holding on to the crumb of Sylvie's suggestion instead, an idea the head of school hadn't dismissed. The Ibsen Intensive. Second year a near possibility.

VII

We began as we always did, along the edge of the light, sweating under our black clothes from an hour spent shaking in the darkness. The difference was we weren't preparing to play, we were preparing to perform.

The cohort entered behind us. We didn't acknowledge their presence, or Judith's either, as she outlined the Collective work we'd been focusing on all term. Instead, we tried to centre ourselves and harness our adrenaline.

There were six pieces in total, a short catalogue, reworked for performance from what we'd done during class. We rose five at a time and sat down again after our allotted three and a half minutes on the floor. A few, including me, performed more than once, so when Emmet went rogue it didn't affect my chances of passing too greatly, although it pissed me off no end. Dylan, however, had one opportunity to impress the staff, and his performance was compromised when Emmet didn't appear beside him as rehearsed, leaving him to improvise. Saxon took Emmet's place, reciting what he could remember from the duologue—a stream of consciousness about war, brotherhood, expectation and loss. It had differed each time Emmet and Dylan rehearsed it, but there were moments, phrases that Judith had picked out, turning points for the supporting cast to follow, as they made repetitive gestures around the space behind the two men. In class, the climax of the piece had been when Emmet broke out of the text to run around the space as Dylan shouted his name. Saxon replicated it as best he could. But key moments had been muddled.

Dylan was devastated.

The space cleared and we debriefed with Judith. If there had been an incident, an accidental misstep, usually she'd address it. But in this case she said nothing; Emmet's disruption of the work was too terrible to acknowledge.

Once she'd left we started to bump out the space. The lights had to come off the rig, the props had to be taken to the storeroom. Dylan didn't move. He stood glaring at the floor, fists clenched.

Emmet hit the ground without any of us seeing how. It was only when Dylan jumped on top of him that we realised what was happening. Emmet didn't defend himself. He let Dylan hit him again and again.

'Don't touch me!' Dylan yelled as Richard pulled him off.

Emmet rolled onto his side and began to laugh. I kneeled beside him. Blood pooled and seeped into my black pants.

'What can I do?' I asked.

Emmet ignored me and spat blood. I recoiled and stood up again.

'No one says a fucking word!' Richard threatened. 'Not to Judith, not to anyone!'

'He provoked me!' Dylan screamed.

'No, he didn't.'

'On the floor! You were all there.'

'Doesn't matter,' Richard said.

Dylan was indignant. 'He needs to be held accountable.'

'Keep quiet,' Richard warned.

'So it's okay for him to sabotage my performance?' Dylan asked. He lurched at Emmet again but Saxon held him back. 'You might not care, but I want to be here!'

Emmet cackled.

'What's so fucking funny?'

'Not a word,' Richard repeated and led Dylan to the door. One by one we followed, leaving Emmet to mop up his own blood.

'Am I wrong?' Dylan asked, once we were outside. He looked like a kid, holding on to the straps of his backpack with both hands.

'I don't know,' I replied.

'Was it bad?'

'He was bleeding quite a lot.'

'Not that,' Dylan said. 'I meant the work.' He flicked his head sideways to shake the curls from his eyes. It was a gesture I'd seen a hundred times before, but now I saw it for what it was: a nervous tic. I understood what he was asking me and why. I'd be anxious too if I were in his position.

'You're fine,' I said. 'The scene was solid.'

Dylan smiled. 'Thanks.'

I'd said what he needed to hear. To continue with a scene when a fellow actor had failed to participate would count in his favour. A company member with that kind of stamina was worth holding on to, if the work was strong. And it was.

—

Half of the company were given warnings. They hadn't failed, but they hadn't passed either. It created an invisible division.

We were aware of the expectations. Do the work. Don't get sick. Don't skip class. Make critique without judgement, back your sentiment on the floor. But it was all subjective and the only opinions that really mattered were those of the faculty. If they believed something was missing, then it was—that *something* being an indefinable quality present in some, lacking in most. The kind of talent that was impossible to turn away from.

In an office on the first floor, I sat before them. The staff talked—of course they did. Nevertheless, it was a shock to hear them comment on my performance in classes they hadn't taught themselves. Quinn mentioned the Collective showing as an illustration of my ability.

'You listen with your body,' she said, 'present and aware.' Then she winked, as though to remind me of the impromptu Juliet performance in the foyer—and my degradation.

There were murmurs of agreement. After that, I knew I'd avoided a warning and held on to the rest of their notes lightly.

I left the room, walking quickly past the company members loitering by the staircase, commiserating with each other.

Imogen grabbed my arm. 'How'd you go?'

When I smiled, her shoulders fell. 'Congratulations,' she said, clearly disappointed. The gap between us in the ranks of the company had widened.

'Thanks.'

She shook her head. 'Don't ask.'

'I won't,' I said, relieved.

'Drink?'

It was mid-afternoon; the Malthouse bar had only just opened when I ordered a bottle of red for us to share. Imogen launched into an analysis of her review with the faculty, trying to piece it together in a way that made sense to her. I couldn't tell her what I really thought: that she was talented but not altogether watchable.

'They gave me the "we want more from you" speech, like I haven't given it my fucking all this past semester.' She lit a ciga-rette, the habit having grown over the course of the term. 'What I don't understand is how they assess us. I mean, how do they, really?'

I said nothing.

'Sorry, sorry,' Imogen said. 'Listen to me: what a bore.'

'You're not.'

'Yes, I am.' Imogen took a drag. 'Emmet says he'll quit.'

I didn't even pretend to be shocked. 'Yeah.'

'Fucking shame.'

'The pressure?' I asked.

Imogen frowned. 'Richard didn't tell you?'

Richard didn't tell me much anymore. 'No.'

'His friend passed away.' Imogen nodded towards the drama building. 'The girl who trained with Quinn.'

I remembered Emmet's argument with Dylan outside the Australian Centre for Contemporary Art, the many hints he had dropped but never elaborated on.

'That's fucking awful.'

'Yeah,' Imogen said. 'She'd been in a bad place for a while.'

We fell silent for a moment, watched the dirt in the courtyard blow about in the wind.

'Why do we do it to ourselves?' Imogen asked. 'Become actors?'

'Because we can't do anything else?'

Imogen laughed so hard she began to cough. 'Fuck's sake!'

Saxon walked towards us. He had his hands in his pockets, shoulders shrugged to his ears. He reminded me of the photo of Bob Dylan walking down the street with a girl on his arm. All I needed to do was insert myself beside him.

'Hi,' Saxon said. He reached for my hand and pulled me to standing. 'I'm going to take this one home before Anya's,' he said to Imogen. 'You okay with that?'

It was strange to see them converse casually like this. They had nothing in common outside drama school and me. Their antipathy was obvious in how their bodies tensed when they were forced to interact.

"Course,' Imogen responded.

But I was worried about leaving her. 'You sure?'

Imogen shooed me away. 'Go on!'

I bent to kiss her, an apology. 'Bye.'

Imogen kept her cheek tilted to the sky. I rested mine against it briefly and felt her savour the softness of it.

I stepped back. Saxon opened his coat. Wrapped in his warmth, I pressed my head against his chest as we walked. I could hear the thud of his heart. It muffled the sounds of the city.

'We celebrating?' I asked.

'You bet,' he replied.

But we didn't stop at a bar or talk about our reviews. We sat quietly and watched the commuters raise their collars against the early-winter afternoon through the foggy glass of the tram window. Then we were at his door, in his bed, our skin exposed to the cool air.

Saxon lay a worn patchwork quilt on top of me afterwards. It smelled of him, of wood smoke and the back of the cupboard. I lay on my back and watched the creeping shadows of the afternoon dance along the ceiling. The embroidery scratched my shoulder: his name in the top right-hand corner of the quilt.

'Who made this for you?' I asked, running my fingers back and forth over his name. I could feel him looking at me, deciding whether to respond.

'My mother,' he said finally.

'Where is she?' I asked carefully.

Saxon propped himself up on his elbow and thumbed the lettering. 'Overseas, I think. I'm not really sure.'

I knew which beer he liked to drink, which writers he preferred, but I still knew nothing about his life before drama school; nothing about the woman in the picture beside his bed.

'Tell me,' I said gently.

'Nothing to tell.'

He kissed my collarbone then rolled off the bed and pulled his jeans on. I heard him walk down the hall and open the fridge. A bottle top clicked against the countertop.

I studied the quilt. The gold stitching was hand sewn, darkened in places from wear. I sat up and looked at the individual squares. Inside each was an embroidered object. A footy. A teddy bear. A heart. I pulled the quilt around me and tried to imagine the woman who'd made it. There was an intimacy in being enveloped in something like that. It made me think of my own family. Of the worth of things.

Saxon appeared in the doorway and handed me a beer. He waited for me to have a sip then said, 'Stay with me through winter.'

'Okay,' I replied, like his offer was no big deal, though we both knew how much weight it held. I rarely stayed the night. Not that Saxon had ever asked me to leave—but he'd never asked me to stay either.

'We should get going,' he said.

I dropped the quilt and exposed myself. 'Okay.'

Saxon stepped towards me and cupped my skull with both hands. I leaned into them, bared my neck.

I watched myself as it happened, as I pulled him back onto the bed and rolled on top of him, as I closed my eyes and arched my back.

His invitation conjuring a lascivious character from the depths within myself.

Stay with me through winter.

—

It was the kind of party that rolled like the ocean. Rooms filled then emptied all at once, a cycle of new faces and abandoned goodbyes.

I felt light as I passed between second years who knew my name. I understood what that meant. Word had got out. I was one of a small group of first years who had excelled that semester. I held value.

Emboldened by the night, I asked if I could try it. Sylvie watched on as Saxon held my hair back, the three of us squeezed into the upstairs bathroom by the staircase of Anya's share house in Brunswick. The powder burned my nose, tasted metallic. It turned to paste and slid down my throat.

'Yeah?' Saxon asked.

'Yeah,' I responded.

Sylvie bent and snorted her line. She twitched her nose at her reflection above the vanity. Her eyes flicked to my own. 'Babe.' Sylvie turned and tilted my chin upwards with the tips of her fingers. Then she positioned me in front of the mirror. Small white crystals clung to the hairs inside my nostrils. I pulled at them.

'Here,' she said and handed me a lipstick from the back pocket of her vintage Levi's. She watched me apply it then took it back, a small current passing between us. Then she reapplied it to her own lips. I thought, *We look alike.* The red matched her shirt, a cowboy-style button-up. A version of Monroe in *The Misfits.* I told her so.

'Thank you,' she whispered and took my hand.

The powder forged a closeness, and we moved through the party like old girlfriends, commenting on everything we saw, a focused intensity to the words that spilled from our mouths. She'd stroke my arm or rest her palm on my chest. 'Yes, yes,' she'd say. Then she'd tap her nose at the precise moment the surge would lull, and I'd follow her. Saxon would be there, leaning against the bathroom door, ready to begin the process all over again.

I felt indebted to Sylvie for including me, for the small act of intimacy that continued to repeat itself.

'Should I give her something? Pay her for it?' I asked Saxon, looking from one golden eye to the other.

He ignored the question and began to recite Poe's 'Eldorado'. Students flanked us where we sat on a calico couch, stained and overstuffed. On the floor, by the fire, along every wall, they smoked and swore and sang along to the music that pumped out of a tinny CD player on the scratched veneer coffee table. Saxon spoke above it.

I pressed my forehead against his. 'Saxon?' But he was in a trance. He quickened the pace of the poem and surged towards the final line with my face in his hands.

Where did you learn that? I wanted to ask. *Who taught you?* I racked my brain for a poem I knew by heart. I couldn't think of one. I felt paranoid and wanted to return to an earlier feeling.

'More,' I said.

Saxon knew what I meant. He smiled and lifted me from the couch. I straddled him as he carried me through the doorway, to space, to cooler air, to Sylvie in the kitchen doing lines with Yates.

'You never took me up on my offer,' Yates said when he saw me.

The coke was cut up on the laminex countertop beside the microwave. Sylvie bent over it, offered Yates a rolled note once she'd finished and took a sip from a chipped mug. I looked around for Richard, for my friends, but we were alone. There was no need for privacy now.

'*The Importance of Being Earnest,*' Yates said when I didn't respond. 'Sylvie joined me instead.'

Sylvie lifted her mug to Yates and smiled. I felt behind me for Saxon. He draped his arms over my shoulders and pulled me into him. Yates looked from my face to Saxon's and back again.

'Did Quinn really find you roaming Carlton Gardens in the middle of the night?' Yates asked Sylvie, though his eyes were still on mine.

Sylvie laughed. 'I wondered when that little rumour might resurface.'

He turned to her. 'That's what you told people, isn't it?'

'That and various other things.'

'Such as?' Yates bent over the countertop again and snorted.

'That I'd been abducted by an avant-garde theatre troupe,'
Sylvie said.

'Imaginative.'

'Thank you.'

Though there was a playfulness to Yates's manner, his questioning felt intrusive. I could sense how much sat beneath the surface.

'So, which is it then?' Yates asked. 'Don't leave us hanging.'

Sylvie ignored him and raised her face to the ceiling. I thought she might be trying to conceal something, to keep tears in their ducts by way of gravity. But then she began to sway, moving to a beat only she could hear. Yates started to clap.

'Are we out?' Anya asked, having appeared from nowhere.

'No,' Sylvie said, continuing with the movement.

Saxon produced a small clear bag half full of granular white powder and shook it.

Anya snatched it and blew a kiss. 'My saviour!' she said and skipped out of the kitchen.

Saxon leaned towards Sylvie and spoke quietly. 'Come on.'

Sylvie shook her head as though trying to release something from it then walked down the hallway carrying her mug.

There were two lines left. Yates pressed the note into my hand. I recoiled. The note fell to the floor. Saxon picked it up and handed it back to me.

'Who says chivalry is dead?' Yates quipped, plucking the note from my hand.

I became inflated with irrational rage. 'How's Scarlett?'

Yates turned to Saxon. 'Control your *fille*.'

'Get top marks for participation, did she?'

Saxon took my hand. 'Juliet . . .'

Yates gave me a scathing look. 'Yes, actually. She did.'

I'd been astounded by Scarlett's interpretation of the maid in *Twelfth Night*. But I understood now that the world-weariness she'd embodied had not been a choice, as I'd assumed. Yates, the vivisector, had impaired her.

Black heart, I thought I heard Saxon say, and I saw the iconoclastic image of Jesus with the flaming heart. 'Yes!' I said with unrestrained laughter. 'Furnace of ardent love, turned to ash!'

Yates pointed the rolled note at me. 'Out of her fucking mind.'

Saxon ushered me out of the kitchen as Yates snorted back the powder. 'Not worth it,' he said in a low voice. 'Don't fucking go there.'

My laughter faded. 'She was so good,' I said.

Saxon intuited my meaning, 'Yeah, she was great.' He stopped me at the doorway to the living room. 'You will be too.'

His assurance like a flare through my centre. Scarlett was forgotten. 'I want you,' I said.

Saxon dipped me into a kiss.

'Knock it off!' Emmet called and we were forced to re-enter the fray. He sat on the couch, bent over the coffee table, emptying the contents of Saxon's bag. He raised it to his mouth and inserted his tongue, eyeing me as he did so. A greeting. We hadn't spoken since the Collective showing, but enough time had passed for it to have lost its charge. Here we were, at the end of a party, our presence proof of our worth beyond the curriculum.

Anya and Sylvie sprawled by the arch of the brickwork fireplace, close enough almost to be licked by the flames. Sylvie handed me her mug as Saxon pulled me to the floor. I gulped some vodka, then rested against his stomach. I'd lost the ability to speak in the presence of my friends; they appeared enlarged and extreme by all I'd consumed. But the feel of Saxon quelled a tension that had started to lock into my joints. He slipped his hands beneath my shirt and rested them against my rib cage, as if he knew.

'Do it for us!' Anya pleaded.

'No!' Sylvie cried.

Anya sat up on her knees. 'Why not?'

Yates appeared in the doorway. 'Why not, what?'

'Sylvie's been offered the role of Nora,' Anya replied, like it was her news to tell.

'*A Doll's House*,' Saxon said, impressed.

'At the Malthouse, next season,' Anya added.

'La-di-da!' Emmet trilled.

Yates hollered, 'Brava!'

'*Isn't there one thing that strikes you as strange in our sitting here like this?*' Anya quoted.

'Don't,' Sylvie whined.

'*We have been married now eight years,*' Anya continued. '*Does it not occur to you that this is the first time we two, you and I, husband and wife, have had a serious conversation?*'

Yates lay on the floor, leaning back on his elbows. 'This is brilliant—how it should be done.'

'Half-cut in the north?' Sylvie asked.

'Half?' Emmet sneered.

'Absolutely!' Yates replied.

'*In all these eight years—longer than that—from the very beginning of our acquaintance—*'

'Have you accepted?' Yates asked.

'I haven't decided yet,' Sylvie said.

'You're insane,' Emmet remarked.

Sylvie smiled. 'Thank you.'

Emmet shook his head. 'It's fucking Nora, for god's sake!'

'—*we have never exchanged a word on any serious subject.*'

'Tad obvious, don't you think?' Sylvie asked. 'I played her for the Ibsen Intensive last year.'

'A privilege,' Yates said.

Sylvie sighed dramatically. 'A bore.'

Emmet took another line. 'Snubbing Ibsen. Can't imagine.'

'Depends. Who's directing?' Yates asked.

'Unconfirmed,' Sylvie replied.

Yates lifted a half-empty wine bottle from the floor and drank from it. 'Interesting.'

'*You have never understood me.*'

'Bargaining tool?' Emmet asked.

'You think I have that kind of leverage?' Sylvie responded coquettishly.

'Yes,' Emmet said.

Sylvie grinned.

'*I have been greatly wronged. First by Papa, and then by you.*'

Sylvie turned to Yates. 'Free mid-March?'

'I'll check my schedule,' Yates replied.

Emmet grimaced. 'Toxic.'

'*You have never loved me. You have only thought it pleasant to be in love with me.*'

'You'll make it work,' Sylvie said.

Yates laughed.

Sylvie took up the text from Anya. '*Papa called me his doll-child, and he played with me just as I used to play with my dolls. And when I came to live with you . . .*'

The room quietened.

179

'I was simply transferred from Papa's hands into yours. You arranged everything according to your own taste, and so I got the same tastes as you—or else I pretended to— '

There was a quality to Sylvie's voice I couldn't place.

'I have existed merely to perform tricks for you.'

Then I realised. It wasn't her voice at all.

'But you would have it so.' Sylvie leaned towards Yates. 'You and Papa have committed a great sin against me.' Space stretched between phrases. 'It is your fault,' she whispered, almost crawling into his lap, 'that I have made nothing of my life.'

The crackle of the fire, the steady breath of a woman possessed.

Emmet exhaled. 'Jesus.'

Saxon tightened his grip on my rib cage.

Anya pulled Sylvie off Yates.

I drained the contents of the mug. 'You should do it.'

Sylvie reached for me. 'I just might.'

Her lipstick was cracked, felt rough against my lips. She kept her eyes open, observing me in the action of the kiss. When she drew away, I saw her, Nora, for a fleeting moment, as though the two of them had conspired to dismantle my innocence together. I can use this, I thought and felt a wave of gratitude for it, for whatever it was I was being let into.

TERM THREE

TEAM THREE

I

That winter, I saw everything as though through the gaze of an imaginary audience. What was the quality of Saxon's breath? How was I responding to it? Where was the repetition, the climax, the denouement of our days together?

The micro betrayed me. I couldn't sleep in the crook of his arm or kiss him in the morning without chewing on a stick of gum first. I kept a clean pair of underwear, a tube of mascara and a toothbrush in a ziplock pouch in my handbag, tidying myself up before he woke (a dress rehearsal), then lying down beside him again (the performance), to begin together.

The macro was far more redeeming. Long afternoons with a heavy, hidden sun, a bottle of red wine, something we could sink into, lulling us from one stretch of wakefulness to the next. I heard their voices, my lecturers, coaching me through those hours as though I could redo something, build on myself, day upon day upon day.

If I came across one of his housemates I'd nod politely. They didn't factor in to my version of our story; there was no need to engage. They were acquaintances. I baited him into an argument about lack of privacy, to see how it felt. Saxon knew; he endured the friction, aware of what lay beyond it—entanglement, our preferred state of exploration.

The rain was relentless; it hit us sideways and kept us mostly indoors, with the exception of Richard's dinner parties. Every couple of days we'd leave Saxon's room for a homemade meal better than anything we'd get from our grandmothers back home. Ravioli; fennel and mandarin salad; beef carpaccio; duck confit. There was always wine and, if Sylvie was around, a little something extra.

In July, I turned eighteen. There was pleasure to be had further down the city's alleyways, deeper inside the bars. No need to look over my shoulder anymore. It was all mine if I wanted it. I told myself that I did.

The rhetorical *what ifs* became a game we'd settle into after midnight on our hunt for *more* through the streets of Fitzroy. Chekhov or Ibsen. St Kilda or the north. Judith or Quinn. Saxon and I would peel away from each other sometimes, interlacing our fingers with those of our friends, and find one another again before sunrise. Last drinks, wet kisses goodbye and the satisfaction of having given it a nudge. We didn't know it'd be different one day, that a winter like that wasn't a given every year.

I pocketed each experience, tallied them. There was before and then there was now, and I told myself, as Quinn had, that the most direct entry point to the work was through living.

—

Fear was contagious.

Dylan ploughed through the crowd and found me by the elevator with Saxon. 'Text! Fuck!'

Quinn's announcement at assembly earlier that morning was everything Dylan had been waiting for—permission to become who he imagined himself to be through the words of somebody else.

Richard trailed behind him. 'It's in the syllabus.'

'Did you speak to the second years about it?' I asked.

'Briefly,' Dylan replied.

My eyes widened. 'Why would you do that?'

Richard placed his head between us. 'Glutton for punishment.'

'Fuck off!' Dylan said.

Richard ignored him. '*Three Sisters*. Every goddamn year.'

'It's a classic,' Dylan said.

'Yes, I suppose it is,' Richard responded.

Dylan tried to shake his nerves out through his fingertips. 'Even so, it's Quinn's method.'

'*Man must work, he must toil by the sweat of his brow*,' Richard called as he sauntered into the lift.

'Blinkers on,' I said to Dylan. 'Right?'

He nodded, and with a slap on the arm from Saxon he brightened. 'Do you think—'

'Stop.' I knew what he wanted to ask. Despite our constant encouragement, the Collective showing had shaken his confidence. 'It's the first day of semester. Plenty of room for—'

'Growth,' Saxon said.

I turned to him and smiled. 'Exactly.'

In the Rehearsal Room we sat like preschoolers in a wide circle on the floor. Barefoot, dressed in black, chins upturned to the woman who would lead us in our foray into text. The ease the second and third years possessed on the floor could only be obtained by learning Quinn's method, a notoriously arduous process for actors in their first year of training.

Quinn sat on a chair with legs spread, knuckles on knees. Her eyes danced over us. 'One of you isn't supposed to be here,' she said lightly.

It was quite possibly a lie, a way to rein in the conceited, but it was still a cruel way to begin. Quinn's presence up until this point had only been felt through others. We'd been able to fool ourselves into believing that she wasn't aware of the weaknesses our training exposed. She knew us not just archetypally, for what we'd been chosen to bring to the company, but what was possible within each of us. Her prerogative was to release it, our talent, through whatever means she saw fit.

'Imogen,' Quinn said.

'Yes?'

'Go to Genevieve, would you? I'd like a coffee.'

Imogen blinked, stood and walked quickly to the door.

'And a scone.'

'A scone?'

'Make it two. With jam.'

Quinn settled her gaze within the void of the circle, speaking only once Imogen had left. '*Three Sisters*. Irina and Baron Tuzenbach. A scene from act four—short, but impactful.'

Quinn allowed time for the assignment to land, for us to swipe through the pages of the play in our minds and remember the scene.

'We will deconstruct the text. Investigate the themes and the characters, gain an understanding of the writer's intention, to form a context in which we can immerse ourselves. The play is a masterpiece, but with such a label come preconceived notions.'

It was the casual way Quinn said 'masterpiece' that frightened me. She'd no doubt witnessed work that deserved the accolade. I had a niggling feeling that no matter how hard I might try, I would never come close to her version of it.

'Will it be cast?' Vivien asked. 'Or are our scene partners self-appointed?'

'Once we've spent a little more time together, I will pair you. The women will play Irina, the men Tuzenbach. I'm sure you're familiar with the roles already.'

The door opened. Heads turned. Imogen re-entered with a tray. On it were the scones and a large steaming mug. She hadn't done anything wrong, but it was an embarrassment to be made to wait on Quinn in the presence of her peers.

'While you're up, Imogen,' Quinn said, 'tell us what you know of Chekhov.'

—

Imogen, Richard and I sat at the picnic table outside Luncheonette beneath a grey, drizzling sky. The whipping traffic, like Quinn herself, was relentless. It set us further on edge.

'Cantankerous old cunt,' Imogen said. 'Pies are her favourite, apparently. The scones were a curve ball.'

Richard guffawed. 'Meat pies? Jesus Christ.'

'*Chekhov laid bare the lives and yearnings of ordinary people,*' I recited. 'Where'd you pull that from?'

Imogen smiled. 'Back of the Penguin Classic.'

Richard was amused. 'Audacious.'

'Compared to Viv?' I remarked. 'Hardly.'

'Come on, now,' Richard said tolerantly. 'She asked a simple question.'

'Outside the order of things,' I replied.

Richard made an exasperated sound. 'Quinn is just another facilitator.'

But that wasn't entirely true. The company needed Quinn's approval. Vivien already had it, and it gave her the confidence to address the head of school like a colleague.

'Emmet wouldn't agree,' I observed.

Richard swatted the air. 'Doesn't matter.'

'Why not?' I asked.

'He dropped out,' Richard said. 'Wasn't for him.'

I frowned. 'Surely it was his best shot.'

'At what?' Richard asked.

'A career.'

Richard stood abruptly. 'I'm getting another coffee.'

Imogen waited for him to leave before speaking again. 'He's still staying at Richard's.'

'I figured.'

Emmet had been at every gathering through winter, though often he removed himself mid-conversation. His belongings had moved from beside the couch to a small study at the top of the stairs. Emmet hadn't mentioned leaving drama school to me, though I'd overheard him threatening it, and I realised I couldn't really call him a friend. More like a conversational sparring partner.

'What a waste,' I said.

We believed drama school was the most direct route to a successful career, and felt privileged to be in training. It was why Imogen didn't object when Quinn asked her to fetch morning tea.

'You won't always be her errand girl,' I said.

In the slouch of Imogen's shoulders, I saw that she didn't believe me.

'And you're not the spare.'

Imogen exhaled slowly. She didn't believe that either.

II

Luna Park was a relic. Saxon suggested we go. An ironic invitation, a pretend date. I said yes.

It took nearly an hour on the tram to get from Carlton to St Kilda. I arrived early and killed time by walking along Acland Street. The people were friendlier here, keener somehow for companionship, or money, or both.

In the fitting room of an upmarket vintage store, I cinched a mustard dress with a wide tan belt. My resemblance to Sylvie struck me. She never divulged where she bought her pieces. It levelled us a little. I asked the attendant to snip off the tag so I could wear the dress now. I'd go hungry for it.

Saxon was sprawled on the grass by the entrance to the amusement park, a longneck in each hand, wrapped in brown paper. He watched the crowd. Another Saturday, people everywhere, bundled up but their clothes brighter than you'd find in the city.

'Beautiful,' Saxon said, as I approached.

I twirled for him, pleased.

He put the drinks down, reached and pulled me into the space between his legs. 'Take a seat. There's time,' he said, though it was falling to dusk. I pressed my nose against his chin, he tapped it with his own.

I was learning to rest inside the gaps, to allow him to speak first. It took effort, leaving thoughts unvoiced.

'Been around a long time,' Saxon said, nodding at the lurid face, 'long enough that maybe we shouldn't risk it?'

'You're not getting out of this!'

Saxon took a swig of his ale and stood abruptly. I fell back against the grass. 'Race ya!'

When I found him, he looked different, tall against the taut lips of the famous entrance. The kid brought to the surface of the man. It was a gift, this sliver of knowledge.

I made a game of it, the long, slow walk towards him. I waited until we were inches apart, lifted my beer and drank it all. He grinned more broadly with each gulp.

'Milady,' he said and took my free hand, kissed it. 'Shall we?'

It wasn't a theatre, a foyer or a bar. It was neutral ground. I tugged his arm and ran towards the queue for the rollercoaster, all self-awareness dissolved.

It was a rickety old machine, barely a ride, certainly not a proper rollercoaster, but the view from up top was unparalleled. We rode it twice to watch the bay darken with the day, bumping against one another, teeth clinking together as we kissed. Lipstick smeared across his lips and mine.

We ate fairy floss off a stick and tossed balls into the mouths of clowns. Saxon won me a fluffy bear. I carried it to a patch of grass outside the entrance. I lay on it and Saxon lay on me. It was dark enough that I let him touch me beneath my new dress with cold fingers.

The stars were out. I found the Southern Cross, smiled up at it. *Are you watching?* Heat rose and fell inside my chest.

We picked up hot chips for the trip home and let tram after tram pass us by. Our reflections streaked past us in the glass doors of the jolting carriages. We were the kids I'd seen inside the park and along the grass. It was no longer a box to tick, but a memory to keep. The experience of St Kilda, of Luna Park, of Acland Street. Of us.

III

Barbara radiated energy. She was a short woman with a penchant for sensible, beige clothing. But when she smiled it was as if she were lit from within.

We lay on the floor in the Rehearsal Room, knees up, palms open as Barbara walked between us. 'When you find your voice, you will find your character,' she said. A Midwestern twang crept into her accent whenever she emphasised a point. It endeared her to us even more than the long list of clients who called her *coach*: De Niro, Pacino and Burstyn. Not that she dropped their names. We'd done our research. Barbara was one of the most sought-after voice teachers in the world.

Phillip sat in the corner, one stocky leg crossed over the other, observing us as we drank in Barbara's every word. He was a disciple of Barbara's method, having trained alongside her in his youth, and he'd invited her to teach some of his classes. She would work with us sporadically throughout her time down under, the reason for her visit never disclosed, for the sake of her client's privacy.

In our first session with Barbara we did little more than breathe, imagining our bodies sliced into parts, allowing a current to connect them. She'd kneel and place a hand on the precise place we stored tension; it was almost telepathic. Though, she explained, 'Our bodies betray us.'

She whispered encouragement and gripped our hands when we responded with tears. 'Life is in the breath,' she said. 'He who half breathes, half lives.'

Quiet revelations, the cracking of interior codes.

'The voice is the servant of your thoughts,' Barbara called. 'Get into the image!' Her proclamations provided clarity. I now understood what Phillip had been prattling on about all these months, what the daily practice had been for; our voices massaged into readiness for an opportunity like this. She would continue to appraise us—it was an institution after all—but the pressure had been removed and our voices were resonant. And Barbara's interest in us felt genuine. After only two hours together, she called us each by name. She treated us like artists and her modesty made us feel as though we were special, though that was far from true; she'd taught hundreds of actors.

Barbara thought we could take on a challenge together.

'Quinn has informed me that you'll be moving on to text this term. I'd like to work on a monologue with each of you, something to add to your repertoire.' Then she stretched her arms out towards us. 'I. Am. Enough,' she said. 'You are all enough.'

I'd have cut out a kidney for her if she'd asked me to.

—

Sylvie sucked on a cigarette outside the Malthouse. 'She's so American.'

'She's inspiring,' I replied.

Sylvie shrugged her faux leopard-fur coat onto her shoulders. 'If you say so.'

'Barbara is highly sought after.'

'That doesn't mean anything.'

'It's a privilege to work with her.'

'Listen to you!'

'It's true!' I said, brittle with frustration.

'Go on, then. Gobble down her rhetoric.'

'We can't all have jobs lined up after third year. Some of us still have a few hoops to jump through.'

'There it is,' Sylvie said, pointing her cigarette at me.

'What?'

'The fight.'

There was no way of arguing with her—she always turned it into a game.

'Lolita,' Sylvie said softly.

'No.'

'Lolita, *yes*.'

I'd opened up to Sylvie about Yates, how he'd propositioned me after graduation. I'd expected her to be shocked. She wasn't. Instead, she started calling me Lolita whenever she'd had a few. I was embarrassed at first but saw no way of getting her to drop it. I tried to work out what she meant by it. She was envious, I imagined, because I'd been noticed by a celebrated artist. Imogen thought it was fucked up. Once I'd read Nabokov's book—in a fever of agitation the month before—I did too.

In the stalls of the theatre's bathroom, Sylvie produced a tiny, clear bag. 'Dregs left, I'm afraid.' She used her key to scrape out the corners and lifted it to my nose, then took some for herself, licking the powder that clung to the plastic before disposing of it in the sanitary bin.

Sylvie took my hand and led me out of the bathroom as the intermission bell rang. We had a couple of minutes left to scramble into our seats inside the Merlyn Theatre for the second half of *I Am My Own Wife*.

'Panama?' Sylvie asked.

'What about the play?'

'I've seen it.'

'I haven't.'

Sylvie brought her mouth close to mine. 'I'll fill you in on the details.' And it hit me: this had been her plan all along. I wasn't her date; I was an accomplice.

Sylvie whispered the famous opening line of *Lolita*. I shivered inwardly with horror at everything it implied as she elongated the words lasciviously.

'Stop.'

'You won't regret it.'

I did the maths. If we left now, we'd be at Panama Dining Room in Fitzroy by ten and I could be in bed by one. I hated myself for not being able to let go, for wanting so badly to do well. I couldn't back up an all-nighter with class. I'd tried. I'd try again.

A tall, unsmiling woman with greying blonde hair approached us. 'Sylvie! Get your agent to call me.'

'About?' Sylvie kissed the woman on both cheeks.

'Yates said yes.'

'I told you he would.'

It became clear to me that this woman held some kind of power here. Sylvie was casual, completely unperturbed. I watched her place a hand on the woman's arm, cast her eyes downwards and laugh flirtatiously. I could see the woman being drawn in, as almost everybody was. I studied Sylvie as she spoke. This was performance, this was skill.

'Maeve is the next Cate,' Sylvie said, taking my hand.

The woman turned towards me. 'That so?'

'It is.'

She squinted. 'You could be sisters.'

'Chekhovian sisters?' Sylvie asked, coy.

'Not for the coming season. However . . .' The woman trailed off suggestively.

Sylvie gripped me tighter. The foyer began to empty.

'Good to meet you, Maeve.'

I nodded. 'You too.'

We waited until she had disappeared into the theatre before walking outside.

'Call Saxon,' Sylvie said.

'Who was that?'

'Let's get a cab. My treat.'

'Sylvie.'

'What?'

'Who was that woman?'

'Gretchen Wells, Head of Casting.'

I gasped. Sylvie laughed; her debt paid for pulling me away from the play.

'Did I seem . . . How was I?'

Sylvie leaned towards me. 'Perfect. You were perfect.'

At Panama, Sylvie bought round after round of vodka. We threw our coats on the floor and danced with strangers at the bar.

The beat of the music intensified, and the bodies before me blurred. I closed my eyes and repeated Barbara's mantra over and over, smiling to myself, 'I. *Am. Enough.*'

When Saxon arrived, he brought me to him and slid the hair off my face with both hands.

'You good?' he asked, kissing me before I could reply.

Yes, I imagined myself saying. *Yes.*

Then the hours slipped away, and I was swallowed by the night.

IV

Dictionaries littered the Rehearsal Room floor, *Oxford*, *Collins*, *Macquarie*, all battered, stained and creased.

Quinn sat, as she always did, at the edge of the space on a chair, her coffee and morning tea on the floor beside her. We were sprawled at her feet, books open, pens scribbling, learning the meanings of words we'd thought we already knew.

The room was quiet. Quinn spoke infrequently, but when she did we raised our faces to her voice obediently.

'The most basic words come with connotations that smear our understanding,' she said. *Never. Troubled. Key. Trifle. Time.* 'We need to remind ourselves of their true meaning before layering Chekhov's work with our own.'

'Did he know?' Dylan whispered beside me.

'What?'

'Did Chekhov know the proper definition of each word he wrote?'

'It was his job to know.'

'But the words might have meant something different then from what they mean now. Then there's the issue of translation; an intermediary making word choices on Chekhov's behalf. And context, *our* context. How do you get to the truth of it?'

I inhaled. 'Dylan.'

'Yeah?'

'Stop.'

'Sorry.' Dylan hunched over his notebook.

Quinn had paired us together. It was comfortable—we were mates and familiar with how each other worked—but until now I hadn't understood how deeply Dylan's talent was rooted in his neurosis. He was compulsive in his approach; he questioned everything, himself especially.

'I'm done,' I said.

Dylan was sceptical. 'You're not.'

'I am.'

Dylan snatched my notebook from me. 'What about *far*? And *see*?'

'I know what they mean.'

Dylan returned to his work.

I peered over his shoulder. 'Jesus.' Dylan had written out the definitions not only for *you* and *in* but for *and, or* and *I* as well. 'You all right?' I asked.

'Why wouldn't I be?'

'This just seems a little ...'

'What?'

'Excessive.'

—

The following week we moved on to themes, given circumstances and beats. You could hide behind text analysis, behind ideas and hypotheticals, but on the floor, you were exposed. No matter how clever your idea, it was nothing without the rigour to bring it forth. The gap between thought and action could be wide.

'Rupture the imagination,' Quinn told us.

'*Rupture the imagination*,' Dylan parroted back to me.

'What does that even mean?' I asked.

Dylan blinked at me and jotted the phrase down in his notebook.

Later, at the Malthouse, lubricated with alcohol, we confessed to each other that we didn't have a clue. But in class everyone nodded and wrote down every word Quinn said. I watched as my company did their very best acting, moving forward like they *knew*. No one gave anything away, though I searched for it, asked my friends after class, *Do you get it?* Few were prepared to admit that they didn't.

—

The next part of the process had us utilising our breath work, sitting on the floor cross-legged, eyes closed. Our scene partners were to feed us our lines one by one. Once we'd imagined and internalised the world of the play in the context of our characters' lives, we were permitted to repeat the line sotto voce. If we couldn't imagine it, we were to recall an event in our own lives to draw parallels that we could later use as stimulation. Quinn's process, like many modern acting methods, drew heavily on the Stanislavski System.

Dylan had spent hours scribbling down his responses to almost every word. I moved more quickly but Dylan's constant questioning made me nervous. I slowed myself down, resisted my impulses.

'Are you sure you want to move on, Maeve?' Dylan asked.

I opened my eyes. 'Fuck's sake. Yes.'

Dylan looked concerned. 'Fine. *Wife*.'

I burrowed deep into my subconscious, to turn-of-the-century Russia.

'*Wife*,' I said. It didn't sound right. *Wife*. I knew how many times it was mentioned in the scene. I knew my character's gender identity and religion, her preoccupations. But what was the secret to saying *wife* as though I were promising to marry a man I didn't love?

'*Wife*.'

'Come to a close,' Quinn said from the front of the Rehearsal Room, bringing us back to the present.

'Well done,' Dylan said. 'Got there.'

'Don't think so, but thanks,' I muttered.

'We'll pick this up again tomorrow,' Quinn called.

Dylan fidgeted beside me. 'We do this with every script, every role?'

'Apparently.'

'It'll become second nature, right?'

'I hope so.'

'I'm going to ask her,' Dylan said. 'Let's do it together.'

'Ask her what?'

'For clarification.'

I was still sitting on the floor. I wanted to retrieve what I'd felt, take some time with the experience. 'I need to finish this.'

'Yes, right. Sorry. I'll ask.'

He was beside Quinn before I could stop him. She didn't acknowledge him at first. Dylan spoke quickly, but even before he'd finished Quinn looked him in the eye and said, 'Enough.' Then she left the room. One of us would have to take her plates down to reception, put her chair away and sweep up the crumbs she'd left beneath it.

'Dylan,' I called. *'Dylan!'*

He ignored me as he gathered his belongings, making a show of an equanimity he didn't truly possess.

—

The best conversations happened *afterwards*, as if he alone could release me from inside myself.

'I can do it on my own,' I said from his bedroom floor. Always the floor. Chairs were foreign to me now. 'Say the lines like they're mine.'

'They are yours,' Saxon replied. 'Do what you like with them.'

'Oh, how I have dreamed of love,' I began, *'dreamed of it for a long time now, day and night, but my soul is like a fine piano that is locked, and the key is—'*

'Don't rush it.'

I paused and tried to retrieve what I'd felt when Dylan had fed me the line that afternoon. When I'd internalised it, imagined the world my character lived in, what it felt like to be lost.

'Lost.'

'Just like that,' Saxon said.

A gust of cool air pushed through the gap in the window seal. It hit my cheek, and I raised my face to it. We were nearing spring, but winter felt far from over.

Saxon took a joint from the dish by his bed and lit it. I watched the smoke float from his lips and wondered what I looked like to him. When he passed the joint to me, I turned to face myself in the reflection of the window. A far cry from Monroe. Just a girl with mussed hair, wide eyes. No glamour. I was disappointed.

I turned back to Saxon. 'If Dylan could just relax a little . . .'

'You would too?'

'Yes.'

'We all sit differently inside the work—that's what makes it ours. Don't blame Dylan.' Saxon was right, of course. He spoke infrequently, but always with intention, so when he decided to share an opinion, those around him listened. 'He has his own way.'

Saxon's phone rang. When he picked up, I sensed instantly it was someone he'd rather speak to in private.

'Go,' I whispered.

Saxon nodded and opened the bedroom door, walked into the hallway and out of the house. I watched him pace along the pavement outside the window. I had a toke and lay on the floor again.

'Who was that?' I asked when he returned.

'No one,' Saxon said.

'No one?'

Saxon took the joint from me, inhaled deeply and blew the smoke out in rings. 'A friend checking in.'

'Okay,' I said and pulled him to me. 'You need checking in on?'

Saxon studied my face as though the truth lay there. He nodded at the photograph beside his bed.

Then he told me.

His mother was an actor. She floated from project to project, state to state, depending on where the work was. When he was small, Saxon went with her. As he grew, she left him behind.

There weren't any grandparents left, only a neighbour—a man about the age of Saxon's father, if he'd had one. The man helped out when he could, walking Saxon to school some days and overseeing homework. But like most people in Saxon's life, the neighbour moved on. In his place, a revolving door of his mother's friends played house until summoned away by their own obligations. Some of them he could trust, some he could not. He learned to keep things to himself.

Saxon's mother told him elaborate stories about the man his father might have been. A drummer, a pilot, a soldier. She wasn't entirely sure. He indulged her stories until he was old enough to call her out on the lies. It revealed what she'd hidden from herself—the boy had grown up and learned about the world without her.

The irony wasn't lost on him: attending drama school, training to become an actor himself. Saxon had done everything he could to avoid it. But it was in him, as his mother liked to say. *Can't deny the calling.*

The voice on the other end of the line Saxon wouldn't give up, but he revealed the person knew a little about where his mother might be, after so long of being owned by the stage.

'She's home.' Apparently the pantomime she'd been working on in Britain had closed. 'She never wanted to be a mother,' he said. 'She told me that once.'

I saw it then. The boy who'd found out who loved him and who didn't a little too early. The knowledge had coloured everything. The books he read, how he interpreted them. The films he loved. The people he spent time with. The roles he gravitated towards and experimented with. The version of himself he could have been if things had been different.

'I won't tell a soul,' I said, eyeing the framed photograph of the little boy over his shoulder. 'And thank you.'

'For what?'

'Sharing something like that with me.'

'Juliet,' Saxon said. A decoy. It felt like he was taking it back.

'Don't do that.'

Saxon sighed and lay back on the floor. I crawled on top of him.

'*Here you know everyone, everyone knows you, but you're a stranger.*' I knew it was too much, but the weed had loosened my mind and I wanted to make a moment of his openness.

'Don't quote to me,' Saxon said.

'Chekhov's right.'

'Not now.'

He pulled me to the bed, trailed kisses down my abdomen and buried his head between my thighs.

From then on, he mentioned his mother occasionally, but only when we were alone. I shouldn't speak of her myself. But she was present, always, in the shape of who he was. The more he said, the more I saw it: the artist he was capable of becoming.

V

An Arts Centre opening night brought together myriad characters who would otherwise never socialise. Benefactors, actors, crew, industry folk and a handful of dedicated subscribers. Yates demonstrated his importance by securing four seats for Vivien and her friends to *Doubt*, a privilege normally reserved for the director of the company.

'Look sharp,' Richard said, thrusting a glass of red into my hand. He was dressed impeccably in a vintage tux; the rest of us looked dishevelled by comparison.

'Ta.'

'That's all you can muster? Darling, drinks are as important as the play.'

It was an opportunity to be seen, to talk about the work with people who understood it, who might listen to our opinions, remember us and cast us one day.

'I can't shake this feeling,' I said. 'Can you?'

Richard raised his glass. 'Catch up.'

'It was chilling,' Anya admitted.

'Yates was brutal,' I agreed.

Richard sipped his wine. 'Wasn't he just.'

'He'd like that,' Vivien said. '*Brutal*.'

'Tell him,' Richard suggested, devilish.

Vivien smirked. 'Yes, tell him.'

I thought about my previous interactions with the man. 'No.'

'You're right,' Vivien said. 'He'd enjoy it too much.'

We turned to where Yates stood at the bar, surrounded by a group of women, all draped in fur, all adorned with diamonds.

'Buttering up the benefactors,' Anya said. She drained her glass. 'Let's get more before the comps run out.'

She pulled me with her through the throng of guests. As we drew closer to Yates, I heard him declare: 'Without *parable* tacked onto the title, *Doubt* would not be interpreted as it was intended to be.'

'Which is?' a woman beside him asked.

'A warning!' Anya called.

Heads turned in our direction.

I tugged at Anya's wrist. 'What are you doing?'

'Stealing his thunder,' she replied.

Yates beckoned her over and planted a kiss on each of her cheeks. 'Anya! Thoughts?'

Anya smiled archly. 'It was brutal.'

Yates waved a hand at her dismissively. 'It's just a play. There'll be another.'

Anya bristled. 'For you, yes, but not for everyone.'

I realised she was right; only the privileged few were in a position to take the work for granted; I was irked by his flippant dismissal of it.

'*You* were brutal, is what she means.'

Yates eyed me, intrigued.

'Are you always?' I asked.

'Depends on the role.'

'Or the cast,' I said daringly.

Anya tipped her face to the ceiling and suppressed a laugh. It felt like a win.

'Thank you for the ticket,' I said.

'Thank Vivien,' Yates replied with offensive frankness.

'Spectacular!' Barbara inserted herself into our circle.

Yates regained his poise. 'Whatever did I do to deserve such a compliment?'

'Cut the bullshit!' Barbara slapped him playfully.

Yates laughed and embraced her affectionately. 'It's bloody good to see you!'

They slung private jokes back and forth. Anya and I stood back politely and waited to be drawn into the conversation.

'Vivien mentioned your stint at the institution,' Yates said. 'She's thoroughly enjoying it.'

'Following in her father's footsteps. There's a career there, I'm sure of it. And these two . . .' Barbara smiled at Anya and me. 'Forces, both of them.'

'Indeed,' Yates replied. 'Have you selected their pieces yet?'

'Scenes for the second years, yes.'

'And the first-year monologues?' Yates asked. 'I have a suggestion for Maeve.'

'Shoot,' Barbara said.

Yates paused dramatically. '*Miss Julie.*'

Barbara stared into my face. 'Yes. Let's try it.'

I focused on the floor, felt the hot glow of anxiety.

Anya grasped my hand. She hadn't forgotten.

'You can thank me later,' Yates said into my ear. 'Just remember to visualise the man Miss Julie is speaking to. *Be specific.*'

I smiled, nodded, melted into the crush of people behind me, grateful for their protection.

I picked up as many glasses as I could carry from the bar then returned to Richard and Vivien. 'Drink these and let's go,' I said.

'What about the evening?' Richard asked, taking two glasses of white from my hands.

'No one cares about us.' I gestured to the crowd. 'They're preoccupied with themselves.'

'She's right,' Vivien said.

'Fine.' Richard threw back his drinks and deposited the glasses on the floor by our feet.

'What did he say to you?' Vivien asked.

'Your father?'

Vivien nodded impatiently. She watched me with narrowed eyes as I searched for a way to explain how her father made me feel.

'Jesus,' she said. 'Maeve?'

The moment was slipping.

'He made a point, that's all.'

'About school?'

'About me.'

Vivien breathed in my response. She took me by the arm and pulled me towards the exit, then turned on her heel abruptly, as if struck by a thought. 'Congratulations, Papa!' she called. 'Another stellar performance!'

The crowd parted and Yates peered at his daughter, who responded by lifting her middle finger. After a series of gasps and murmurs, Yates began to laugh, and the room relaxed.

Anya caught up to us outside the theatre. 'You vanished.'

'I'm going to do *Miss Julie*,' I said.

'Good for you,' Anya replied.

'Monster of a piece,' Vivien said quietly.

'That it is,' Richard agreed.

We threw the lines at one another on the street, the monologue split between three voices. Richard interjected every so often but mostly let us scream into the cool air like banshees—'A Freudian dream come true,' he bellowed. It was a joke now, my interactions with Yates. I told myself it was better that way, that it softened things.

We made it to Hell's Kitchen. I'd drunk too much, I couldn't speak. I tried to listen to my friends as they moved from one topic to another, but all I could hear was Yates. *Be specific. Be specific. Be specific.*

VI

She made a show of her laughter, eyes closed, back arched. I felt the gaze of commuters walking down Degraves to Flinders Street Station.

'Sylvie,' I said. And again. 'Sylvie!' I held her in a monkey grip over the gutter that ran through the street. A table of kids drank macchiatos beside us. 'Come on,' I pleaded, but I was laughing myself, the spectacle an event I'd relish in the recounting.

'You kill me,' Sylvie said, regaining balance.

There was a smattering of applause from the boys along the wall of Degraves Espresso. Wait staff who looked like artists. They knew talent when they saw it.

'I asked a simple question,' I said.

'Well, don't.'

Sylvie walked further down the laneway and leaned against a graffitied wall, beckoning me towards her with a pre-rolled cigarette.

'Look,' she said, 'the method doesn't always apply, okay? Goldoni, for instance. There's no subtext. The words are there, they explain everything.'

I'd been interested in how rehearsals were going and made the mistake of asking her about the process. Sylvie's company was continuing the tradition of mounting a commedia dell'arte play in third term, a scheme that attracted audiences and casting agents alike. It was light entertainment, the kind the masses liked.

'Isn't that against the rules?' I asked. 'Speaking out against our indoctrination.'

'Yes.' Sylvie snickered and lit the cigarette.

'So what do you do?' I asked, searching for enlightenment.

But Sylvie wouldn't oblige.

'Imagine sitting at a desk all day,' she said, eyeing passers-by.

They smelled heavy, of wet wool and stale breath, striding along with heads down, eyes up. Rushing to get home or to a restaurant or to a distraction from their day. We heard clipped conversations, but mostly the sound of motion. Boots stamping through puddles, suit fabric swishing between legs, umbrellas crumpling beneath arms.

'I don't know,' I said, thinking about my father. 'This could be their dream.'

'Dim, don't you think?'

She wanted an ally. Someone to go along with her way of thinking. So I stopped imagining what these people might have— stability, a home, a career—and tried to hear the question she was really asking. *Have we chosen the right path?*

'You're right,' I said.

Sylvie hugged me and slipped her hands up my back, beneath my clothing.

'Jesus!' I squealed.

'Cold hands, warm heart,' Sylvie replied, removing them.

'*The Servant of Two Masters*,' I said, envisioning Sylvie in the title role.

'Torture.'

'You don't mean that.'

Sylvie smiled. 'Don't I?'

It meant so little to her, being a third year. It wasn't black and white like it was for the rest of us. There were variables like upbringing, age, connections, exposure to art that made a difference to how receptive you were to the work. I saw it in her then, all the variables I'd never noticed before. All the experience. The chasm it created between her and me. I wanted to close it.

'Is that Emmet?' Sylvie asked.

It was. He was standing by the door of a shop on the other side of the laneway. Turning the lock, double-checking that it was secure.

I darted around the fast walkers and men with phones pressed to their ears. 'Oi!' I called.

Emmet recoiled. 'Holy shit! How about, "Hello, Emmet. How are you?" Fuck.' It was clear he wasn't pleased to see me.

'Hello, Emmet. How are you?' I mocked. He groaned and slipped into the crowd, I followed. 'Hang on,' I said. 'I just . . .'

He spun around. 'What?'

'I just wanted to see how you're doing.'

'Good. I'm good.'

'You should come back,' I said, and regretted it immediately. The look on Emmet's face was one of utter disgust.

'Are you high?' he demanded.

'A little,' I admitted.

'Emmet!' Sylvie said, pulling him into a hug.

He stepped back, glanced between us. 'Makes sense.'

'What?' Sylvie asked.

Emmet tapped his nose.

Sylvie lowered her voice. 'Want some?'

'From you? Nah, I'm good.'

Sylvie cooled. 'Never had a problem with it before.'

Emmet crossed his arms over his chest, threw his head back to indicate the store. 'Did Richard tell you?'

'No,' we replied in unison.

'Feel superior, do we?'

'About what?' I asked.

'An actor needs an audience,' Emmet responded disdainfully. 'Without one they're nothing but a reduction of themselves.'

'Nothing wrong with working in a shop,' Sylvie said. 'I have, from time to time.'

'And what about you, Maeve? Do you work?'

'I'm a student,' I said.

'Guess not. Thanks, Daddy.'

Sylvie whistled. 'Mate.'

'Well, I *do*,' Emmet said. 'I have a job. I have a *life*.'

'You know what?' I retorted. 'Fuck you. I was just trying to be nice.'

'Nice?' Emmet spat. 'There's your fucking problem! Nice doesn't mean shit.'

Then he turned and walked away, another body draped in black, as the rain set in.

I looked at Sylvie. 'What did I do wrong?'

'Nothing.'

'Did I hurt him somehow?'

'No. You were just *there*.' Sylvie brushed past me towards the arcade. 'I'm getting a drink,' she called over her shoulder.

I hurried after her, and noticed she was grinning as she bolted across Collins Street. Cars skidded to avoid impact. When she made it to the other side unscathed, she lifted her pink woollen coat and satin dress beneath it to flash her lace underwear at the honking traffic.

Sylvie lit another cigarette and passed it to me when I reached her. 'I let them take over a little bit, if I can't use the process.'

My body trembled from the confrontation and the cold. 'Who?'

'The character,' she said, picking up the conversation from earlier. She'd erased the episode with Emmet. Her lesson to me in uncaring. She took my hand and led me through the city, ducking beneath open umbrellas, separating couples and leaping over gutters, embracing how drenched she really was.

'That's yours, right?' Sylvie asked, pointing to a tram, ending whatever escapade we were on.

'I might walk,' I replied, hoping she might change her mind.

Sylvie just shrugged. 'Suit yourself.' She turned and strolled beneath the awnings that ran along Bourke Street. When I called her name, she ignored me, and leaped up a stairwell to The Carlton.

At the Vintage Cellars on Little Bourke, I chose a fourteen-dollar bottle of cabernet sauvignon. I took quick swigs from it and walked through the rain to Lygon Street. I didn't stop outside my building, crossed Princes Street instead, and meandered through the tombstones at Melbourne General Cemetery, imagining myself as Irina. An enormous clap of thunder sent me sprinting to the exit. I slipped on the wet pavement and swore in frustration at the sight of my jeans, and the skin underneath, torn.

Try again.

Beside the busy road, I squatted. Soaked through. A small voice somewhere: *You need to dig deeper.* I shook it away, felt a smattering of stones on my thigh. Realised they were coins.

'Get a hot meal, love,' a man barked and continued walking.

This wasn't Irina. It was a poor impression of Sylvie.

I stood slowly and walked to the crossing, leaving the coins where they lay.

VII

On day one of blocking, Dylan and I stood against the back wall of the Rehearsal Room.

The company blinked at us from the other side of the studio; a single row with Quinn at the centre. I kept my eyelids soft, jaw too. Open, but aware also of the passing of time and the pressure Dylan was under in releasing the first line. He'd insisted on going first, keen to prove that he wasn't afraid of failure. But of course he was. We all were.

Unsure how to prompt my scene partner into beginning, I addressed him directly. 'Okay?'

We both waited a beat, cautious. Then Dylan nodded, closed his eyes, inhaled and released his breath on an extended *ah*, brave enough to exercise his vocal training, uninhibited by Quinn's presence.

Dylan opened his eyes. He looked calm, centred. '*That*—'

'Again,' Quinn interrupted.

Dylan stood erect. 'Sure, sure, sure.'

'Don't talk,' she scolded.

Dylan nodded at the floorboards.

Quinn inhaled deeply and motioned for Dylan and me to do the same. 'In your own time.'

The company shifted.

I knew how literally Dylan took direction. *In your own time* could mean now, or it could mean in twenty-five minutes. He erred on the side of caution always, feeling his impulse once, then waiting to feel it again. It went against the definition of the word as we'd come to understand it and let old habits creep in. Dylan would manufacture something to quell the voice inside his head that screamed, *Don't fuck this up*, and I'd be left working opposite a mannequin.

'Dylan?' Quinn asked after several minutes.

'Yes?'

'Breathe.'

Dylan shook his hands and jumped on the spot. He stopped abruptly and took a sharp breath. '*That seems—*'

Quinn tutted. Dylan turned to her.

'No! Give it to *her!*'

Dylan spun back to face me. '*That seems to be—*'

'Again.'

'*That—*'

'Again!'

Dylan nodded at the wall behind me and lowered his voice. '*That seems to be the only man in town who's glad the officers are leaving.*'

'Yes,' Quinn said before I could respond and swivelled in her chair to address one half of the group, then the other. 'Dylan moved into the world of the character, and we in turn felt that this young man was on the precipice of revealing something meaningful.'

'Thank you,' Dylan said.

Quinn shot him a blistering look.

I knew what the company were thinking. *Thank fuck that isn't me up there.*

'Again,' Quinn said.

Dylan nodded once. '*That seems to be the only man in town who's glad the officers are leaving.*'

'*It's understandable,*' I replied. '*Our town is going to be empty now.*'

Dylan's eyes widened in panic. 'Um, line?'

'You dropped out of the moment,' Quinn said.

Dylan addressed Quinn but spoke at me in a monotone, like a robot. 'I did, you're right.'

Quinn twirled a finger in the air. We clocked it in our peripheral vision. *Again.*

Dylan jumped straight in. '*That seems to be the only man in town who's glad the officers are leaving.*'

'*It's understandable. Our town is going to be empty now.*'

'*Dear . . .*' Dylan shut his eyes, inhaled. '*I'll be back shortly.*'

'*Where are you going?*'

We didn't make it to the end of the scene. Quinn called it midway through and asked for insight from the rest of the company.

'Lack of connection.'

'Physically inhibited.'

'Reporting the event.'

It was to be expected, but it stung all the same, your peers slinging feedback before they'd given it a go themselves. It was a common tactic. Break someone down in case you muck up too. We all did it; no one was entirely blameless.

'Next time,' Dylan whispered as we walked off the floor.

'Next time what?' I asked.

'I'll be able to. Promise.'

'Get out of your head.'

Dylan was stunned. 'Sorry.'

He had proven himself unpredictable. I'd never be able to prep for it, and I wasn't strong enough in that moment to let the revelation go, to hide my frustration and encourage him instead.

Dylan sat cross-legged in the row of students to Quinn's right. He dug into his bag and retrieved his journal and a pen.

'Sit with it a while,' I said.

'I need to get it out,' Dylan replied, focused already on the blank page before him.

We were replaced by another pair who moved quickly through the scene, their version completely different from ours, with a darker, less apologetic Tuzenbach.

'Do you think it's clearer?' Dylan asked me quietly.

'Stop comparing,' I said.

But Dylan was fixated on the other actors and was loud in his appraisal. 'Of course the baron would do that.'

'Dylan.'

'Makes far more sense.'

'Every Tuzenbach will be different,' I said, my voice laced with irritation. 'Every Irina too.'

'They're six lines further ahead than us.'

'It doesn't matter.'

'Yes, it does.' Dylan abandoned his journal and brought his knees beneath his chin. He began to rock back and forth on his coccyx. 'I can do that,' he said. 'I can *do* that.'

Quinn interrupted the work on the floor. 'I hear voices.'

'Don't,' I pleaded.

Dylan stood. 'Can we go again?'

Quinn was amused. 'No.'

'But I understand now where the fault was. In the scene.' Dylan looked between Quinn and me. 'I can get further. We can get further.'

'It isn't about getting further; it's about being present,' Quinn replied. Dylan opened his mouth to speak but Quinn raised a hand in the air to stop him. 'Where is your respect for the work, for *yourself*?'

'Fuck, fuck, fuck, fuck,' Dylan muttered, sitting down and crossing his legs again.

'If we are driven by ego, the work is lost,' Quinn said.

'It's not my ego,' Dylan replied.

'Isn't it?' Quinn twisted in her chair. 'You want to feel good up there?'

'Yes.'

'Then this is the wrong profession for you. Adrenaline obscures the vision, good or bad. You can't serve the work if what you're striving for is a *feeling*.'

'I understand that,' Dylan replied.

'No, you don't. And I wonder, are you worth my time? Are you willing enough, strong enough to retain my direction?' Quinn paused. 'Stand up.'

Dylan obeyed.

'Let me look at you.' Quinn floated towards Dylan, circled him. 'Private school education, prim parents, a little girlfriend on the side. Have you broken her trust yet? Drunk yourself into oblivion?' She tousled his curls, laughed slyly. 'I sense a little desire to, a little hunger for *more*. But more of what exactly? Go inwards, seek those base feelings I sense lurking beneath your *projections*, and release them. I want truth from you, nothing less.'

Dylan trembled, and I looked away, repulsed by how our head of school had exposed him.

Quinn turned to face us. 'Where were we?' she asked rhetorically, and she motioned for the actors to pick up the scene again.

Dylan took up his journal, a coil of tension. He made notes at every pause in the work, whispering Quinn's words back to himself, a kind of self-flagellation.

When class was over, I waited for the company to file out of the studio. Dylan ignored me and continued scribbling. I gave him space; he was upset. But after watching him fill page after page I decided to intervene.

'Dylan?'

'What?'

'Let's debrief.'

'No need.'

'Don't you think it's important to investigate what went on up there?'

Dylan closed his journal with finality and sat up on his knees. 'I've felt it now.'

'What?' I asked.

'Imperfection.'

He looked blankly at my forehead, unable to lie to me directly.

'You didn't do that on purpose,' I said, angered. 'That wasn't *Method*.'

'No?'

'You had a moment. Don't call it something different to save face.'

Dylan looked away, studied the cover of his journal. 'I'm not.'

'All right,' I said, 'you fucked up. Let's move on.'

His internal struggle was clear, and I can't deny it gave me pleasure to watch him squirm after the mess he'd made of our scene.

'I didn't fuck up.'

'This is a partnership—'

'I didn't fuck up, Maeve!'

'What you do up there affects us both!'

Dylan brought his hands to his head and screamed. 'Take it back!' He pounded his fists against the floorboards. '*Take it back take it back take it back!*'

His panic was primal. He tore at his shirt, at his skin, as if to remove something—the memory of what had taken place on the floor.

Disgusted, I took hold of Dylan's hands and pinned them. He fell forward and lay his tear-streaked face against my thigh.

'Dylan, *stop*,' I implored. 'We have time. Assessment isn't for a while yet.'

He shuddered. 'We have time.' His breathing slowed. 'Say it.'

'What?'

He turned his face up to mine pleadingly. 'That I didn't fuck up.'

'Come on,' I scoffed.

'Say it, Maeve. I *need* you to say it.'

'No! Jesus—'

'Please. *Please.*'

I surrendered. 'You didn't fuck up.'

Dylan exhaled. 'Thank you.'

The fluorescent lights of the studio became brighter as the evening grew late, and I re-dressed him—socks over toes, shoes onto feet. T-shirt, jacket, scarf.

Dylan held on to me. We left the building together as security were beginning their rounds.

'Think you could walk me to Flinders?' Dylan asked, hobbling slightly.

'Sure,' I replied.

He was behaving like an invalid, and it was difficult to work out just how hurt he really was, if his stilted movements were a true manifestation of his fear.

'Let's run the lines,' Dylan said. 'Please.'

I felt guilty, partly to blame for calling him out, for making it clear that there would be consequences to his actions, a revoking of my respect. 'Fine.'

Dylan pointed to a suit as he crossed the street in front of us. *That seems to be the only man in town who's glad the officers are leaving,*' he said, as though the line was a continuation of the conversation we were already having.

Quinn would have been pleased.

—

There wasn't a moment's reprieve. Each company had their projects and were torn equally between serving the work, serving the director and serving themselves.

'I have no clue what the play is about anymore,' Anya told us over drinks at the Malthouse.

'Common this time of term,' Richard responded. 'Be patient.'

Anya passed me her cigarette. 'Take this,' she said, 'and this.' Her glass. 'I'll show you.' She pulled a script from her bag, rose from the cement barrier we used as a seat and stepped into the dugout with reverence.

We were a lonely trio. Richard recruited less and less these days, a midweek hangover not being as acceptable as it once was. There was little room for error in third term. The serious drinkers did so at home, poring over a script, making illegible notes for the morning.

'It's fucking freezing!' Anya said, blowing breath into her hands. 'If the cigarettes don't kill me, Melbourne will!'

'Get on with it!' Richard called.

'Hecklers won't be tolerated!' Anya yelled back.

Richard chuckled. 'You're a ham!'

Anya closed her eyes and inhaled exaggeratedly, mocking our daily practice. Then she spoke the text. Her voice was thin with so few bodies to buffer it against the weather, but it didn't dissuade her. Anya gave it to us, accent and all.

At the close of her short monologue Anya dropped character. 'And so it goes. See what I mean? Maeve, I'm lost.'

'You're not,' I replied.

'It's Pinter,' Richard said. 'Make a choice.'

'Ah.' Anya took her drink from my hand. 'But which choice is the right one?' Then she gulped the wine and started the section again. I took a drag from her cigarette and nestled closer to Richard.

Anya had been cast in *The Homecoming*, to be directed by Judith. Of the three contemporary plays allotted to her company for assessment, Ruth was the most intriguing female lead. Anya was a realist. She saw the role as both a gift and a threat. Judith had cast her on the one hand so that she might meet her potential. And on the other, to reveal her weaknesses. Either way, the stakes were high.

'Notes?' Anya asked.

'You'll have clarity in a week,' Richard said. 'What does Judith say?'

'Busy with the boys.'

Richard sniggered. 'I bet. Jealous?'

'Honestly? A little,' Anya replied. 'But it allows me a certain amount of freedom.'

'Bullshit. Her partiality is crippling your instinct. Never have you asked me for notes on a role!'

'Are you serious?' I asked.

'It's true. In all the years we've been friends—'

'About Judith.'

Richard turned to me. 'And here I was thinking Miss Queensland was fully grown.'

The image I'd buried of the exchange between Saxon and Judith in Genevieve's office came back to me. 'She'd never pursue a student.'

'She doesn't need to,' Richard said. 'They pursue her.'

The gravel churned with the wind. The courtyard was deserted. Only the truly committed patrons remained outdoors.

'I'll never live down failing twice,' Anya said.

Richard stood. 'You won't. Show me the script.'

They huddled together over the pages.

'I fucking love this play,' Richard said.

'So do I.'

'Try it again,' I said impatiently.

Richard gestured for me to wait and continued his dissection of the script. Anya tugged her short hair distractedly, mumbled responses I couldn't hear.

I sighed into the darkness; tried to cast my anxiety about Judith there.

Richard began to unbuckle his belt and spoke the first line of Ruth's text in a high-pitched, breathy voice.

Anya hit him with the script and laughed. 'Sexist pig!'

Their playfulness pulled me away from my thoughts and into their performance, newly found.

—

Inhale, ribs, abdomen; exhale, abdomen, ribs.

You were told one thing, instructed to do another. Each class another version of the next. There was a flash of understanding occasionally and you took it with you, tried it out then threw it away. Not everything worked every time.

Was it the teacher, the work, or was it you?

Inhale, ribs, abdomen; exhale, abdomen, ribs.

Yoga became a part of our daily practice, replacing some but not all of our Movement classes with Freya, though she was our teacher still. She said yoga might serve us well. And it did. You saw it in the work and the class after. Even the less nimble could relax into the postures without too much difficulty. There was no text, no curriculum, no Quinn.

Inhale, ribs, abdomen; exhale, abdomen, ribs.

No one to impress but yourself.

—

Barbara called for me to present *Miss Julie.*

'On top of the lines?' she asked.

'Yes.'

'Good. You're up.'

I stood and found a place for myself in the centre of the room, but without the protection of my peers I hesitated.

'Maeve?' Barbara's face was open. She nodded reassuringly. I expelled the fear I held through my breath and began.

'*No, I don't want to go yet.*'

I spoke ready for interruption and breathed into the phrase that followed with the permission of Barbara's silence.

'*You think I cannot stand the sight of blood. You think I am as weak as that—*'

My tension melted away. And I saw him, Jean, a man I'd crafted from Dylan, Yates, Saxon. A target for Miss Julie's frustration, discomfort, lust. Visible to me only, above the heads of my peers at the furthest wall. It made the moments sharper, more clearly defined. *Be specific*, Yates had told me. I was trying to be.

'*I think I could drink out of your skull, and bathe my feet in your open breast—*'

I wished the faculty were in attendance, that they could see the ingenue replaced with this other woman. If I could show them, there might be potential to explore other roles in second year, and in my third I wouldn't be stuck running the gamut of my archetype as I'd seen happen to the third-year company. There was only a small window for exploration before the faculty locked you into the version of yourself that was easiest to access, the name of the school more important than your own.

'*—but the lackey's line goes on in the orphan asylum—wins laurels in the gutter and ends in jail.*'

The final words were a whisper, not at all how I'd rehearsed it.

'You felt that, didn't you?' Barbara asked.

Freedom. 'Yes.'

'Excellent work, Maeve.' She gave thoughtful, considered feedback. Notes on breathing, diction and alignment. The feeling in the room was one of warm acceptance.

Barbara called another name.

As the next student began, I repeated the monologue back to myself surreptitiously, savouring the sensation of flight.

VIII

The gardens inside the National Gallery of Victoria were an oasis almost unknown to the public. The exterior of the building was austere. It was hard to imagine from the street just how expansive the grounds were, how lush and inviting, no matter the weather. Of course, Richard was the one to alert us to their existence. He seemed to have copious amounts of free time to roam, always on top of what was happening in his adopted city of Melbourne, unperturbed by the burden of the work. When he invited us to join him there it felt like he'd been keeping it from us until he felt ready to share it.

We started to use it as an extension of the school. The fresh air cleared the mind, brought perspective and calm at a time when we were hitting the floorboards hard.

It was one of a handful of crystal winter days. Richard and I lay on our coats, eyes closed to the sun. Dylan and Imogen were running lines, marking the new blocking of the *Three Sisters* scene between sculptures and symmetrically cut hedges.

'It works,' I said. 'It bloody well does.'

'Stop preaching,' Richard said. 'It's unbecoming.'

I rolled towards him. 'You agree, though, don't you? Barbara's process is kinder. She gets more out of us because of it.'

'Debatable.' Richard pointed in Imogen's direction.

'She's the exception.'

'*You* might be the exception. In reverse.'

'Can't you relent just once?'

'To appease your ego? Never.'

'Imogen's under pressure.'

'And it serves her.'

I raised myself up on my elbows and watched as Imogen fed Dylan his lines. She was patient with him in a way I struggled to be. It surprised me, the lightness that had come into her work since the beginning of our time with Quinn. She was kinder with herself and others.

'What does she say about it?' I asked.

Richard shrugged. 'She's determined. Doesn't let on.'

Quinn had continued to belittle Imogen by sending her on errands. We weren't brave enough to speak up on her behalf. Thankfully, we didn't have to. After a few weeks of this routine, Imogen began to smile when called on, as though it gave her grit, something to work against. Perhaps Quinn knew that was exactly what Imogen needed.

'Where's Saxon?' Richard asked.

'No idea.'

'Big of you,' he said.

I liked having places to go without him, being able to tell Saxon I was busy. It gave me freedom, autonomy. I told myself it meant I was mature, but really I hoped it would make him miss me, want me. Make him call more often.

'They're doing well, he and Viv,' Richard said.

'Very.'

'I like watching them together.'

'So do I.'

It was true. They were a natural pair. When they rose to take their places on the floor in Quinn's class for development, the room fell silent. You could learn from observing sometimes, if the work was strong enough. But there was a part of me that was jealous. I wanted to stand beside Saxon not just outside the drama building but inside it too. To be seen as his equal. I wondered if Quinn knew and kept us apart deliberately. It was too easy to pair people who were already courting; part of our training was to create chemistry from nothing.

'Does Saxon ever rehearse with Sylvie?' Richard asked, out of nowhere.

'Not that I know of,' I replied. 'Why would he?'

'No idea.'

Then I knew. It was like being kicked in the guts. And suddenly it was as though I'd been expecting it.

'Are you baiting me?' I asked.

'Into what? An argument? No. I'm simply passing on information. I care about you, darling.'

'Did you see them together? Alone?'

'No.'

'Then what the fuck are you talking about?'

Richard sat forward and nodded towards Imogen. 'Ask her.'

I was beside her in an instant. Afterwards, I would wonder if I'd manufactured the event instead of responding like it was something that was actually happening to me. As if I'd seen it somewhere and slotted it into my life.

'You've always hated him,' I said, wrenching Imogen out of her rehearsal with Dylan.

'What?' she asked, trying to free herself from my grip. She looked past me towards Richard. Her face softened with realisation. 'I wanted to tell you myself.'

'But you didn't think I'd believe you?'

'No.'

'They're friends.'

'And aren't we?'

My heart quickened and I let go. 'What did you see?'

'You should talk to him.'

'I'm asking you.'

There was pity in her eyes, the kind I was certain she'd seen in mine more than once.

'Your jealousy is sickening,' I said.

Dylan stepped in. 'Come on, Maeve. Don't say things you can't take back.'

'Like you can talk,' I threw at him. Then it dawned on me. 'You knew as well.'

My rage should have been directed at Saxon. But he wasn't there, and I wasn't ready to break something I couldn't name. Had we ever talked about being exclusive? I couldn't recall. I'd assumed our intimacy implied it.

'How long ago?' I asked Imogen.

'Does it matter?'

'Yes.'

'A couple of weeks,' she replied. 'In the meeting room on the first floor. Running lines—Goldoni, I think. They looked . . . very comfortable.'

'You waited all this time?'

'I hoped he might say something.'

'They were just rehearsing, Maeve,' Dylan said uncertainly.

'You really believe that?' I asked.

My friends looked at one another. They'd already leaped to conclusions apparently. The work bled into reality so easily sometimes.

'I don't know . . .' Dylan said.

I pressed my palms against my eyes and saw stars. 'How fucking embarrassing.'

They let me rant for a while. We'd all been broken at some point. Perhaps it was simply my turn.

'That's enough,' Richard said from behind, his palm between my shoulder blades. My cheeks were wet, my throat raw.

'Maeve,' Imogen said softly. 'Maeve?'

'Breathe,' Dylan urged.

'I'm fucking trying,' I wept.

We weren't entirely alone. Patrons were dotted throughout the gardens, all of them now turned in our direction.

I wanted to run, to find him, and at the same time to crawl away. 'I don't know what that was.'

'Yes, you do. Don't skirt around it,' Richard said. I was surprised by the authoritative tone in his voice.

'And channel it,' Dylan suggested. 'Don't waste it.'

I looked at him sadly. *Channel it.* The excuse, the reason, always.

We sat down exactly where we were, a small circle in the shade of the building. They let me leave it there, my ebullition, and we returned to our usual talk of Quinn, the second years and our training. I felt a surge of gratitude, though I didn't thank them.

I lay back when Dylan and Imogen started rehearsing again. Richard did the same and took my hand. The cool sky was a tonic. I watched the clouds pass quickly beneath it as Chekhov's words floated towards me, the voices of our scene partners caught on the wind.

—

The preview of *The Servant of Two Masters* was that afternoon. My friends pulled me up, got me a drink, then another. I walked into Studio One with the kind of heavy-headedness that came with drinking during the day. It brought on a nihilistic feeling I couldn't shake.

We weren't late but the seating bank was almost at capacity. Dylan, Richard and Imogen climbed it ahead of me, searching for a space to squeeze into. The faculty were spread throughout, pads in laps, ready to take notes. And there was Saxon beside Judith in the centre aisle.

'Juliet!' Saxon called.

Imogen turned back. 'Want me to come with you?'

'Definitely not.'

'I don't mind,' she said.

But I did. I wasn't ready to let rip, despite Imogen telling me I should.

'I'm fine, honestly,' I said.

Imogen sighed. She wanted a fight. 'We're here if you need us.'

When I reached Saxon's row he pulled me onto his lap. 'Missed ya.'

Judith patted my thigh. 'Don't get caught up in the drama.'

Like a needle through the heart. *She knows*, I thought. 'Sorry?' I looked between them, ready for Judith to launch into a lecture about how to harness heartbreak on the floor.

'With Dylan. I've been informed that it's affecting your work.'

It was a peculiar comfort to realise Judith was talking about *Three Sisters*. It would have come from Quinn, but the mention of it in front of Saxon felt pointed. It polarised our aptitude. Just the way she liked.

'I won't,' I said.

'Good girl.'

I stood up. Saxon kept hold of my wrist. 'Hey, stay a while.'

The others in the row jostled along at Saxon's command, and I settled into a seat of my own. He was being chivalrous. It took effort not to thank him, to remind myself of exactly why I felt the way I did. I steadied myself by focusing on the set in front of me, an Italian square bathed in warm light.

'Seen a Goldoni before?' Saxon asked.

I shook my head, twisted my cheek between eye teeth. 'You?'

'Yeah, in Italy.'

'Didn't know you'd been.'

'Is that an accusation?'

'Yes.'

Saxon laughed and bit my ear. It blatantly marked me as his. But I could feel Imogen watching and waiting for my response. I did nothing. It was worse than violence almost, an insult to us both after the hours she'd spent consoling me.

The overture blared through the speakers and the Italian square began to bustle.

The audience knew from the first word exactly what they were getting. *Victory* had alienated the school's usual audience; *The Servant of Two Masters* would draw them back. Relief swept through the seating bank and the students became raucous, keen to show support and make clear they understood the action.

It was a habit of mine, formed in that theatre, to turn my head and observe the audience as they took in the first few moments of a play; their faces, either blank or whipped with emotion, indicated how willing they were to receive it. And though the audience contained my peers, who were accustomed to her talent, when Sylvie entered every pair of eyes was drawn to her and turned golden by the light of her presence. When I looked at her myself, I saw no sign of our late nights together. Her work never suffered, no matter how much she consumed. I realised I'd hoped it would. Had I always? Or had that afternoon's revelation brought it out in me? It was difficult to tell; the searing betrayal had burned through many layers.

My teeth slipped inside my mouth, and I tasted blood.

'Sorry, sorry.' I was up, brushing past sets of legs and running down the stairs. The emptiness of the foyer enveloped me, and I stood very still, acutely aware of my lack of resolve. Fleeing helped nothing. I'd have to sit through the play again and be punished by viewing Sylvie's work twice.

Like a taunt, I heard her voice. It hit me with a gush of cold air from the theatre as the doors opened again, overridden only by the muffled sound of laughter.

'What's going on?' Saxon asked.

I had been ready to surrender to self-loathing, to steal a bottle of wine from the bar and lie down alone in the Botanic Gardens.

Saxon punctured the romantic vision I had of drowning my sorrows by running a rough palm along my throat and turning me to face him.

'I just . . . I can't.'

Saxon frowned, concerned. 'What is it?'

I opened my mouth and blood trickled out of the corner.

'Ah,' Saxon said and smudged it into my skin. He dragged his thumb to my chin then lifted it off, holding it between us for a moment before placing it inside his own mouth. Proof, I'd reflect on later, of his investment in us. 'Come back inside.'

I shook my head.

'Want something for the pain?'

'Yes.'

Then her voice again, more laughter, and Richard and Imogen slipped through the theatre doors. Richard looked expectant and Imogen anxious.

There'd be rumours now. Four of us leaving mid-performance would not go unnoticed. The other students would whisper, concoct stories. It might be to my benefit, create a mystique around me like the one that swirled around Sylvie. Or it could be the beginning of a slow decline, depending on what I did next.

If Saxon was aware of the presence of my friends, he didn't say. I smiled weakly at them over his shoulder then turned away.

'Where exactly in Italy did you say?' I asked, taking Saxon's hand and leading him towards the exit.

'I didn't.'

'Go on then,' I said.

As we stepped through the glass doors the cold hit me like a shock. But Saxon saved me from it: he wrapped his coat around my shoulders, and we left.

—

After class, after debrief, after drinks and dinner, after we'd hurried back to his house in a desperate lurch of intimacy and undressed, after he'd let me curl into the groove of him, I'd find my nerve and ask him to *speak to me*. And he would. His Hamlet, piercing the dark. Never the same soliloquy, always a surprise. How I bathed in his voice, relished his *exposure*. It meant something. *I* meant something.

Often, much later, he would call out in his sleep, and I'd be startled awake. Not Shakespeare. A child, asking for his mother. An unearthed instinct would take hold of me. I'd stroke his hair and say, *It's okay*, made self-important by his need for me.

IX

'Fucking yes!' Richard screamed, head tilted back, face to the night sky. 'Darling, you were a vision! A *vision!*' He didn't hand out compliments often, so to hear it from him, for us to witness it, must have felt grander than a glowing review in *The Age*. Anya was deserving of it too. She'd held her own beside the men, imposing in their numbers on the bare stage. She'd risen to Judith's challenge, worked hard and proven she was capable of being a lead. It was inspiring to watch her transform between roles, from a scene study to a Shakespearean play and on to a contemporary one. It proved that the training worked.

Anya keeled over laughing, then rose and saluted her friend with a glass of red. 'Thank you!' Her modesty lasted a mere second before she launched herself forward and ran around the dugout, wine splashing.

Winter lingered but we were joined by the company members above us. After a long stretch of their absence, the Malthouse courtyard felt full. There was a feeling of camaraderie now the plays had opened, and I couldn't wait for the surge of energy the second and third years felt to transfer to me off the back of performance. They spent their days recovering as much from their evening shows as from the drinks afterwards, while the first years continued to labour over the *Three Sisters* scene.

Saxon stroked my hair and talked to a third year as I watched Anya and Richard collude across the courtyard. Dylan and Imogen were discussing Pinter with Vivien. It felt almost like the beginning, before we really knew what was expected of us.

My friends did me the courtesy of feigning amnesia when it came to Saxon. They looked away when they saw us together and nodded sympathetically when I thanked them drunkenly for their friendship. *I'll ask him about her soon*, I'd promise, but we all knew it would take something momentous for that to happen. As for Sylvie, I avoided her completely.

'Hear ye, hear ye!'

A man's voice echoed through the courtyard, having the desired effect of drawing everyone towards it. Yates moved into the light and plonked himself down beside his daughter. He took her glass, had a sip and held on to it.

He was a familiar presence to us now. Casts from various venues around the precinct appeared often at the Malthouse post-show. But Dylan joined us so infrequently after class that to see Yates in such a casual setting stirred something in him. 'I'm going to talk to him,' he said.

'Absolutely not,' Imogen replied. 'You're drunk.'

Ignoring her, Dylan stood, steadied himself and walked towards Yates.

Vivien shook her head as he approached, a silent warning. *Don't.*

It was too late: Yates was aware.

'Show me,' he said as Dylan stood before him.

Dylan froze. The students and patrons in the courtyard stilled.

'*Show me,*' Yates said again.

'What would you like?' Dylan asked, his anxiety clear.

'This is an opportunity, son,' Yates said. 'I'll be casting *Lord of the Flies* for a limited season at fortyfivedownstairs.' He paused, allowing curiosity to swell. 'Show me the monologue you've been working on with Barbara.'

There was no way Yates would cast someone over drinks. He'd scout openings, ask colleagues, hold auditions to create a careful blend of recognisable names and up-and-comers; Dylan was neither. This wasn't an audition. This was sport.

Dylan inhaled and began quietly. '*When my cue comes, call me, and I will answer.*'

'Bollocks!' Yates bellowed. 'Make it watchable, lad!'

A bubble of laughter.

Dylan spoke above it. '*My next is "most fair Pyramus". Heigh-ho.*'

We leaned closer, careful not to disturb the gravel beneath our feet or gulp from our glasses lest we be noticed and called upon to join in. It had the effect of driving focus towards Dylan, allowing him the illusion of our support.

'*I have had a most rare vision. I have had a dream past the wit of man to say what dream it was.*'

A Midsummer Night's Dream—fitting, for all that it alluded to. Dylan's Bottom echoed his own earnestness.

'For god's sake, endear them to you!' Yates called.

Dylan was desperate for acceptance, and his confidence built with our attention. Patrons wandered closer, lured from the street by the vibration of his voice. They began to respond with laughter, to punctuate the text with applause. The crowd grew.

Yates stopped heckling and began to direct with sincerity—not for Dylan's sake, but his own. 'Draw them in, lad, draw them in!'

Dylan turned slowly, acknowledging his director's note through action, with open palms, meeting the gaze of the audience surrounding him. '*The eye of man hath not heard, the ear of man hath not seen—*'

There were cheers, whistles. The circle tightened around him. Yates had to stand like the rest of us to keep eyes on his actor. He continued to call out, but it was clear that neither Dylan nor the audience regarded his presence as necessary anymore. So Yates pierced the fourth wall, stepped into Dylan's space so that actor and director were together on show.

Dylan was too far in now to be intimidated. He'd caught the energy of the piece and rode it with the support of the patrons. '*It shall be called "Bottom's Dream", because it hath no bottom—*'

Yates couldn't assert his power now by flipping the monologue into a demonstration of his own talent. All he could do was wait for it to end and declare afterwards that he'd drawn this performance out of the drama student.

But his ego was larger than reason. As Dylan soared towards the final line, Yates gripped Dylan behind the neck and brought their foreheads together.

'*Peradventure, to make it the more gracious,*' they roared at each other, '*I shall sing it at her death.*'

Yates let go and Dylan fell backwards.

Applause bounced off the brick walls of the Malthouse and transformed the courtyard into an arena. There were calls for more. Yates bowed, shook his head. 'Not tonight,' he repeated until the cheering petered out. Dylan stood and tried to catch the eye of his director, but Yates was besieged by the crowd, carried inside to the bar. Dylan watched his idol drift from sight.

'Did you see me?' he said to no one, to everyone.

Yes, we screeched.

My friends gave Dylan gentle feedback and congratulated him on his courage. I was alone in my annoyance at what I saw as Dylan's flagrant need for approval, my perspective informed by what I knew about my scene partner from working with him in private. I wanted to puncture his buoyancy. 'Didn't quite make sense, though, coming together at the end.'

'On the contrary,' Richard said. 'I found it poetic.'

'Yes!' Imogen agreed. 'Opposing versions of the same man.'

Saxon placed a hand on my spine. It brought me back to my surroundings. He was the only one who knew the true source of my frustration.

'I suppose it could be interpreted that way,' I mumbled.

'Papa *has* played the role before,' Vivien said at the same time, and my comment went unheard. We could all jump on Yates now and unite in our indignation at how, in a public setting, he'd made such a show of Dylan's vulnerability.

''Course he bloody has!' Richard exclaimed.

'Opportunist,' Anya said darkly.

'You did good, Dylan,' Vivien said. 'Really.'

Dylan's face softened with the acknowledgement. 'Thanks.'

I did not join in with the compliments; I sat there feeling sour. I sensed Dylan searching for me in the darkness, my silence as pointed as praise.

—

I breathed in downward dog as the company trickled into the Rehearsal Room, taking their place on the floor and beginning a daily practice of their own.

Freya had been right, yoga did serve me, and I let the image of her drift through my consciousness as I moved through each posture. I had underestimated her, our Movement teacher, and realised that she wasn't any less of an artist just because she wasn't currently working on the main stage. I'd not considered that teaching might have been a choice, a way to serve her practice, bolster her art. How ignorant I was. A creative life could evolve.

I'd come across a framed photograph of Freya on the first floor, in a third-year production of *Cloud Nine*. I learned that after her training she'd gone on to work for the Sydney Theatre Company, Belvoir and Steppenwolf in Chicago. If I'd known earlier, I might have taken her approach to Movement a little more seriously. Now, in third term, I felt as though I'd wasted an opportunity.

When she entered at ten past nine, I came to attention and waited patiently for instruction. She unrolled her mat and sat in lotus. I mimicked her as though luck had no place in my future, had no place in hers either, as though the course of our lives would be determined simply by how hard we worked. Or, contrarily, how little.

Inhale, ribs, abdomen; exhale, abdomen, ribs.

—

Barbara insisted on there being no audience for the monologue showing. To work towards an end point so early in our training would be counterproductive. The rush of adrenaline that comes with the presence of an audience might revert us to our former selves, the ones who'd got us into the building but would never be allowed to leave.

There was an order, alphabetical, to keep things even between company members, but really no one was nervous. The afternoon would be an extension of Barbara's classes, with a final round of notes at the end.

So it came as a surprise to see Yates slip through the Rehearsal Room door. We all turned at the click of the handle. Barbara winked at her old friend without pausing her speech, the last one she'd deliver before she left us.

'Leave yourself open to discovery. Do not settle into the familiar!'

Phillip pulled a chair from a stack at the back of the room and placed it behind us for Yates to sit on. I realised, with a flutter of excitement, that he was the only person I truly wanted to share the piece with, that his was the only opinion I cared about. It felt fortuitous that he should witness it, my last attempt at *Miss Julie*. In hindsight, I realised it had been his plan all along.

'Finally, I'd like to thank Phillip for permitting me to take over his classes with you. The techniques you are learning in Voice will allow you to connect to your thoughts and feelings more deeply, and connect in turn with those of the characters you play.'

We applauded. Barbara smiled and applauded back as though *she* were grateful to *us*. Perhaps she was. We'd given ourselves over to her so willingly, put into practice the method she'd spent decades perfecting.

My name was called, and I took my place on the floor, settling my gaze just above Yates's head. As I stood there, conjuring a world to step into, I replayed his phrase: *Be specific*.

'And breathe,' Barbara prompted.

I closed my eyes, inhaled through my nose and opened my mouth to speak on the outward breath.

'Wait,' Yates said.

My eyes flicked open.

'Barbara, I apologise,' Yates said earnestly, placing a hand upon his chest.

Barbara shook her head. 'Not at all.'

'It's just—a thought has occurred to me.'

'Always a dangerous prospect,' Barbara deadpanned.

Yates smiled, spoke gently, 'Well, why talk to a blank wall when you could use *me*?'

The company tittered. It felt almost as though it were at my expense.

'This piece in particular could use a body as stimuli,' Barbara mused. She turned to me again. 'Maeve, respond to the physical offers you receive from Mr Yates.'

'I will,' I replied, preoccupied with the thumping inside my chest that turned Yates into a wavering vision. I closed my eyes again, and when I opened them he was barely a foot away.

'Begin,' Barbara said.

The truth was, I'd never delivered the speech to anyone before—it had always been conceptual. To have a man, Yates in particular, to bounce the lines off changed everything. And he knew it; there was pleasure to be had in being implicit in the undoing of a woman, inside a character like Miss Julie.

'*No, I don't want to go yet.*'

The voice didn't sound like mine. It had a guttural quality. It surprised me and my thoughts split between Miss Julie's and my own. But I stayed with it, stopped chasing what I'd experienced the last time I'd worked the text, to yield to what Yates was offering.

The space between us seemed to vibrate. Any movement he made had the effect of jolting me backwards or compelling me towards him. When he finally touched me, taking my wrist tenderly with both hands and turning it over in his palm, I felt a shock so disturbing I had to stop before delivering my next line.

'*You think I cannot stand the sight of blood. You think I am as weak as that—*'

Yates leered threateningly. It was just as I'd imagined Jean might do at that precise moment and I thought, *He's done this before.* That, or Yates was capable of imperceptibly shifting out of himself and into the skin of another.

There were no wrong choices, Barbara had always made that clear, but the words I spoke were so contradictory to the physical that I felt I had to regain some kind of power. I pulled my wrist from his grip.

'*—and then I shall tell everything!*'

Yates leaned closer and I slapped him. The room took one sharp, collective breath and held it, suspending all of us inside the scene. I hadn't humiliated him exactly; I'd met him on his level. Maybe it was one and the same.

He was acting now, caught in tableau, hand to cheek, bent over at the waist. The only movement came from his eyes. They turned slowly in their sockets to stare at my feet. If this were to be played out in real life, his response to mine would have been far more violent. He'd go for my throat, chase me until I was his.

The alternative was far worse.

Slowly, very slowly, Yates raised his head and stepped closer. I withdrew. The room receded to a fish-eye vision, and I winced when my back hit the cold wall of the Rehearsal Room. He removed the distance between us, came so close I could smell his sweat, could read the years in the lines on his face. He spread my legs with his knee and planted a soft kiss on the underside of my jaw.

'*Oh, but it will be good to get an end to it—*'

Against my thigh his erection was firm, and my body responded with breath. I gulped it in, down to my pelvis. *There it is*, I thought, *at long bloody last.*

Yates panted hot air with excruciating restraint. 'Be specific,' he uttered.

I became very still: '*—if it only be the end.*'

Yates groaned. With the jarred sound came more breath, Miss Julie's words carried upon it, until finally, he rose to face me for the final line through a serious of quick adjustments, like the cracking of knuckles.

'*—wins laurels in the gutter and ends in jail.*'

There could be no natural ending. No resolution without Strindberg's finale. It was intolerable, sinking into one another's gaze like that, waiting for Barbara to call it.

'Rest,' she said finally.

The room boiled over in a tentative fit of laughter, releasing Yates and me from our roles. But I could feel his eyes roaming over my body, daring me to voice the secret he'd hidden within the performance.

He took my shoulders in his large hands and pressed downwards. 'We had fun, didn't we?' he said, then let go. It felt like being tossed aside.

The conversation that followed was full of congratulatory feedback. The insertion of Yates, my peers emphasised, allowed for a more authentic interpretation of Miss Julie. But those charged final moments were inseparable from my own feelings, and I was desperate to perform the monologue over, to reclaim some kind of ownership of it.

The next student was called. Yates didn't offer to stand in. He settled into his chair again and conversed cordially with Phillip as the first few lines were spoken. I sat on the floor and searched for Saxon. He smiled at me and mimed applause. But it wasn't as reassuring as a nod from Vivien, a little further along.

—

'Red?' Saxon asked, leaning against the doorframe.

'Sure.'

He knocked on the wall with his knuckles in affirmation, and disappeared down the hallway, taking all warmth with him.

Alone in his room, I looked at it anew. The books on the mantelpiece, the collection of ticket stubs and bottle caps on the side table. Evidence of where he'd been, what he'd done without me. Traces of Sylvie, perhaps.

Had he brought her here? Would it matter if he had? If they'd been physical, yes. But maybe their rehearsals required it. It was excusable. Almost.

'Shame you missed it,' Saxon said, catching me thumbing the program of *A View from the Bridge*, abandoned by the window.

'I was . . .' But I couldn't remember where I'd been that evening.

'With Imogen, you said.'

'Right.'

We stood in the darkness. The white light from the streetlamp through the window pane caught the underside of his chin. I resisted the urge to trail my finger along it, wanting instead for him to ask me what was wrong.

251

Saxon offered me a glass. 'You must be drained.'

'You as well.'

'I wasn't up there with Yates.' He moved in front of me and leaned against the windowsill. 'What did it feel like?'

'Real.'

'That's the goal,' he said and tapped his glass against mine.

I couldn't match his enthusiasm. 'Aren't we supposed to protect a small part of ourselves?'

'For what?'

I wasn't sure exactly. 'For the sake of our sanity.'

'I'd rather what you experienced.'

'And what's that exactly?'

Saxon drained his glass. 'Immersion.'

I did the same and asked for another. He gave me the bottle. I sank it while he talked about Arthur Miller. I liked listening to him form opinions about things, catching each thought as it sprang from his subconscious. It felt like an extension of trust, to be included in these musings. What we shared publicly was almost always already formed.

'Miller turned down Hollywood, worked in the theatre, honed his skills there,' Saxon said.

My anger slipped away. When it resurfaced, I wasn't able to recognise it as mine. The afternoon had morphed all feeling into a haze I lay beneath, of Miss Julie's character and my own.

'That can't be true,' I said sometime later, placing the empty bottle on the bedside table next to the photograph of Saxon as a boy. 'Five days?' I ran my finger along the frame, collecting dust from the glass above his little face.

'Legend has it.'

'Imagine having that kind of confidence.'

'You do,' Saxon said.

I laughed and absorbed the compliment. 'Thank you.' I closed my eyes and felt the bed against my back without meaning to fall. The sheets smelled the same; there was comfort in that. I could sense him above me and waited. A hand on my chest, lips on my neck.

'Miller's first play, written in'—I paused, enjoying the sensation of his rough chin on my clavicle—'five . . . days.'

I was drunk. The *Miss Julie* monologue rushed through me. I stopped the words as they bristled on my tongue, and I imagined Yates watching from the far corner of the room.

'You were really present today,' Saxon said, snapping me from the vision I'd slipped into. 'Beautiful to watch.'

I sat up on my elbows. 'I think I really hurt him, slapping him that hard.'

'It was necessary,' Saxon replied. 'He was testing you.'

We were on the precipice of something. I could feel myself leaning into it, looking over the edge. Did being present mean I could do what I liked? I was present now.

I lifted my hand, pulled it back. Saxon caught it before it hit his face.

'That was beautiful too: watching you decide,' he said. He rolled off me, onto the mattress.

'No, I don't want to go yet.'

The first line, out there, inside Saxon's room.

'Go on,' he said.

I threw my leg over his body, straddled him and brought my mouth close to his ear. *'I think I could drink out of your skull, and bathe my feet in your open breast—'*

I undressed him, he undressed me, and the monologue continued. Another version, softer but just as real.

I made him wait until the final line, revelling in my power over him. The feeling lingered long after release.

We'd crossed a line, and each time that followed there would always be the question of whether we'd slip back into that world together.

'Again,' Saxon said after an hour of quiet.

Yates's face floated in front of his. The deep lines and penetrating stare. It aroused me.

'No, I don't want to go yet.'

I'd never be able to release her, Miss Julie. She'd forever sit inside me, like a Russian doll, encased in the skin of the character that would come after her, and the one after that. I'd only ever get to play her again in ways like this, with Saxon, the ending never complete. Yates may have hijacked the monologue, but he'd gifted me a slice of Miss Julie and brought her to life.

—

The following evening, Vivien stood beside her father on the other side of the Arts Centre foyer, the pair of them surrounded by his fans. She held her face in soft reproach, upturning the corners of her mouth slightly whenever a head turned towards her. It could be mistaken for a smile by the encircling women. I knew better. Underneath she was seething.

The play had only just finished, and the bar was crammed with people ready to gulp down cheap wine and throw their opinions around the room. Red cheeks, stained lips. It was that kind of evening. Anya, Imogen, Richard and I had separated ourselves and claimed a stretch of the bar where service wouldn't be interrupted by our presence. We were drinking greedily, one of us always waiting in the queue so that there would be no chance of sobriety.

I stopped listening to what Richard and Anya were talking about, didn't offer my thoughts on the performance of the lead when Imogen asked, 'What did you think?' I was too engrossed in observing the woman I knew from class, the girlfriend of my mate, my rival on the floor.

Vivien had been cold towards me from the outset. It had never occurred to me to ask her why. I skirted around the tension between us, and sometimes criticised her in a vain attempt to diminish her talent.

Yates paid Vivien no attention, turning his back on his daughter as he flirted with his admirers. She stared into her glass, her lips moving slightly. Was she counting? Yes. Five inhalations. She shook her hair from her face and leaned towards her father, gestured towards the bar.

Yates acknowledged her with a throwaway gesture, a swat.

I didn't look away as she turned in my direction, and when our eyes met across the room I saw a flash of fear before she replaced it with what I'd come to think of as her mask.

The conditions of Richard's friendship with me made sense all of a sudden, as did the negative way Vivien responded to my work. It had little to do with me and everything to do with what she knew about women. I was competition, not just on the floor, but for her father's attention too. And I realised she'd been groomed to believe, as most women were, that there wasn't enough room at the table for all of us.

But since the opening of *Doubt*, I'd imagined that perhaps we could be friends, and if not friends then at least allies. She'd acknowledged something that night, cracked my vision of her as the villain in my story. She was more than that—she was an artist trying to create space for herself.

I should have kept this revelation to myself, but I ached for Vivien's approval; I hadn't understood until then that I always had. When she approached, I took her hand. 'Can we talk?' Whether she was intrigued or merely tired I couldn't tell. Either way, she accompanied me to a quiet corner of the foyer.

'I get it now,' I said.

Vivien knew what I meant without explanation. 'You've seen a glimmer, Maeve, you've not lived it.'

'It must be impossible being his daughter. Having to prove yourself all the time.'

I gestured in the direction of her father with my wineglass.

Vivien took the glass, drank from it and handed it back in one fluid motion. 'Don't feel sorry for me. I know what I want, where I want to go and what I have to do to get there.'

'You can talk to me.'

'Is that so?'

'Yes.'

Vivien's face became blank, wiped clean of emotion. She studied me and, as she did, I saw inside her, through each iris, the full life she had already lived in the presence of artists. She could play anyone with the knowledge she'd acquired. Male or female, it didn't matter. Brutus, Hedda Gabler, Abigail Williams, Stanley Kowalski. We would never be equals. She'd had a head start.

'I like boundaries,' Vivien said, blinking quickly and casting her gaze across the room. 'Everyone wants to work with Papa.'

'I don't.'

'*Everyone.*'

'Well, the offer is there.'

Vivien contemplated her father. 'You know, I've never seen anyone stand up to him like that before.'

The foyer seemed to fall away, and for a moment we were the only two people on the planet. 'Miss Julie?'

'Yes, her,' Vivien murmured. 'I saw it, Maeve. The choice you made.'

I looked at my Cons, battered from wear. 'Thank you.'

'No.' Vivien's voice was commanding; I looked up at her again. 'Thank *you*.'

It was nothing more than a moment, a glimpse of what our relationship could be in the future. Like a flash in the dark, gone again in an instant.

'Now, let's get buckled and get the fuck out of here,' Vivien said.

The next best thing to friendship.

X

The woman before me looked undone. Not beautifully so, not like Sylvie, but freshly wounded. Bloodshot eyes, mascara tracks. Flushed cheeks, ears and neck.

The locker rooms were empty but would soon fill as students finished up for the day and prepared for their evening performances. I had hurried out of the *Three Sisters* showing to clean up, to leave before running into anyone. But now I was paralysed. Stuck on the image of myself. This woman, this stranger who peered at me through mirrored glass.

'What do you need?' Imogen asked, her face appearing beside mine. She spun me towards her, and I crumpled to the floor.

'That didn't happen,' I said. 'It didn't.'

Imogen placed her hands on my back. 'Stand up,' she said. 'Stand up, Maeve.' But I couldn't. I was flooded with shame.

—

A confidence in Dylan's and my ability as a duo had bloomed since his performance in the Malthouse courtyard. He'd taken what he'd learned from Yates and delivered it with Barbara. It was insight into what my scene partner needed to really soar: attention.

We rehearsed in the evenings, fleshed out every possible choice our characters might make, so that if we steered off course we'd be able to come back to one another. And I listened. The answer wasn't inside myself. I couldn't work any harder to know Irina. The connection to her, to the world of the play and to the baron, existed in the space between Dylan and me on the floor.

The *Three Sisters* showing had been closed to the rest of the school. It was faculty and company members only. But my mind wandered to Yates—he might appear again. It was him I thought of when Dylan delivered his first line. I lost my bearings and could find no way of replying. In the extended pause that spread between us I had the acute feeling of floating outside myself. The walls were too white, the quiet too loud, my peers too close for me to be able to move freely.

There was an unspoken rule that no matter what happened during a showing or a performance, the actor must stay inside the scene. No matter whose line it was, whether it had been dropped or skipped or replaced entirely. It's what we were in training for, to live and respond in the moment, for the knowledge to settle like silt within us and expand the boundaries set in place for our characters.

I tried to bring myself back. *Your name is Irina Prozorov. It is nearing the turn of the twentieth century. This is the baron. You live in a provincial town in Russia.*

I couldn't voice the text. The rhythm was lost. Without rhythm there were no beats. Without beats there could be no meaning. Like a dog chasing its tail, I'd never recover the scene.

'Can we start over?' I asked.

Strange, I thought, *that my body should speak on my behalf.*

The room fluttered. Quinn remained completely still, almost unsurprised.

'No,' she said. 'Pick it up from where you were.'

I vibrated with panic. 'Can I take a moment to centre myself?'

'No.'

'*Please.*'

'Pick it up,' Quinn said, each consonant crisp, 'or get out.'

'I can't,' I choked. '*I can't.*'

My footsteps were percussive against the floorboards as I fled. I could hear Quinn's voice but couldn't make out her words. And then I was through the door, running along the passageway to the stairwell. The metal railing against my rib cage; the dizzying drop below. The beating of my blood beneath a Hollywood score. Which heroine? Madeleine. Falling from the bell tower. *Vertigo.* A scream: my own. Then another.

The hysteria sent breath to places I'd only ever been able to access on one other occasion. With Yates. I closed my eyes, held the railing and shook with fury. He wavered there with Miss Julie. I heard myself scream again.

'Maeve.' Freya's voice was tender. 'Maeve.'

I slid to the concrete, my body wrecked, heaving.

'Maeve,' she said again and spread her hands across my shoulder blades. '*Inhale, ribs, abdomen; exhale, abdomen, ribs.*'

'I can't—stop—' I stuttered.

'I know . . . *Inhale—*' she instructed gently. '*Ribs—*'

It took many repetitions of the mantra to ease my breathing.

'They're waiting for you,' she said eventually.

I turned my face to hers. 'What do you mean?' I asked sharply.

'Finish it, or you'll be asked to leave.'

I stared at her in stunned silence. 'Can I try again tomorrow?'

'Now, I'm afraid.'

'But—'

'Shall I call your parents? Ask them to collect you?'

The fear of being forcibly removed coaxed an answer from me. 'No,' I said. 'I'm okay.' Trying to believe it.

Freya understood. We walked back along the passageway together and waited for the voices inside the Rehearsal Room to rise, denoting a break in the scene work. She held open the door, and I waited for permission to re-enter.

Silence.

Quinn turned in her chair, her avian features more pronounced in anger. She threw one tasselled end of an ivory pashmina around her neck and pointed at me. 'Are you quite finished?'

I dared not search for comfort in the faces of my friends. 'Yes.'

'Then *get on the floor.*'

I drew in a quick, shallow breath.

Quinn laughed bitterly. 'Your preparation leaves a great deal to be desired. *Move.*'

I walked without consciously choosing to. Dylan scrambled to standing. The edges of my vision darkened so that I could look nowhere but at his open, adolescent face.

'Begin,' Quinn demanded.

Dylan hesitated. Quinn stood, and with her movement Dylan spoke his first line as though taking up a challenge. The threat of physical intervention spurred me on, and I responded.

Quinn guided us through the scene with affected weariness, directing me to step, to speak, all my impulses having fallen through the floor. I was lost up there. Completely and utterly lost.

Pretend, I told myself. *Fucking pretend.*

When it was over, Dylan was kind—far kinder than I had ever been when he'd wavered off course.

'Wasn't at all how we'd rehearsed but it still made sense, I think,' he said when we resumed our seats on the floor beside our company.

I felt worse for it. I deserved to bear the brunt of his anger. But he had none. Dylan was growing into an artist. I was being left behind.

—

The locker room was beginning to fill now. Steel doors opened and closed; students loitered for a glimpse of me. I would have done the same. Another breakdown, nothing particularly special. A vague warning. *This could happen to you.*

'How did I get here?' I asked Imogen.

'Physically or metaphorically?'

'Both,' I replied.

'I can't answer that,' Imogen said. Her voice was soothing. I wanted to curl up inside it and forget myself.

'I'm so sorry I didn't watch your scene,' I said.

'You did.'

'Not really. How was it?'

She pulled me towards her. I felt the steady rise and fall of her breath and hoped that she would tell me it had gone terribly, that I would have someone to wager my worth against in the lower rung of the company.

'Good.'

It was a simple, honest response. I flicked my face upwards and saw a lighter version of my friend. She looked settled, satisfied. The pressure of Quinn's presence had served her well, just as Richard had said it would.

I began to cry. Imogen tried to quiet me with words, to soothe me with touch. I sobbed against her cheek. Her mouth slid onto my lips. I became silent when her tongue pressed against my teeth. I released my jaw, opened myself to her and for a blissful moment forgot who I was.

Your name is Irina Prozorov. It is nearing the turn of the twentieth century. This is the baron. You live in a provincial town in Russia.

Imogen's eyes remained half closed as she pulled away. There was a quick, quiet acknowledgement of how vulnerable she'd made herself to me.

'So,' she said without apology, a warm smile creeping across her face. When I said nothing, her chin quivered, and she looked at me imploringly. 'Better?'

No, I thought, feeling a sense of loss I couldn't place. Then I saw him standing behind her as my field of vision widened, and I returned to where I was.

His name caught in my throat, and I had a moment to choose the kind of person I wanted to be. I left my friend on the floor and followed Saxon out of the locker room, through the hallway and down the spiral staircase. Students lingered in the foyer as

I tumbled past, and I wondered if they knew how horribly I'd behaved from the words that trickled out of my mouth. *Please. I'm sorry. Come back.*

The full force of the afternoon hit me as I stepped outside into the cold. Fatigue settled in my chest and spread to my bones. I felt drunk with it.

Saxon was waiting for me on the kerb. When I approached, he began to walk. I followed him to the corner of the building. He stopped there, lit a cigarette and waited for me to speak.

I reached for his hand, but there was a distance between us now. He took a step back and I was reminded, through the embarrassment of being denied, of the anger I had been harbouring towards him.

'You've been fucking her,' I said, with venom in my voice.

It pleased me to see Saxon's features sharpen in admonition. I deserved what was coming after that; I was asking for it.

'Who?'

I stalled. I had expected him to deny the allegation, the details of which I didn't really know.

'You've been rehearsing together,' I said.

Recognition flashed across Saxon's face. 'Ah,' he said and nodded towards the drama building behind me. 'So that's what that was. Retaliation.'

My face burned. 'You admit it?'

'Yes,' Saxon said plainly. 'Sylvie and I have been rehearsing together. She asked me to keep it quiet.'

I believed him. Saxon was loyal; Sylvie had an image to maintain. She wouldn't like anyone knowing that she'd needed assistance in building the character she was getting so much praise for in the Goldoni. It diminished the persona she projected; revealed a corner of the woman she truly was. The woman I'd refused to see.

'You haven't been together?' I asked.

'Not in the way you're imagining.'

Saxon took a drag of his cigarette and passed it to me. I twisted it and inspected the small flare. I could press it against my wrist, I thought, dull the crazed feeling in which I was floating.

'You and me,' Saxon said.

'Are fucking.'

Saxon flinched. My words were coarse and I could see that they hurt him more than they did me.

'Exclusively,' he replied.

The relief felt like a flood. I could swim back through it, regain ground. I took a drag of the cigarette, blew the smoke out through my nose. I'd been practising.

'What do you think we've been doing?' Saxon asked.

'With what?'

'Us!' he shouted in frustration. 'I want to be with you. It's that simple.' He stepped back and gestured at my head. 'But there's this whole other world you're living in.'

His words sliced me apart; I knew they were true. 'I—aren't we—aren't you in it?'

'Where?'

I looked around me, clutched at my chest. 'Here?'

'Nah, I don't appear to be.' He turned to the drama building with a pained look. 'Imogen is in love with you.'

'No, she isn't.' A vision of Imogen left alone in the locker room came to me. I shuddered at my own cruelty.

'Stop deluding yourself, come on.'

'She can't be.'

But I knew he was right. Saxon saw the truth of people, while I saw only how they behaved in relation to myself. 'I ruined the scene,' I said, disassociating.

Saxon glared at me in disbelief. 'There'll be others.' He took the cigarette from between my fingers, drew in smoke and stubbed it out. A door had been closed, a part of him shut off.

'For you, maybe,' I replied, too scared to apologise for the damage I'd caused.

Saxon looked at me sadly. 'I remember watching you at the auditions. Couldn't take my eyes off you. You had no idea how strong your instincts were back then.'

'And now?'

He didn't answer.

'Can I come back to yours?' I asked, desperate. If I could touch him there'd be connection. It could all be erased.

Saxon dragged a booted foot against the kerb. 'Not tonight.'

The wind began to howl, scattering what little remained of my dignity. I kissed him hard on the mouth, put my hand on his crotch. He didn't kiss me back. When I pulled away, he looked injured.

'Juliet—'

'Take me to your place,' I pleaded.

I waited for him to respond as the weather whipped around us, but time tracked on without a word.

'I'm done,' I said, not meaning it, wanting something to hurl myself at after the humiliation of the afternoon. Of getting so much so wrong.

One beat, two beats, three.

I made the quick decision to abandon my possessions. I couldn't walk inside the drama building without someone asking me how

I felt. I didn't trust myself to keep quiet. Like a thread, the *Three Sisters* scene could unravel it all.

I turned my back on Saxon and walked briskly along the street. I hoped he would follow me, wrap his jacket around my shoulders like always. I slowed my pace and finally turned at the corner near Kings Way, expectant. But the shape of him had already dissolved into the inky Melbourne night.

We'd never talked about love, but the dizziness I felt at the immediate loss of him was everything I'd ever read about.

This hurts, I wanted to scream. But the city already knew. Heartbreak was as common as the cold.

—

I wore my rehearsal blacks, no make-up, hair pulled back off my face. Ashamed and serious and sorry.

'You need a break,' Judith said.

I was experiencing deja vu, surely. The same room, the same number of chairs, the same faculty members sitting in front of me for the end-of-term review. Only this time, instead of receiving praise, it was the opposite.

'To pull out of a scene like that . . .' Quinn trailed off, allowing space for the disappointment I felt in myself to permeate my body. She leaned forward, prised my journal from my hands and began turning its pages with casual authority.

'We're concerned, Maeve,' Ford said. 'Go home for the break.'

'Have I failed?' I asked.

Freya couldn't look at me directly. She opened her mouth to speak but was silenced by Phillip's laughter. 'Dear girl!'

'There's still fourth term,' Judith said.

It wasn't an answer.

'Where did you go?' she asked.

'I don't follow,' I replied cautiously.

'You were so hungry. So focused. *Where did you go?*'

Searching, I imagined myself crying out. 'I *am* focused,' I said instead. 'Hungry.'

Quinn looked up from my journal. 'Prove it,' she said with disdain, and I was dismissed.

The rest of the day passed in a wash of grey.

I approached no one, and I was left alone even through the final assembly of the term, until Sylvie put her arms around my waist and whispered, 'My place.' She kept them there as she shouted over my head to her friends, 'See ya tonight! Ten pm!' Her touch was reviving, and I forgave her for the things she had been at fault for in my mind.

—

At Sylvie's place, we laughed about it, the absurdity of my thinking her and Saxon had got together. But it was a performance on my part; I missed his intensity, longed for it to be set on me once again. Without it I felt lustreless.

'I could fuck him, sure,' Sylvie said. 'But not, like, date him.'

'Why not?'

'We're too much alike. We'd hurt one another, and for the sake of it too. For the *experience*. You, on the other hand . . . you, Lolita, fuel him.' Sylvie picked up a plastic straw from the kitchen benchtop and used it to snort back a line. 'Jesus, fuck,' she said, standing abruptly and pulling at her nostrils.

I took the straw from Sylvie's grasp and bent over the powder. She held my hair off my face. 'And he you.'

I did one line, then another, chasing the feeling of the first.

'By second year, you'll be paired together,' Sylvie said. 'I have a sense for these things. And through whichever play it is, you'll make amends, fuck one another to dust and subvert the story. Critics will love it. The faculty too.'

'What about now?' I asked.

Sylvie tapped my nose mischievously. 'Be patient.'

There was a knock at her door.

When she opened it, Richard, Vivien, Anya, Imogen, a bunch of second years and almost Sylvie's entire company streamed in.

She lived alone in a small cottage in Northcote. One bedroom, a gable roof and an untidy courtyard of tumbling ivy. It was freezing out there, but most of the guests were smokers.

The music was turned up. Vodka bottles passed between us. It didn't taste like anything or feel like anything, blunted by the cocaine.

'Honey,' Vivien said, taking a hold of my hip bones and admiring the chiffon dress I was wearing. 'New?'

'No, it's Sylvie's.' All of it in fact, from the brass earrings to the thigh-high stiletto boots.

'Steal it,' she said and walked past me to the kids shivering in the cold. 'What are we dealing with here?' she asked and was presented with a plate racked up in lines.

Richard and I watched her from the doorway. 'Viv's on the rampage,' he said.

'She got the all-clear, surely,' I replied.

'Of course. But Quinn mentioned Yates.'

'In her review?'

'Told her to step out of his shadow.'

'She didn't,' I said, mortified on Vivien's behalf.

'Indeed, she did. I had my ear pressed to the door.'

Richard kissed my hand, moved into the courtyard and dipped his head to the plate. I avoided Imogen's eye, went inside for another drink.

I scanned the room, knowing already that Saxon wasn't there. I'd have felt him. It seemed like a waste, the buzz, the booze, without him to witness it coursing through me. He hadn't called since the night after the *Three Sisters* showing, and neither had I.

'Drink,' Sylvie said, thrusting a tall glass into my hand. 'We're leaving in twenty.' She ground against me to 'Let's Dance' and held my hands behind my back to playfully trail her teeth along my collarbone.

I felt bright, almost sober. 'I want another line,' I said and was instantly presented with one.

No one bothered to pretend anymore. We were almost there. Almost second years, almost third years, almost graduated. One more term to complete. Fuck sipping drinks politely. Fuck hiding in bathrooms for coke. We were artists, animals made to recreate the lives of others. We could live a little in our own skin. We were at Sylvie's, after all.

The house was left, door open. A tram sped past, another followed. Like zombies, we banged against it: *Stop! STOP!*

The light blistered my mood, and the movement of the tram brought it all up. Laughter, anger, vodka and all the powder, now sludge.

Imogen called my name. I knocked on the glass doors, they squealed open, and I ran, vomiting against the closest tree in Carlton Gardens. Groans from passers-by, a faint stab of embarrassment

270

and another murderous convulsion. The tram dinged, and the horde continued towards their destination without me.

'Hey.' A gentle voice beside me. 'Hey, it's all right.'

Imogen sat on a gnarled limb of the tree.

I couldn't speak. My throat burned, and so did my eyes.

'Can you walk?' Imogen asked.

'No.'

'That's fine. Let's just . . .' Imogen eased me backwards. I thought I'd never hit the ground, but I did, and she lay my head on the soft flesh between her chest and shoulder. 'Don't think about how you might smell or who saw you or how you might get home,' she said. 'Let's just lie here for a moment and breathe.'

The city rushed by, ready for release. Pent-up anxiety, fear, jealousy, hurt, to be extinguished—or at least muted—by a drink or two. But that rarely happened. The next day was always hell because one or two became five or six plus a bag.

I wanted to apologise for being a shitty friend, for being insensitive to Imogen's feelings and ignoring something that was probably always there. *Next term*, I thought, as words started to echo inside my ear. Faint but beautifully delivered words:

'and, when he shall die,
Take him and cut him out in little stars,
And he will make the face of heaven so fine
That all the world will be in love with night
And pay no worship to the garish sun.'

'Juliet,' I said.

'A cliché is a cliché for good reason,' Imogen replied, acting, but almost indiscernibly so.

271

The sky wasn't clear; clouds hung high, cloaking the moon. Melbourne swirled around me, Imogen continued with the monologue, and somewhere between *so tedious is this day* and *every tongue that speaks* I blacked out.

TERM FOUR

TERM FOUR

I

I wanted to leave, to go home, to be bleached by the sun. For every conversation I'd had, substance I'd taken, class I'd participated in, to be washed away by the ocean. To breathe above breaking waves into the deep pockets of myself recently made available and forget my friends and what I blamed them for.

But the choices had been mine. The lies wouldn't crystallise.

I'd been the one to divert, to steer my moral compass away from the girl who stared at me now, tacked to the wall of an apartment that felt like the residence of a stranger. The smiling face, so much younger than my own, though the family photograph had only been taken the summer before.

Go home for the break.

I didn't look up from the pavement or the torn carpet of the bus. My slow feet took one step, then another, up onto the plane. The streets widened into the freeway and the city disappeared beneath me, became a blemish on the patchwork of browns and greens without me truly noticing. To do so would be an admission, and I wasn't ready for hindsight. Though the moments were there if I could look, ready to be strung together like bulbs, fragile and illuminating.

I knew I was home by the heat. Queensland made a joke of Melbourne, asked why those disembarking the plane looked so serious. The blue sky oversaw everything, making dark corners bright. Making things clear.

'Where did you go?' my mother asked when I straightened up in the car park. We hadn't spoken properly in weeks.

I heard Quinn, Judith, Saxon. I heard Richard, Vivien, Dylan, Imogen, Sylvie and Yates.

'I don't know,' I replied.

She hugged me. 'Yes, you do.'

I was enveloped by her smell, the salt air mingled with it, a comfort I'd forever taken for granted.

Suddenly I was in my bed, staring at the ceiling, listening to the sounds of the house I'd wanted so desperately to grow out of, to play the characters I'd read about, women I'd watched onscreen, onstage, on the street. A small betrayal of my family, of my mother particularly, who'd guided me with such care towards the goal that had been drama school. I'd dismissed her opinions, held others in higher regard because of what they'd achieved, how they'd lived. But she knew things they never would. I hadn't realised that until now.

My father was quiet, resigned, couldn't meet my eye, and I knew he was letting me go. The cracks in my character were noted, but the paths were mine to tread. On my second night home, he sat on the edge of my bed beside my worn-out body and read aloud from *A Fortunate Life*. When he left the room, I cried silently for his poorly concealed disappointment in me.

The grime wore away after a week of sand and salt. I didn't wash it off. I liked to chew the ends of my hair while I read. The fishy tang of it something to ground me as I sailed through the text of Patrick Marber's *Closer*, our project for fourth term.

Something resurfaced, a shimmer of an old self, quietly reassured with each day spent at home. As the break petered to an end, I worried she might disappear when I donned rehearsal blacks and started to wear shoes again, to walk on concrete instead of sand.

I'd been so quick to agree that Victoria was superior because of the coffee, the culture and the cold. But Queensland wasn't backward at all. I saw now that the people here were rooted in their strongest selves, unswayed by objects or opinions. The wide blue sky made sure of it.

—

Imogen met me by the entrance of the drama building. We didn't loiter. She took the lead; we walked inside and found a seat for the start-of-term assembly. She helped me bat away the questions. *Where were you? What happened?*

'She was with me,' Imogen said.

And it was true. I had been. Passed out beneath a tree in Carlton Gardens.

She slipped in and out of conversation with students from other companies as they passed on their way to empty seats. In between, she was matter-of-fact; there wasn't time to tread softly, and I got the impression she wanted it over with. 'I stole it from you,' she said, looking ahead, not at me. 'I wanted to know what it felt like, to take.' *The kiss.* 'And you were there.' She was a woman in full possession of herself. The *Three Sisters* scene had been a turning point and the break afterwards time enough for the confidence she'd found in her performance to cement. 'You don't care, do you?' she asked, shifting focus as Richard and Vivien bent to air kiss our cheeks.

I wasn't sure that I did. All the same, her curt explanation cut swiftly and deep. I felt deserving of it, the pain, and it was easy to accept that I'd been an experiment. Though the care she'd shown in getting me home and showered after Sylvie's party belied her words.

The sound inside Studio One grew. I settled into it and pretended to listen to my friends as they talked about their holidays, circling around the information Imogen had planted between us.

Then Saxon arrived.

We locked in on one another for a beat, then he broke it by turning his back and sitting on the steps of the seating bank. It left me winded.

The faculty were a small procession. They quietened the space as they entered and took their seats in the six black chairs that faced us: Genevieve, Freya, Ford, Quinn, Judith and Phillip. I watched their faces as the curriculum was outlined and found myself responding agreeably like my peers, though I felt none of the usual excitement. I was preoccupied with an urgency to get started, to be on the floor, making up for the *Three Sisters* scene as though it could be erased and forgotten.

'Shall we continue?' Quinn asked.

She took pleasure in announcing the plays for the term and went about it slowly, hinting at who the playwrights were before resting happily in the clamour that escalated with the names of Sam Shepard and Ferdinand Bruckner. The second years would be split between *A Lie of the Mind* and *Buried Child*, while the third years would immerse themselves in a new adaptation by Judith of *Pains of Youth*.

The first years already knew about *Closer*. It had been revealed to us on the final day of third term. Four characters between us, two scenes each. The knowledge gave us time to research over the break—an annoyance to some, a welcomed distraction for me. The play had never been performed at our drama school. We thought ourselves special to be the first.

'On your feet!' Phillip called and led us to the floor. We brushed the walls, a wide circle, every student in attendance. To be present for the final start-of-term assembly was a sign of respect to the third-year company, and Phillip's vocal warm-up a kind of salute.

We were one undulating spine, one resonant voice, though each of us moved slightly differently. My vision was soft, but I became alert with every new addition to the practice, glancing between students on the curve of the circle. Some closed their eyes as they worked; others chose not to participate at all, waiting to pick up the next exercise once the current one had come to an end. I could read the first years, knew precisely how they'd work, but the second and third years were anomalies to me, grounded and self-assured.

I stood between Oliver and a second year I knew only from the stage. He'd never so much as made eye contact with me. I wanted to impress him, to get him to turn in my direction. The remnants of what I'd absorbed up north ebbed like the tide against the harshness of the space, pulling me back to who I was before, sloshing me towards who I wanted to be. *Forget the second year*, I thought and was returned to Phillip's practice just as it was coming to an end.

'Thank you,' Phillip said.

There was soft applause and Oliver wept, spreading emotion around the circle. The place meant far more than we ever let on, transformed as we were by what we'd experienced within it.

It was routine to acknowledge your peers after a group warm-up. But that morning it took longer than usual. Each set of eyes met mine silently for a moment of connection. We held what we knew of one another before being set adrift.

The circle split. We were free to make our way to class. I was pulled into a flurry of conversation that veered back and forth between *Closer* and who'd coupled up over the break. My friends were as entitled to my personal space as I was to theirs. Everything was emphasised with touch, and I was ashamed by how villainous I'd made them out to be. They weren't conniving or cruel, they'd simply extended invitations to places and people and experiences. I'd said yes. I could blame no one but myself for how it had altered the work. I wanted to apologise. Instead, I let their energy guide me along the familiar path to the Rehearsal Room.

At the door, I watched as my company spread themselves throughout the studio. Tethered by our training. For a little while longer, at least.

—

Two hours slipped by. I followed Freya's figure as it bent and rounded, using all my strength to stay focused, though I knew exactly where Saxon was at all times. The Twenty Movements of Jacques Lecoq was another of her specialties, and we would spend the next eight weeks learning them.

The class ran over. We weren't permitted a break. Phillip stomped in and immediately began to pass around printouts of the phonetic chart as we shovelled muesli bars and dried fruit into our mouths. He allowed it for a moment, then scolded us for eating while he was speaking.

'Reading phonetics will be like learning a new language,' he said, and for the first time it felt like being in a lecture hall at a proper university, a professor before us with a flair for rhetoric.

After four hours in the studio we were heavy with information and my friends walked out without turning back. I lingered. Saxon was tying his boots, and I had the sense that he was waiting for the room to clear.

'Hi,' I said softly, though it echoed through the space. The sound reached him, and he responded as he always did by repeating the greeting back to me.

'Hi.' He left it there. We waited, two lonely islands at opposite ends of the floor. Finally, his voice swam towards me, but the words were sharp. 'You never called.'

I was confused. Hadn't I needed his permission to? For a woman to reach out first was desperate: that was the lesson I'd absorbed growing up. Now the rules were unclear. *You never called.* A little spark that set me in motion.

I crawled towards him and pressed my lips to his. The offer wasn't innocent. After a morning on the floor, our bodies had been worked into readiness. I stood, knowing he'd follow. In the alcove where the chairs were stacked, Saxon threaded his hands through my hair and kissed the nape of my neck.

'Are you sure?' he asked. 'I don't want to hurt you.'

I removed my shirt and slipped my pants to the floor. 'You won't.' But I couldn't be sure. Physical need replaced rational thought.

The wall was cold against my back. I turned to face it and was relieved by his force. I shut out our surroundings and focused on the heat of him, the quickening of his breath. If someone came in, I'd keep going. It would be impossible to break apart. We were a machine, moving parts made to fit.

'You're shivering,' he said, when it was over. I waited to hear the zip of his fly before turning to him.

'I'm not cold.'

Saxon picked up my shirt and pulled it over my head. He was careful with my hair and held my pants for me to step into without meeting my eyes.

'Juliet,' Saxon said.

And I knew it was the last time.

'Do you think they'll cast us together?' I asked, raising my chin to keep pooling tears from falling.

He played along. 'That'd be something.'

'Wouldn't it?'

Saxon nodded at the floorboards. I reached forward and brushed my thumb against his lips in a gesture I'd seen an actress make somewhere. I caught myself, pulled back. The girl he'd watched in the audition room had retreated. I needed to be undistracted to draw her out again.

'Are you sure you're not hurt?' he asked.

Every inch of me ached with longing. 'Yes.'

He took my hand, kissed the knuckles. 'Tougher than me, mate.'

We walked out of the Rehearsal Room and along the corridor together, connected by the tips of our fingers.

⁓

I lay fully clothed on my bed and watched the darkness between the blinds deepen. The remnants of the day wafted off me; it smelled like the sum of my existence. Sweat, dust, alcohol and

Saxon. Tomorrow it would be different. Sweat and dust only. It had to be.

That evening, shame had prevented me from drinking more than one glass with the rest of my company. Red wine, the usual antidote, brought on a feeling of nausea that grew stronger with each sip.

My friends had pontificated on the scene choices from *Closer*. The further into the play, the darker the world, and those who'd been allocated the scene between Larry and Alice at the strip club read it as a sign of their ability. The cast list had made a mockery of my aspirations. Quinn had given me one scene instead of two. Half a scene, really, at the beginning of the play. Act one, scene two, between Anna and Alice. Vivien would work with me, which insinuated that I might need supervision. I was Vivien's third scene, a small burden, but one she was more than capable of carrying.

The only way to recover was to work. I reached for my bag below the bed and felt for the cover of *Closer*, the top corner fraying already from overuse. I flipped to the scene, re-reading it in the hope of uncovering some hidden meaning that might paint me as an exception instead of an example. I could find none. But I was optimistic. The floor might illuminate something, the silver lining being that there was no one to compare my scene work against; I was the only student to receive it. The other five scenes would be viewed multiple times at the end-of-term showing, as the roles overlapped.

Saxon would play Larry opposite Vivien as Anna, a continuation of the partnership they'd explored the previous term. I'd hoped that I might draw close to him again through the work, but that possibility had been disallowed.

I shook the feeling of Saxon from my bones and kept reading. I had to put my energy into the character on the page; I had to prove to my parents, to *myself*, that I was capable and that the work was worth it.

—

On top of Voice class, Movement class and *Closer* with Quinn, there was generative writing with a playwright from Finland, an introduction to mime with Freya, and essays due on the rehearsal process of the second-year productions. There were gallery openings, preview showings, reading lists and midnight movie sessions. All of it was an extension of the work, and the conversation afterwards as important as a post-class debrief.

Our notion of performance continued to expand and our concern that society had little use for it was something we argued over often. Without art, how were we to console ourselves, where was society to turn? We grounded ourselves in the belief that art wasn't frivolous, it was necessary. Our training had given us the confidence to verbalise it, and we flung our ideas around liberally.

Work sprouted across the city in bursts. You had to be quick to catch a run of something. Don Nigro's *Scarecrow* was playing at a dilapidated warehouse in Coburg, recently transformed into a performance venue. Vivien had already attended the opening with her father and permitted Richard to invite me along, since it was a public event. We raced to the showing right after class.

I was grateful for the invitation, though I didn't know the play. All I'd heard was that it was unmissable and an ex-drama student was in the cast. It was only once we'd taken our seats that I read the program. It sent a shiver of embarrassment through me to see a small portrait of Emmet on the page. I hadn't got over his hostility the last time we'd spoken.

'We were lucky to get these seats,' Richard said. 'They're trying to extend the season.'

'You never told me Emmet was working,' I said.

'Didn't I?'

'No.'

'I thought if I did you'd make an excuse not to come,' he confessed. Richard took my hand. 'But I didn't want you to miss the chance to see a Don Nigro performed outside the institution.'

We looked around at the stragglers filing in, cramming into the standing room section. The space was electric with anticipation. I wondered how Emmet had managed it, to be cast in something that had the potential to overshadow a main stage production.

'Can you keep a secret?' Without waiting for my response, he went on, 'Emmet's been cast in a play at the Sydney Theatre Company next season, but the cheeky bugger won't tell me which one.'

'He's really done it,' I marvelled.

'Done what?'

'Proved me wrong.'

'By working without a degree?'

'Without any training,' I corrected.

'Ah,' Richard said. 'Stronger without. Wait and see.'

Darkness descended over the audience. The sound of static was amplified to crackle through the mass of bodies that padded the venue. Two lighting rigs on either side of the space bounced light off the floor and walls, giving the impression of being inside a furnace. It was a nightmare, and Emmet embodied it, a constant presence on the stage. Richard was right, as he almost always was. Emmet was beyond our training, capable already of sustaining an imaginary world. Drama school had stunted his abilities, but working drew them out.

After curtain call, the actors remained where they were, and the audience flooded onto the stage. The lights remained dim and heavy metal replaced the static. The world of *Scarecrow* spread between patrons. We felt like survivors of it.

'Every night!' Richard yelled. 'Immersive, right?'

I nodded as a woman passed me a bottle of red. I gulped mouthfuls down, afraid I might not come across another. The pact I'd made to steer clear of alcohol receded to a far corner of my mind. A potential encounter with Emmet required lubrication.

'Man of the hour!' Richard pulled his mate into an embrace.

The men held one another and those milling about turned in their direction. When they stepped apart there was applause, and Emmet nodded solemnly, tears in his eyes.

The crowd grew, the warehouse hummed. People had wandered in off the street to join the party. I watched as Emmet and Richard talked, unable to hear them over the racket of voices and music and movement. I was too nervous to interrupt. When Emmet finally turned to me, I was prepared for another onslaught of criticism. 'Thank you for coming,' he said instead, with unexpected warmth.

'Phenomenal work!' I shouted back.

'Keep going, Maeve,' he said, leaning close. *'Promise me.'*

I felt patronised by his solicitude and laughed.

Emmet looked momentarily aggrieved. 'Promise me,' he repeated, and snapped his fingers at me impatiently until I gave my assent.

'Okay,' I said stiffly. 'I promise.'

Satisfied, Emmet turned back to Richard. The men came to attention and saluted one another before Emmet was drawn away by a sea of limbs, his value to the horde having increased exponentially since his standing ovation.

Another bottle was passed between guests, wet around the rim, and I watched as it was emptied by the collection of artists in attendance. It was an amalgamation of worlds, but a jolt all the same to see Judith stride towards Richard. She placed a fresh bottle in his hands and made a moment of watching him drink from it. They looked like cast mates on leave from a film, carrying their beauty with indifference.

It was strange to move on from working with her. Our time in Collective felt very far away, almost as though it hadn't been me who'd participated in the work but someone else. In a way, that was true. I felt branded by Judith. And though a masochistic part of me craved to be alone with her again, just us in her office, I had a niggling fear that she might exploit my vulnerability.

To see her now, outside of school, was sobering. I tapped Richard on the shoulder and pointed towards the exit.

'Stay!' Richard cried. But Judith regarded me coolly.

I blew him a kiss. 'Be good!'

'Always!'

The party had escalated. It was an effort to reach the door. Before stepping through it, I turned back, to witness my teacher licking wine from Richard's lips.

—

The process was quicker than it had been with *Three Sisters*. We moved through definitions and script analysis at speed, before slumping into the steady breadth of imaginative work. We hadn't experienced Introspection, or the stretch of time it allowed. It had been left out of Quinn's method in third term—too advanced for a first-year company to begin with. We'd had to build towards it through the *Three Sisters* scene.

Introspection was permission to play out the characters' lives and to explore the subtext, the expectation being that when you spoke in front of an audience, the character's interior world would glisten beneath your skin.

With only half a scene, and having exhausted all other entry points, I spent hours auditing the work of others inside the Rehearsal Room. The music of Arvo Pärt played through the sound system. Black plastic covered the windows, the walls made perpetually golden by freestanding lamps. Their light illuminated the floor, strewn with random objects and broken furniture. A derelict set; the world of *Closer*.

A preview of Quinn's process had been offered to us throughout the year, in the form of rehearsals and showings, and it was only now that I realised how everything had been moving towards this point. The hours I'd stolen from my schedule to watch the second years rehearse Ibsen months before directly informed what I was witnessing now—Saxon and Vivien, weaving their scene into one another.

Saxon was an actor absorbed. It was a lesson to me in how to perform, how to live. I'd have traded places with Vivien in an instant, to be on the receiving end of his intensity. He stalked her on the floor. She tore pages from a paperback. The words came slowly, the words of Anna, and sometimes Saxon responded with his own lines quickly, as though he couldn't contain them a second longer. Then the hours would stretch and melt, reminding me of the imagery of Dali, clocks turned to wax by the passing of time.

After almost eight hours on the floor, Quinn brought the work to a close. I wandered out of the studio as the trio debriefed.

The other pairings had been left to their own devices and I scooted around them as I walked along the passageway. Melodrama was spread across the script of *Closer*, but it wasn't to be played as such. Without supervision, the risk of flailing towards it was inevitable. Saxon and Vivien were the benchmark; their work would be viewed more than anyone else's, perfected to showcase the method. I hoped to be protected by association.

In a quiet corner on the second floor I spoke the text aloud, Vivien's lines and mine both, and considered the pain I might inflict in order to understand the truth of our characters.

'It requires the same focus, the same intensity, as living does,' Anya had told me about Introspection. 'Like being inside two lives at once.'

'Does it hurt?' I'd asked.

'It's eviscerating,' she'd said.

From what I'd witnessed, I knew it to be true.

—

The following week, Vivien stopped me between breaths. I accepted it as humbly as I could and tried to deliver the line with the intention she wanted to hear. Really, it was futile. The meaning would shift once we were on the floor.

'Again,' Vivien said.

I exhaled and delivered my line. Satisfied, Vivien delivered hers.

The Rehearsal Room door swung open. Two women walked out, one in tears. She brushed past us, and I watched her move to the lift. Vivien paid her no mind and stepped into the space. It was dark and it took a moment for my eyes to adjust. The set was exactly as it had been for Saxon and Vivien's scene work, but the furniture was placed differently, the objects a little more battered.

'Choose what you'd like,' Quinn said.

Vivien and I wandered through the space, selected items and rearranged the furniture to our liking. There was nothing to go on but our own specific understanding of the play. After the embarrassment of *Three Sisters* and my panic attack afterwards, the expectation to deliver hampered my choices. I could trust only the certainty of time passing; that in a handful of hours I'd be free of the floor.

I took my cue from Vivien. She closed her eyes and stood completely still amid the detritus. I didn't want to hold her up so I did the same, instantly criticising myself in the darkness for being led by someone else's impulse.

'Begin,' Quinn said.

We started with walking, but our pace steadily increased so that we were running by the first line.

We kept up the speed and the text was released from us through movement. I forgot myself and found parts of Alice I could use to shape her character by playing out the options that lay beneath the text, recalling and exploring repressed memories. Quinn's voice would bring me back, a lifeline to reality, directing Vivien and me towards one another whenever we drifted from meaning or ventured too deeply into the subliminal. She always knew if a word required more space. 'Repeat,' she'd say, or, 'Again.' And we'd fulfil it through touch. Pressing, stroking, hitting, kissing. Sometimes an object, sometimes each other. The word would lift out of us through action. We'd apologise for the accumulation of bruises afterwards, for the cost of tending to an imaginary world under Quinn's instruction.

When it was finally over, four hours later, I crawled to the edge of the light and lay still. Quinn allowed it. No matter my inability to perform the previous term, there was recompense in absolute compliance to the method. Vivien held my ankle, with her free hand writing the notes we were to embed into our work. I listened. The air between Quinn's thoughts was as rich with meaning as the words spoken, just above a whisper.

Introspection was over, and like a snake shedding its skin we had to let go of what we'd experienced on the floor and allow it to be alive in our delivery for blocking. Trust was important, for the method and our partnership both. I'd hurled myself at *Closer* for Quinn, for Vivien. For the sake of my first year.

—

Spring was upon us, though we'd barely felt the change. Being inside all the time meant we only ever saw the beginning and the end of its days. Daylight was a surprise after the depths we'd been inside of; the novelty of the sun drew us to it.

Vivien and I lay on the grass and squinted into the afternoon, anonymous between the runners and suits on their way through the Botanic Gardens. We pulled her jacket over us like a blanket, hoping the extra warmth might solidify the work we'd done, like a kiln.

'It was satisfying,' Vivien said.

'I'm terrified of losing it,' I replied.

'You won't.'

'Can't be sure.'

'No,' she said and rolled towards me, her face hovering above mine. 'But fear will cripple you if you let it.'

We'd said little to one another after leaving the Rehearsal Room. Voicing our own thoughts felt like a betrayal of the women we'd been inhabiting only a half hour before. Who we were to one another was suddenly difficult to differentiate.

'It'll cripple *us*.'

I remained still beneath her and imagined myself exploring the word *cripple* in front of Quinn, extracting every possible meaning it might hold.

If I fucked up like I had in the *Three Sisters* scene, Vivien's credibility would likely take a hit. I'd been entrusted to her to coax the best out of me. But in reality her investment in us was an investment in herself.

'Clear?' Vivien asked.

'Crystal.'

Her threat kept me pinned to the lawn long after she left to meet Richard. Dusk brought a bright sky, and I distracted myself with the colours until night stole all heat and evicted me from the gardens.

II

'You were concerned for my welfare,' Dylan said, 'and it ultimately led to your own downfall!'

It wasn't true, of course, but it was better to pretend. Dylan had taken to analysing my subconscious as though I were another character in one of Marber's plays. He'd come away clean from the *Three Sisters* scene. If he hadn't, we wouldn't be speaking now. We both knew it and ignored the sharp fact on which our friendship balanced.

The steps beneath me were cold, but we wouldn't be staying much longer. The break between classes was short. So I indulged Dylan as I watched the flow of students drift inside the building from Luncheonette.

They were an apparition, and I admired it, the trio strolling towards us. Richard, Judith and Saxon. They were casual with one another, though it was palpable, their collusion. I wanted to trail behind them and pick up the scraps of their conversation, to help me make sense of this place now that I'd been cast to the periphery.

I caught myself, averted my eyes and fixed them on Dylan. He grew more animated with the attention, and I felt suddenly weary of filling the gap Saxon had left, though I was grateful to Dylan for trying.

'Maeve,' Judith said.

I snapped my head towards her.

'A tutorial,' she said.

I scrolled through my knowledge of what that might mean. 'For *Closer*?'

'Yes. Tell Vivien and ask Genevieve to book a space for next week.'

'Will Quinn mind?'

'She's asked me to lend my support. We don't want you to have another *episode*.'

My insides curled with unease. 'But we've already finished Introspection.'

Judith pursed her lips in the specific way she did whenever someone challenged her authority. 'A precursor to blocking.'

She slipped an arm around Richard's shoulders and they resumed their conversation. But Saxon hung back. He knew as well as I did that Judith's expression of concern was intended as a belittlement of my skill. A tutorial meant standards weren't being met. He was offering his support.

I kept my head down, proud of my stoicism. Saxon took the hint and walked inside.

'Do you think they're fucking?' Dylan asked when Saxon had gone.

The question was like being shaken awake.

'In the beginning, I mean.'

It took a moment to realise he was talking about *Closer*.

'I think so,' I said slowly, and Dylan pulled me to my feet. We leaned into one another like siblings.

—

We sat on the floor of Richard's lounge room. The coffee table was set for four. We had gathered in Emmet's honour, to mark the occasion of his being cast in an independent film shooting in Perth. It was a small role, but the majority of his scenes would be played opposite a name, one we feared saying aloud in case the offer evaporated. Emmet couldn't give away too many details, so he picked up his favourite topic to rip into instead: the curriculum.

'Too difficult for a first-year company,' Emmet said. 'The division between love and pain is so thin, if it isn't managed properly the characters will flatten into stereotypes.' He slapped the coffee table, vehement. '*Closer*, for god's sake, requires skill!'

'That we don't possess?' I asked.

'Not yet,' he replied.

Richard considered Emmet's point, and so did Imogen. They were treating Emmet with a new reverence now.

'I agree,' Richard said finally and resumed serving the radicchio salad with his hands. '*Closer* is a challenge.'

'It's better suited to a second-year cast,' Emmet opined.

'We aren't playing every scene,' Imogen pointed out.

Emmet smiled sardonically. 'No, just bearing the emotional weight as though you were.' He tore into a hunk of bread with his teeth and nodded as he chewed, building towards a tangible climax. 'It's for her. Quinn's fucking with you. A few people will rise to the occasion, and she'll use them as an example of her process. The rest will be broken by it.'

'You can't know that,' Richard said.

'I can.'

'How?' I asked.

There was no way of skirting around a question so plain. He had to be open with us now.

'Because of Lexi.'

Richard and Imogen shifted uneasily. They knew more than I did about the woman Emmet metered our treatment by. I wanted to be let inside the circle; to understand, as they did, the root of Emmet's hatred for our head of school. 'And?'

'*And* Quinn reduced her to a shell of a person.'

In the past he'd been elusive, drip-feeding us morsels of gossip, most of which we'd dismissed, disbelieving. But the work had changed him, and he'd proven the system wrong.

'Lexi could have been someone,' Emmet said, his voice volcanic. 'She wanted to contribute!'

'It's all subjective, isn't it?' I asked him.

'No, it's a kind of pillaging, what Quinn does. The person might retain their talent, but they won't be able to harness it once she's done.'

Emmet launched into a tirade about Quinn's misuse of power. How she belittled students and used their personal histories against them; encouraged promiscuity between scene partners; laughed at alumni seeking guidance; and overtly favoured students who willingly gave themselves over to her process, enabling those company members to live out the fantasy lives of their characters without reprimand. He painted Quinn as a megalomaniac, one we were bound to through the work.

'If you define yourself by your art and are exploited by the one person who's supposed to nurture it . . .' Emmet allowed space for our minds to wander. There was no answer, though we retold the stories that shaped our understanding of the school, justified Quinn's behaviour. But with Emmet's perspective all the warning bells began to clang.

'But what's in it for her?' I asked. 'What does she gain by it?'

Emmet and Richard exchanged a look and shook their heads at my naivety.

'Quinn doesn't perform anymore,' Richard said. 'Can't. All her talent goes into the process she's created.'

Imogen was quietly indignant. 'Cycle of abuse.'

'Richard told me she left you destroyed after *Three Sisters*,' Emmet said, gratingly candid.

I turned to Richard in shock. He wouldn't meet my eyes.

'Now she gets to piece you back together,' Emmet explained. 'You're just her type. Don't confuse her attention for admiration.'

Imogen mumbled, 'For fuck's sake,' under her breath.

'And what, men are exempt?' I asked, wounded.

Emmet understood my insinuation. 'No. But I wasn't prepared to lose myself any more than I already had for that place.'

He lifted a bottle off the table and took a swig, moving on, his reason for leaving drama school made clear. He had the success of *Scarecrow* to wash his behaviour away with. He was superior; what he'd achieved was the goal.

If you define yourself by your art.

I excused myself shortly after and stood before Richard's bathroom mirror, searching for what it was that signalled my archetype so plainly.

Juliet.

Each day, each year, had primed me for the roles I'd be allowed to play. No amount of effort, no storehouse of talent, could change

297

that. I'd forever be at the mercy of others' perceptions. Emmet knew it and was trying to prepare me.

—

It was more than a tutorial. It was a test. I didn't completely understand this until I was stuck inside of *Closer*, three hours in. Opposite Oliver, a ring-in. A male energy.

The Rehearsal Room had been made available to us in the evening, midweek. We were depleted, but not enough to be distracted by the promise of the weekend. Still, we were pliable, less concerned with what bruises might appear on our skin. If it were Monday, we might have taken a little more care with our bodies, and they knew it.

The evening mirrored my audition. Oliver and I connected immediately. This time, we were the backdrop, the context to Vivien's psychodrama. We played out the literal, simulating sex and violence while Vivien stared into the lens of an old disposable camera and drew from it the text. The words she spoke were full of meaning.

But Quinn wanted more.

We were building towards the moment Alice asks Anna to take her picture. Options were dwindling. I was exhausted, ready to claw myself out of the scene. But I held on to the emotion and kneeled before Vivien, crying while Oliver stroked my hair.

Judith paced the floor and called direction. 'Go further.'

Quinn stepped past her and into the light, piercing the world of the play. What Judith had tried to procure on her behalf wasn't enough.

'Envision your father,' Quinn said.

Vivien's lip twitched, the only clue to the terror I knew she buried deep—that her place in the school was not based on talent alone.

Quinn put two fingers under my chin and lifted my face for Vivien to look into. 'Watch her, with *him*.'

In each session I had audited, Quinn remained seated and called direction to the actors from outside the scene. No one ever stopped working; we were to integrate the note and remain immersed. With Quinn's bony fingers touching me, I did the same.

'Stand up, Maeve. Oliver, push her against the wall.'

An alarm sounded in my head, but I obeyed. It felt familiar. In the obscurity of the work, I didn't realise what Quinn was asking. It was only once the wall of the Rehearsal Room was firm against my back that the memory cracked open and Oliver became Yates. I gasped, transported beneath the weight of his body.

'Are you watching, Vivien?' Quinn asked. 'Give her your line, Maeve.'

But my voice had vanished.

'*Maeve.*'

The room was silent except for Oliver's laboured breathing. I writhed, caught between realities. I couldn't remember Alice's next line, had lost my place entirely. But something primal took over, and I called for *help*. Within the breadth of the process the plea still served the scene. Help could mean anything. All the female characters I'd played had asked for it at some point.

Vivien responded by swivelling upwards, and I saw the beauty of our Feldenkrais training in the fluidity of her motion. She came to standing. Shoulders above thighs, thighs above knees, knees above feet. Jaw relaxed. Textbook perfect.

'Stop,' she demanded in a quiet voice.

Oliver released the pressure on my body.

'Thank you,' I murmured.

'Vivien, his choices have paved your path,' Quinn said. 'What does that feel like?'

Vivien held me in a look that connected us as the women we were playing both on and off the floor, then dropped it and left the studio.

Quinn called after her as the Rehearsal Room door slammed shut.

Judith told us to rest. Oliver pulled me down onto his lap and crossed his arms over my chest to contain my ragged breathing. 'Well done, doll,' he said, cutting through Quinn's voice as she raged. They ignored us and I realised none of it had been for my benefit after all; I'd been used to draw from Vivien the anger Quinn wanted to cultivate.

I saw it all now; flash cards before me. Yates on one and Richard on another. Every class I'd ever taken with Vivien, every scene we'd participated in together, every interaction. And now this. Quinn knew everything that had passed between us, and that was the true reason for our pairing. Alice and Anna.

I remained inert as Oliver rocked our bodies back and forth. I shut my eyes to the burst of fluorescent light that flooded the space as the women left: the facilitators I'd bled and bruised for over the course of the evening.

Oliver debriefed with me quietly, a long soliloquy that ended before Quinn's insertion into our scene. 'We'll pick it up from there another time,' he said. But neither of us could be sure when that might be, and I knew I wouldn't be able to bear it if we did.

—

I couldn't find Vivien. I'd waited too long, indulging Oliver's observations. There was truth in them, but I knew it was just his way of placating me, fearful of being implicated in any wrong-doing himself. Any good work I'd done had been overshadowed by the way the session had ended.

Oliver kissed my cheek and sashayed across the street as a tram skidded noisily through South Melbourne. Outside the drama building I stood still with nowhere to be.

The air was warmer than I'd anticipated and smoke-scented. I breathed it in, comforted by the whisper of summer. Fourth term would soon be over, the year finished with.

The scene had followed me to the street, and I saw everything through the lens of what I'd just worked through. I imagined walking slowly around the city, finding Saxon and making him watch while I flirted with someone else.

'Maeve,' Judith called. I swung my head towards a red dot glowing by the brickwork. She inhaled, the end of the cigarette flaring, and blew the smoke like a lure. I approached cautiously. The world of *Closer* wouldn't dissipate, and when I spoke it was as though someone else had scripted the words.

'That wasn't teaching,' I said.

Judith nodded, drew again on the cigarette. 'What was it, then?'

'I don't know, but I wouldn't call it safe.'

'Going to report it?' Judith asked, unconcerned. 'Risk failure?'

'And say what? No one would believe me.'

Judith crossed her arms and turned towards the skyline. 'It's a kind of magic. Folding into the lives of others. An audience doesn't care how we do it, just that we do.'

301

Her eyes were following something, someone behind me as she spoke. 'The patrons, the board don't care either. Don't understand. They choose to look away when confronted with the specifics of the method. On paper it makes up the curriculum. On the floor . . . a world, that most people believe you can just step out of and into real life.'

'Doesn't work that way,' I said.

'You're learning.'

'Quinn went too far.'

'She did.'

'Why didn't you stop it from happening?'

Judith smiled. 'Because sometimes it's worth it.'

I slid into a sickening helplessness as I realised who stood behind me. I spun around and, caught between them, I suddenly had nothing else to say.

'Hey,' Saxon whispered and took my elbow.

Laughter steamed in my gut and erupted in sharp bursts. I shook free of him, enjoying the power of it. But the feeling turned to remorse at the sight of them together. It was pathetic and perfect, like I'd manifested it.

'I fucking knew it,' I hissed and turned away from them, my walk quickening into a sprint.

'Juliet!' Saxon shouted, but he didn't follow me.

Imogen answered straight away when I called.

—

The Night Cat was busy. Imogen sat on a vinyl couch by the window. She swatted away drinkers trying to claim the space as theirs. On the table in front of her were four glasses, two short, two tall. Without speaking, she gave me a short one first. The whisky burned my throat, but it felt right. Soon my lucidity would give way because of it.

Next Imogen passed me a pint. I drank half and slumped back. The centre of the sofa gave out and we were pressed together. The closest we'd been in weeks.

I told her everything. The session, Vivien's abrupt departure, Saxon's arrival. The Night Cat thumped around us, but Imogen's attention never wavered from my face, even when late-night drifters began to encroach.

'There's been rumours,' Imogen said. 'About Judith.'

'I know.'

'I warned you. Many times.' But she'd made a false accusation before. Sylvie and Saxon were no more than friends.

Imogen's eyes flicked between my lips and forehead, demanding a reply. But I had nothing left; I was spent.

Her place wasn't far, and we walked through the dark streets arm in arm.

She lived in a house full of women, the heritage-listed cottage rundown but cared for. Imogen's room was sparsely furnished. A queen bed, a single side table and an antique desk by the window that overlooked a bin-lined laneway. Everything in its place, nothing unnecessary. It was like looking inside her skull.

But beside her bed was a stack of books, with Marber's small collection of plays on top. It had never occurred to me to research the writer, to investigate his technique. It was smart, and she displayed the collection for no one other than herself.

'I can't believe I've never been here,' I said.

Imogen removed her shoes and jeans and climbed into bed, raising the sheet like a tent for me to join her. 'I have asked you.'

'I'm sorry,' I said. 'For—' I stopped myself. For forgetting her. For using her. She already knew. To voice it would be unkind.

Imogen kept a gap between us as we drifted off to sleep.

In the morning I was awoken by the bright sound of a magpie and found myself nestled into Imogen's side.

To wake her would be a beginning I wasn't ready for. She had shown me true support when I'd come to accept duplicity as the norm. If only I'd been receptive from the outset.

'You can leave the embrace alone now, I reckon,' she said, groggy with sleep. 'Chalked up enough experience to draw from.'

Recalling Initiation, I covered my face with my hands, embarrassed.

'Hey,' she said gently, 'it was brave.'

'Desperate, more like.'

Imogen pulled my hands away. 'Let's go with endearing.'

I smiled at that. She'd forgiven me.

—

Phillip liked to use Vivien as an example. Her resonance was unusual for a woman. She could project her voice further than anyone else in the company after a year spent releasing it from her pelvis.

He looked between us. 'Where is she?' Phillip stepped in front of Richard's chair and snatched the leaflet from his hands, a phonetic breakdown of Sylvia Plath's 'Ariel'.

Stunned, Richard snatched it back. 'I don't know,' he replied, back straight, neck long.

Phillip couldn't protest; Richard's alignment was perfect.

The room continued to pass phrases around the circle while Phillip stood in the centre, fiddling with his moustache, fuming.

'Keep going,' he ordered.

Multiple company members rolled their eyes at the back of Phillip's head as he left the studio. The poem was dropped with the sound of him hurrying down the stairwell. I leaned forward to get Richard's attention.

He shrugged at my inquiring look. 'Viv? No idea,' he said.

Phillip never returned to class. I imagined him scurrying like a rodent from office to office, demanding an explanation for Vivien's absence, as though she were the cornerstone of his process, proof he was capable.

Soon enough it would get around, the story of our tutorial the night before, its shape shifting and changing like wildfire.

We trickled out of the performance space and into the Rehearsal Room to begin second period with Freya. But instead of stretching as we always did when Movement class was due to begin, we were halted by Quinn.

'Sit down and listen,' she said. Freya hovered behind her.

We took the direction and landed exactly where we stood, bodies scattered at random across the floor. It felt unnatural; we almost always formed a circle at the beginning of class.

'Vivien has taken ill,' Quinn said. 'It is unlikely that she will return.'

The space had been cleared; there was no visible remnant of the night before. But there was a new scratch in the floorboards, a metre long, near the far wall, where Oliver had dragged a chair through the space with me on top of it at the beginning of last night's session. Whatever happened, there was proof of me there.

Quinn looked out through the windows at the white sky of the south. 'However, she has promised me she will take part in the *Closer* showing.' She closed her eyes and didn't open them again until she'd turned towards the door, as though to extinguish us from her mind, from all memory.

We stood slowly and removed our shoes. Freya stood completely still, concentrating on a ball of dust by her feet. It was a long time before she began to instruct us.

'One,' she said, and we started to move through the twelve of the Twenty Movements we'd perfected. Freya seemed vacant as she walked between us. Usually uncompromising in her critique, she said nothing and released us early. Vivien's absence had ramifications, reminded everyone of the cost of our training.

Imogen took my hand, threw my bag over her shoulder and walked me back through the passage, down the stairwell and across to Luncheonette.

'It's not your fault,' she said, when we were out of earshot of our peers.

'Then why do I feel like it is?'

'*They* did this,' Imogen said. I could feel her bristling. 'They put you in the centre of it.'

'What about Vivien?'

Imogen ordered and paid for us both—a flat white and a toasted sandwich each—then took my shoulders in her hands. 'She'll be fine, but you might not be.' The deli buzzed around us. 'You hear me?' Imogen added. '*You might not be.* Stay focused.'

I nodded.

'Repeat it,' she demanded and placed the warm food in my hands.

'Stay focused,' I said.

Satisfied, Imogen reached for her coffee and gave me mine. 'Now let's retrieve what you worked through last night.'

—

Each pairing was allocated time with Quinn to block their *Closer* scenes. With Vivien absent, I was permitted to audit while the rest of the company waited outside the Rehearsal Room for their turn. I used the opportunity to observe the missteps and minor victories of my peers. They'd ask for my opinion during the lunchbreak as if I were able to channel Quinn's thoughts. It gave me an air of authority—the irony being that I wouldn't have the chance to work in front of her again: Vivien had stipulated that if she were to return for the showing, she would no longer rehearse with Quinn.

So in the evenings I stayed behind. The Rehearsal Room was ours; Genevieve had given us a special dispensation because of what had happened. The reputation of the school was at stake.

Quinn was replaced with Oliver. Vivien and I trusted him enough to guide us. Our characters bloomed without the pressure of our head of school. All options were explored, and we settled on a rough structure. On the day, we could adjust it organically, depending on how the scene played out.

The sessions were short and intense. Vivien said little and never stayed longer than she needed to. Afterwards, Oliver and I would walk to the tram together.

'Has she failed?' I asked him one evening. Our friendship had developed from one-sided admiration on my part to something more like mutual respect.

Oliver laughed. 'Doll,' he said, 'no. Is that what you think?'

'I just figured . . . her attendance.'

'There are exceptions, and she is one of them.'

'But she might not come back.'

'Oh, she will.'

The number 1 approached.

'Coming?' Oliver asked me.

'I might walk.'

Oliver shrugged and waved the tram down. 'Sleep well, Maeve, my dear!' he said in a parody of the old screen sirens, then jumped on board. He blew a kiss to me from the back window of the carriage.

St Kilda Road was quiet. I stopped outside the Arts Centre and gazed at the golden spire before crossing the street. It looked like the Eiffel Tower, a carrot dangling at the end of a rod. A career, the main stage, consistent work.

'It's garish, don't you think?' Vivien said, a lone figure against the railing of the tram stop.

It shocked me to come across her, this ghost, my scene partner, in a place other than the Rehearsal Room.

'Shouldn't you be home?' I asked.

'Kind of you to wonder,' she replied sarcastically.

'I only meant—'

'I know,' she said and waved away the rancour of her jibe.

A car passed slowly, the sound occupied us.

'Thank you for staying with the scene,' I said.

'You're welcome.'

'Can't be easy.'

'It is actually. I like the play. It's everything else that's the problem.'

We waited for her tram together, trading insights from what we'd learned on the floor with Oliver. It was completely different from any other interaction we'd ever had. We were like professionals almost, dissecting a scene.

Her tram approached. She held the door as I sped towards the end of my thought.

'They could have been friends,' I said, meaning our characters. 'I don't think so,' Vivien replied, and retracted her hand from between the doors of the carriage. She leaned against the glass panels and watched me as the distance between us grew.

III

Our essays on the process of the Shepard plays were due. The invitation to attend rehearsals had been open to us all term, but I was often the only company member there. It wasn't a priority. Even so, I liked the darkness, the swell of words that rose to meet me from the floor without the pressure of having to hold on to them myself. Witnessing a production taking shape alleviated my fear. It was a huge undertaking, but a manageable one when you broke it down, all the hours spent on the floor.

I sat alone at the back of the seating bank, beside the tech desk. In the front row, the director's head bobbed between the actors and a notepad on his lap. The frequency with which he was peering down indicated that the actors had gone off course.

A Lie of the Mind required restraint, and the second-year cast possessed very little of it. Rather than trusting the dynamism of the text, the students were simulating emotion, becoming parodies of the American families they were trying to portray.

But Anya held her own as the character of Beth, and I saw how *The Homecoming* had been a building block for her. She'd grown more confident during that production, and it was reflected in the choices she made now, in the lilt of her accent and her altered physicality. Beth was a real person. She could walk off the stage and onto the street, Anya gone forever, enmeshed in the interior world of her character. It seemed a shame so few people would witness it.

'You could remount it,' I said when the director ended the session. We were in the locker room and Anya was dressing.

'There's still a week until previews,' Anya called from behind the fabric of her shirt. 'The play could shift entirely.'

'It won't,' I said. 'And you could recast.'

Anya's dishevelled head emerged. 'With whom?'

'Anyone.'

'How wicked of you,' Anya said. 'Imagine the reaction to *that*.'

The halls were empty, the building closed.

'Come for a drink,' Anya suggested. 'Sylvie's been asking after you.'

'She has?'

Anya nodded. 'Do you good.'

I knew it wouldn't, but my ego had been boosted, and I wanted to know what *come for a drink* meant. We could go anywhere, be home anytime, the city a blank canvas.

'Can't stay long,' I said.

'Liar,' Anya smirked, and I knew immediately where we would go.

—

We gathered at Sylvie's house, a small crew who knew one another intimately. I might have behaved better if I'd been surrounded by strangers. Instead I was cajoled by the fairytale of friendships cemented on nights just like this one.

It had been weeks since we'd seen one another, but Sylvie's firm embrace in the doorway told me she'd been unaffected by my absence. It would have hurt less if she'd been displeased.

'A little Method,' Sylvie said and winked, slinking down the corridor towards the kitchen in a 1920s flapper-style dress. *Pains of Youth* was close to production week.

We crowded into the small kitchen: Richard, Anya, Sylvie and me. Sylvie slung red into mugs and was careless in racking up—fat white caterpillars that sharpened to a point.

The familiar zing of that first taste triggered an immediate hunger for more. I waited as patiently as I could, watching the plastic school clock above the fridge. After ten minutes I asked for another line, and my friends obliged.

That's better, I thought and picked up my mug of wine, blunted enough not to care about the conversation or myself.

I was jolted out of my passivity by a figure striding into the kitchen, a man who had let himself in without knocking.

'Chekhov's gun,' I said aloud, and Anya reached for me.

Yates held a bottle in one hand and a script in the other. 'Revisions!' he called.

Everyone cheered.

Sylvie kissed the pages, took the wine and abandoned both by the sink. She cut a line for Yates, who dived straight into a monologue on his vision for *A Doll's House*.

'So it's going ahead?' I asked.

Sylvie prodded my torso. 'Where have you been?'

'Working,' Anya replied for me and squeezed my hand.

Yates removed his wallet and rolled a fifty. 'A late addition to the program,' he said. 'The subscribers loved it.' The line disappeared in a flash of movement.

My equilibrium lost, I slipped out onto the street, hoping to dissolve into something familiar. I leaned on the little fence that divided the footpath from Sylvie's sliver of a garden and looked up at the moon, a bright slash against black. It seemed to vibrate. I emptied my mug and threw it towards the road. It shattered against the bitumen. A dog barked, and the moon stilled, just a little.

He must have seen it as an invitation when I left the kitchen alone.

'Could be you one day,' Yates said, 'under my direction.'

A cheap compliment that meant nothing. We were alone together now. The rest was inevitable.

'Miss Julie,' he added quietly.

I missed Saxon so deeply in that moment that I surrendered to the distraction of this other man. When I turned towards him, his features slid, and I couldn't see who I was looking at anymore.

Yates read my silence as assent. He trailed a finger along the curve of my jaw. I couldn't stand the intimacy of it; I jutted my chin and was met with an open mouth. There was no synergy, though I tried to be as hungry for it as he was.

My back strained beneath the pressure of his stance. I kneeled and pulled him down into the garden bed to breathe. Yates keeled beneath my palm, his body angular atop the flowers.

Time was elastic. The longer I held him, the less I partook. A voyeur. I reminded myself this had never happened before, though there had been times when he'd been present, when I'd roused the memory of him as I'd lain with Saxon; fodder for

313

experience. It was really happening now; hadn't I envisioned it? For the life of me, I couldn't think why. Then I saw Saxon with Judith. Sylvie on stage. And I heard Quinn. *She needs a little more . . . life.*

Yates shuddered into my hand, and I shook away the thought. He twisted and pounded the dirt with a clenched fist.

'Jesus,' he said, his accent broad and unaffected. *So that's how he really sounds*, I thought, and wiped my hand on the flowers.

Voices drifted to us from the kitchen through the open doorway. We turned towards it but didn't stand.

'The threat of being caught . . .' Yates said as he lifted his buttocks to adjust his pants. 'Quite the aphrodisiac.' Then he flopped against the soft earth with a long, satisfied groan.

My knees ached from the pressure of supporting my own weight. I got on all fours and lay down. Yates didn't offer me any kind of physical satisfaction in return. He simply nudged my head with his bicep, and I lay back on the thick barrel of his chest self-consciously.

'There you are!' Sylvie called from the doorway. The relief of her made me want to cry. Light refracted in the crystals that dangled from her dress, a kaleidoscope of colours that grew against the house as she skipped towards us. Sylvie flung herself down beside Yates. He lay between us, a cliché. I felt my extremities tingle as they gossiped about the other actors in her company, the ones who wouldn't make a career of it.

A shadow hovered above us, a woman in a wide stance. Like chastened schoolchildren, Yates and Sylvie got up and raced to the house. *It was them*, I wanted to shout. But Anya knew.

She pulled me to my feet and handed me a bottle. The vodka tasted like a memory, a warning from an earlier time.

From the tilt of her head I knew she wasn't disappointed, just resigned, which somehow felt better. And I realised by the way she copied my grimace as I clenched my jaw against the bitterness of the booze that she'd sought me out to offer solidarity. She'd been me once, and now I was her. No matter how many times Anya had tried to avert my eyes, I'd landed exactly where she'd hoped I wouldn't: with Yates. To her credit, she didn't say *I told you so.* She pushed her palm against mine and interlocked our fingers.

A taxi arrived; the driver called my name. Anya slid a scrunched-up twenty-dollar note into the front pocket of my jeans and bundled me into the car. A small kindness; she'd say my goodbyes for me.

'I can't leave Sylvie,' she said before shutting the cab door, and I knew exactly what she meant. Sylvie would succumb to Yates more quickly if she wasn't there.

It felt strange to be alone after so much touching. I could still feel the mark of him on my body. I wound down my window and called out to the empty streets, an open-throated cry that terrified me and the driver both, though he didn't reproach me. He let me be and passed a box of tissues between the seats when we arrived outside my building.

IV

I had never taken a sick day. In June, I'd caught a terrible cold, and persevered through a haze of Sudafed which didn't feel all that different from being high. When I ran out, the aches came, my nose ran. Even then, I went to class. It never occurred to me to stay home. To keep going was a sign of strength, a measure of commitment. If the rest of the company fell ill because of me, so be it.

But all my previous efforts seemed for nothing because here I was, immobile, wet and naked, wrapped in a doona on my single-seater lounge chair. I'd caved, and not because of something I'd caught, but because of something I'd done.

My forehead was numb from pressing it against the glass, observing the comings and goings of the people on the street below. Imagining their lives in miniature made the night before seem cleaner. People got fucked up, they hopped on a tram, they bought coffee and croissants and painkillers. I wasn't so bad. The clothed ants were proof. They were worse because they went about their day as though the night before had never happened.

I hadn't slept. I needed to sweat out the night in privacy, then sleep would come, and I could work. That's what I'd moved here for, wasn't it? *To work.*

I watched the rising sun colour the north and with it the Valium set in. I'd been impressed by Anya's forward planning. Below the scrunched-up note had been a little pill. I'd swallowed it dry after coming out of the shower.

My heart rate began to slow. I drilled the lines from *Closer* and when a tiny head tilted upwards from the street I ducked like I'd been caught out. Had I placed the emphasis on the wrong word? Confused the meaning of a phrase? Or spoken the lines of the wrong woman, the wrong character, from the wrong scene?

The trams sped along Lygon Street. I calculated the time by the distance between them. When the gaps widened along the tracks, I knew class had begun. There would be questions about my absence, a doctor's certificate to be sought. I hoped Richard might spin a story. That it might trickle down, become something solid to strengthen my image and not the opposite. Please not the opposite. *Please.*

—

The swelling exaggerations in my mind subsided after two days spent alone. On the third, I was plunged into the cracking clarity of sobriety that sprung me from the lounge chair and into my rehearsal clothes. I'd wasted days. There weren't many left.

On the street the warm air burned my lungs, and for a moment I confused my surroundings with home. I waited for the city to part for me. It didn't. I moved quickly to catch up.

I halted at the glass doors of the drama building, ignoring the smokers on the front steps. The foyer marked a threshold. To step into it would be an acknowledgement. There was only one way to work: *from where you were.*

I smiled at everyone and interacted with no one. When I reached the Rehearsal Room I found a place on the floor, closed my eyes and started my daily practice, motivated by the threat of failure.

I was anchored by my tutors. Freya first, then Phillip mid-morning. There was freedom in movement and satisfaction in the smallest of sounds. My body remembered, and I marvelled at what I was capable of.

At lunchtime, Imogen sat with me on the pavement, our feet outstretched to the cobblestoned street. The sun was strong. We basked in it and passed a pair of cheap sunglasses between us whenever one of us wanted to look up at the sky.

I didn't say much. Imogen filled the gaps and passed me a copy of *Slouching Towards Bethlehem* for the downtime. She understood. Empty evenings from now on. I couldn't trust myself with the extracurricular.

I audited Quinn's class and waited for Vivien after hours. She said nothing, though I assumed she knew everything. Any respect she'd had for me was lost; I felt it in the friction that existed between us on the floor. She pushed a little too hard, took every opportunity to hurt me as far as the subtext allowed. Biting sometimes, scratching and tearing at my clothing, laughing when my body became exposed and bloodied. But it was her disappointment that injured me the most, as though to have given in to her father was the worst kind of sin.

Oliver mediated as best he could without intervention, and the work grew stronger.

On the tram ride home, I thought of Saxon. I granted myself the time it took to travel along Swanston before the carriage turned onto Elgin to luxuriate in the memories of us. When I stepped off the tram, I chose to forget. To focus and think only about what was in front of me.

The days followed this pattern and an earlier wish was realised: my bookshelf filled. Second-hand paperbacks that came via Imogen and hardbacks I'd bought instead of food. I trailed my fingers over their spines—an accumulation of knowledge that spanned the course of one year. I could feel the ideas I had wanted to absorb and remembered who I'd been when I read each of them. Then, in a blink, those girls were gone and I arrived in the present.

V

By the end, we'd taken to spending each lunchbreak on the steps outside the entrance. All three companies, rolling cigarettes, sharing lunches and trading stories with an ease we'd not felt before. We were almost second years, and these last pockets of time with the companies above felt like the passing of a baton.

While the *Closer* scenes consumed us, it seemed insignificant compared to what the second and third years endured in the evenings. They threw banalities at us to appease our anxiety, to move on to lighter conversation. But in their sideways glances I saw their concern. They had been us once; it would soon be our turn.

By fourth term we'd found out through the Shepard plays which second years were capable of transformation and which weren't. Most reverted to habit; only a handful surpassed the preconceived notions of their ability. Anya's Beth received attention from a noteworthy theatre blogger. She was marked as one to watch, the heavy shadow of having repeated finally shed.

The third years drew crowds in Judith's adaptation of *Pains of Youth*, but few enjoyed it as much as the players themselves, who sustained the dark world of the play well into the early hours of the morning.

I ushered it three times, and each night it was different, though the text was the same, the blocking almost identical. When I asked Oliver about it, he said, 'Rehearsals are for you to find it. Then you play.' *Play.* I'd forgotten what that felt like.

The third years were such a stark contrast to the people they portrayed in the evenings that I was certain they'd all go on to great things. But that wasn't true. There was still agents' day—a showing that reduced each company member to a short paragraph, their talent highlighted in a three-minute scene. The agents and directors relied on the showing to recruit. It seemed unjust to me that these people, the ones who drove the industry, might never see their future clients in a production like *Pains of Youth*. Or that a role beneath a name might make someone more valuable than their peers, even if the actual performance had been uninspired.

—

There was a woman at the entrance with long dark hair, greying at the roots. Her floral dress fell to the cement and billowed in the wind. She held it down with one hand and smoked a cigarette with the other.

'First year?' she asked.

I took a step back and smiled. 'Yes.'

The woman squinted as she sucked the nub.

I know you, I thought, but was interrupted before I could identify her.

'Could you show me the way?' she asked, already walking through the doors ahead of me.

In the lift, I listened to her talk about how Melbourne was now overrun with outsiders. When we reached the second floor I said, 'Here we are.'

The doors opened but the woman paused so long they began to close. She stuck her hand between them, they jolted open again, and she stepped out. I followed.

'Can I find someone for you?' I asked, but before she could respond we saw Judith approaching with open arms. I watched the tangle of limbs, and then the women stood back and took a good look at one another. Judith gripped the woman's shoulders, and the visitor wiped her eyes and laughed. The sound of it reminded me of Saxon.

I turned towards the Rehearsal Room and saw him through the open door, bent at the waist with his fingers threaded through his toes. The woman stood beside me as Judith entered the room and rubbed Saxon's back. His head shot to the side. He stood slowly.

Saxon walked through the door, and the woman reached for his face. There was an affinity between them, no matter what he'd told me in private. The woman placed her cheek against his and I saw her back shudder with suppressed emotion. Saxon looked helpless and relieved. His mother had come for him after all.

She was permitted to sit in on Movement class and while she observed all of us, her attention was focused on her son. Illogically, I wanted to build on who I could be to her and gave more than was necessary on the floor. But Saxon worked as he always did, any adrenaline he felt contained. An artist in rehearsal, undistracted by the anomaly of an audience. That, more than anything, would have impressed her.

I sought him out at the end of class. I searched every studio, every hallway. Eventually, I found him standing alone at the base of the stairwell, staring at the polished cement beneath his bare feet. He didn't hear me approach, and I watched him, a breathing statue. In and out. In and out.

'She's back,' I said softly, and Saxon winced. It was an error to mention his mother so soon after her arrival. I knew he'd prefer to mull it over and come to terms with it alone. But I longed to ease the pulse of his pain with my own, proof of an old loyalty.

'She'll stay with Judith,' he said.

Saxon waited for me to connect it. Him, Judith and his mother. His familiarity with our tutor, the phone call in winter. Knots of understanding loosened, and I felt guilty to be encroaching on what would become the memory of his mother's return.

He lowered his voice but still the words echoed and bounced. The building held them and seemed to laugh. 'It hurts, you know? I couldn't find a way to explain it to you,' Saxon said, clearly conflicted about his mother. Pitiful that I was asking him to spell it out for me now.

'But I saw—'

'What you wanted to see.'

'You're not together?'

'No, of course not.' Saxon smiled sadly. 'Judith is Mum's best mate. I've known her all my life . . . She's the only family I've got, really.'

The words tumbled out of me. 'Can we start over?'

His face became brimful with sorrow. 'I don't think I could take it.'

'What?'

'Us falling apart again.'

323

The leather jacket he wore, all the black. Beneath it were soft edges. I'd realised it too late, coloured his intentions darker than they truly were to fit into a narrative of my own.

My voice swelled with tears. 'I'm really sorry.'

Saxon regarded me kindly. 'Yeah, me too, Juliet.'

A student ran down the stairs and approached Saxon from behind. We talked to him like we weren't in the middle of something major. The guy said, 'Chookas for *Closer*,' then headed to the foyer. We couldn't pick it up again, our broken conversation.

'I heard about'—Saxon paused and I clenched my jaw in anticipation—'your scene.'

I released the tension, spared the injury of hearing Yates's name. 'And?'

'Solid, I'm told.'

I wondered by whom. 'We'll see.'

Saxon lifted his hand and moved it towards my collarbone. An old impulse he couldn't follow through with. He dropped it, and we watched one another until the gap between us closed. The embrace felt organic, fully realised, like the first.

—

We were waiting for Vivien, sitting quietly on the floor, dressed in black, props in hand. Quinn sat behind us on a chair with the faculty on either side. Everyone leaned towards the door as it opened, and I knew she'd planned the performance of her arrival.

Vivien took her time undressing out of her street clothes. The rustling of fabric and the tossing of shoes filled the space, but nothing vocal, nothing human. She must have prepared at home because she took to the floor without so much as a hum, and I was called upon to deliver our *Closer* scene.

'Maeve,' Quinn said with brusque impatience, 'find a beginning—'

'I will,' I interrupted, focused on Vivien before me. 'In my own time.'

I could feel my peers staring: incredulous, awed. To disregard Quinn's direction was to remove her venerable title.

'The fire, *the fire!*' Quinn laughed dismissively. 'Let's see if Maeve can set it aside and serve the scene.' She looked between the students. 'Think she can? I'm doubtful.' Then she began an impassioned spiel about trusting her process, about allowing the work to be held by our preparation. I took none of it in and repeated a single word to myself, the one I'd come to think of as Oliver's. *Play.* I removed everyone else from my consciousness. Judith, Barbara, Yates. My company, seated obediently at Quinn's feet. No one had put it as succinctly as Oliver.

Play.

With my instincts revived, I spoke the first line of the scene.

Vivien held a camera, but not the one we'd used in rehearsals. This one worked. She began to shoot me with it. A little flash. A new offering that wiped the slate clean.

Like in life, I couldn't recall what I'd said or how I'd said it. There was no ending. I simply drifted off the floor when I saw in Vivien what was happening to me—our bodies relaxing into being our own again.

Vivien remained where she stood and altered herself accordingly when her next scene partner joined her. After she finished her third scene, Vivien left. Nothing was noted, nothing was said. The afternoon continued as though she'd never been a part of it.

There wasn't applause or any acknowledgement of what we'd delivered that afternoon. Quinn released us from the studio with a curt nod. We gathered our possessions in silence as our tutors formed a circle of chairs on the floor we'd made a stage only moments before, to deliberate on our futures.

My company walked together along the corridor towards the stairs and erupted into laughter. From it sprang questions about how the showing had gone and which students had done well. Dylan arched his back and howled like a wolf. Almost everyone else joined in. No one felt self-conscious anymore; our most extreme selves had been given air to breathe. Because that's what had been brought out in us—every corner of who we were, every ounce of who we could be, to blend and change without apology. We were bonded now by the charge of the place, no matter which students progressed or failed.

Vivien was smoking on the steps. Richard ran past me to greet her. Imogen and I held back in the foyer to watch and gasped in unison when Vivien slapped him.

'They're over,' Imogen said.

I realised I'd already known.

We watched through the glass doors as they fought. We weren't worried about them or hungry for gossip. Just weary, vaguely interested, committing to memory for future use the unexpected way Richard heaved as he cried, how Vivien held her mouth as she laughed. They didn't stop as the building emptied, students slowing to eavesdrop on their way to the Malthouse. Phrases drifted towards us as the doors opened and muted again when they shut. I turned to Imogen at the mention of Judith.

She sucked her teeth. 'Come on, you had an inkling, surely.'

I remembered Judith licking Richard's lips after *Scarecrow*. 'He talked about it,' I said. *Through others*, I wanted to add.

'Flying a little too close to the sun,' Imogen said. 'Covering all bases. Brazen bastard. Imagine if it were reversed. Imagine a male teacher, a female student. Richard will be fine. Judith too, probably. If this were a normal institution . . .'

I flooded with shame at the memory of the crumpled flowers and Yates, remembered how harshly we'd all judged Scarlett. I began to speak, but Imogen stopped me.

'Don't compare,' she said. 'Move on.' It was the only acknowledgement she'd ever make that she knew what had happened between Yates and me.

There were drinks, celebrations, but without discussing it we left them behind and walked to the tram. At Imogen's place we watched *The Birds* on her laptop beneath the bedcovers and lost ourselves in the trivialities of another actor's pain, relieved to be done with our own for the year.

—

Summer signified the end. The city wasn't built for it. I felt guilty, sweating on the tram into town, as though I alone had brought it on. I hadn't meant to wish the year away. I'd wanted to absorb it for my training. Now it felt like I'd barely survived.

Squat terrace houses grew into plump buildings, and glass punctured the sky on the edges of the grid. I wanted the change I felt in myself to be reflected in the frame of the city, for the construction sites to sprout into skyscrapers to measure my growth against.

I arrived early. There was no one on the steps, and the glass doors opened for me automatically. Genevieve was at reception, but otherwise the drama building was empty. I took my time walking through the foyer and slid my hand along the rail as

327

I ascended the stairs. I looked up and felt the potential of the place, the ghosts of the characters waiting to be brought to life again. It didn't scare me as much as it once had.

Inside the Rehearsal Room I undressed. Bare feet, black tights, black t-shirt. Free to move through the daily practice I'd cobbled together after months of trying to find my breath, my voice, my body. A combination of yoga postures, Feldenkrais and purposeful stretches that flowed into a short medley of vocal exercises. Alone, I could rest inside each choice without distraction, without worrying about being watched or judged for how I brought myself to readiness. On my back, knees up, eyes closed. Palms open. Jaw slack.

The doorhandle rattled and I became irrationally angry at the sound of someone approaching. I exhaled loudly.

'Ignore me,' Saxon said.

My body tensed and my breath caught. I kept my eyes closed and listened, imagining how he might remove his jacket, untie his bootlaces. The slow, deliberate walk he'd take across the floor, how that would crumple into kneeling. More real to me than my own movement.

'When you breathe here,' Saxon said, 'everything connects.'

His hands spread across my abdomen, an old exercise. The warmth of him, the smell. I softened and expanded to the edges of the space, retracting beneath his palms.

'Again,' Saxon said.

I stopped counting the inhalations and surrendered. Saxon dissolved, and I was present, unencumbered by the weight of myself, of us, of everything I usually struggled to leave at the door.

I opened my eyes. 'Thank you.'

'No problem,' Saxon replied.

We stood. I continued with my practice and Saxon began his. Content to move, to voice sound, for ourselves alone. His opinion mattering less, finally, than my own.

—

Closer came back to me in parts. Never linear, never whole. It was impossible to assess myself through the broken moments of recollection. My place in the company felt unclear. Text redefined our ability. My sliding scale became redundant. But judging by the lack of attention from my peers, I guessed my value lay somewhere in the middle. I was neither a threat nor a hindrance.

We would find out if it had been enough, our varied interpretations of *Closer*, via the post in January, back in our home states, far enough away from the people who'd decided whether we were worthy of returning for another year of training or not.

It made the final afternoon feel like a pretence. No end-of-term review, no panel to front. Only the phonetics exam and the Twenty Movements to complete. To fail Movement, to fail Voice, seemed inconsequential. All of it was in support of character. The real test had been with *Closer*.

Our enthusiasm waned as the hours passed and the buzz from the lower ground grew. It was agents' day; the second years wandered the hallways beyond the Rehearsal Room, making it harder to connect with our work. Still our bodies laboured, and we felt progress in our aching muscles, our loose joints.

Freya and Phillip made no mention of what we'd experienced together in the lead-up to this final day—as though to mention the poetry we'd recited, the shapes we'd made, might undermine the process altogether, detract from where we'd landed. They just said *thank you* and released us. But as I gathered my things and took a moment to look out of the Rehearsal Room windows for the last time, I felt Freya trail a hand along my shoulder blades. 'You made it,' she murmured, and continued through to the passageway. I repeated the phrase back to myself with a small sense of accomplishment as clouds gathered like gauze over the buildings below.

We made up for the anticlimactic end to our first year of training by allowing ourselves to be pulled into the wave of celebrations beyond the studio a little too enthusiastically. Bottles were opened, anecdotes swapped, as we considered how the third years must feel to be leaving the place for good.

In the foyer, the last of the agents' day crowd lingered and between them wove the third years, dressed for a big night out. Black gowns, black suits. Lipstick, hairspray and cologne. Not in rehearsal gear or barefoot. A covering-up of the work, of the roles they'd inhabited. But the tiny imprints were there, blended beneath their make-up. They could never properly be blotted away.

A pair of arms wrapped around my middle. 'Lolita,' Sylvie purred.

She kissed me with her lashes and swayed. It felt belittling after everything she knew about me now.

'How do you feel?' I asked, disentangling myself.

'Fine.'

The elevator doors opened and a pair of students walked out. Pulling me with her, Sylvie moved towards it. A wicked smile shaped her lips. 'Lolita' always meant something.

'Surely there are people you'd like to speak to,' I said, a plea.

Sylvie ignored me and pressed the button for level two. 'Going up.'

The doors shut. I leaned against the wall and watched her fish between her breasts for a vial. Sylvie unscrewed the lid and took a bump then offered it to me. When I refused, she insisted and brought it to the corner of my nose. I flinched and the powder fell. Sylvie tutted.

'Should I be nervous?' she asked.

There was no straight answer, and she knew it. The falsity of our friendship crackled between us. It made me feel embarrassed for everything I'd revealed, the drunken *I love you*'s and all the party favours she'd used to draw them from me.

'Guess not,' I replied. 'You've had one foot out the door all year.'

Sylvie pouted, pleased to have someone to spar with. 'Ouch.'

'Why did you come back?'

She considered me. 'Is that a real question?'

'Yes.'

Sylvie stood upright, replaced the vial and reached for the stop button. The elevator jolted.

'Look at me.' She placed my hands on either side of her face and held them there with her own. 'Really. Look.'

Beneath the harsh lighting she forced me to see the darkness from which her art sprang. It was too awful to articulate, how I'd wanted it once: a shard of the dark to give strength to my own work. It didn't matter. All along, she'd sensed it.

'Did Quinn really have you discharged from a psychiatric facility?' I whispered.

It was an error to ask so directly. Sylvie's face clouded. She dropped my hands, turned away from me in an attempt to deflect. I'd watched her do something similar onstage in *Pains of Youth*.

'Did you really fuck Yates?' she asked, spinning towards me again, changed.

I blinked at her. 'What?'

331

'Concerned, were we? About passing? Hoping he'd put in a good word?' She delivered the accusation with a sneer.

'I didn't sleep with him,' I said weakly.

'Inconsequential.'

'My relationship with Yates,' I said, reaching for my maturity, 'has nothing to do with passing.'

Sylvie laughed at the ceiling. 'Or your career.'

I was used to being led in circles, altering myself to receive her. But I was tired. The year had caught up with me. To shift in and out of the person I was no longer felt worth the cost. I needed the truth, the centre of something.

'Did Quinn really—'

Sylvie stiffened. 'Stop.'

'I just—'

'What?' Sylvie demanded. 'Want to help? Take advantage, more like.'

'No, of course I don't—'

'Bullshit!' Sylvie screamed.

The word reverberated through the small space and stilled us.

'You're really hurt,' I said. 'What happened to you?'

Sylvie's face opened to the opportunity. She reached for the emergency button and held it as she spoke. The trilling sound of it bolstered her performance.

'*I am a seagull,*' she said. '*No, that's not it . . . I'm an actress.*'

My breath hitched at the reference, but I was too enthralled to stop her. Sylvie continued with Nina's monologue, her vulnerability bubbling beneath the words, and I understood that it was an explanation of sorts, of what she'd lived through before drama school and her motivation to return. Here, she had the freedom to rail against the source of her pain and get as close to the brink as

332

possible without the severity of consequence. She could be violent or irreverent, lustful or deranged, it didn't matter. Sylvie was a great actress; her anguish made her so. However she behaved offstage would be excused.

'You can't unlearn it,' Sylvie said, reaching for me.

'What?' I asked cautiously.

Her fingers trailed my collarbone and rested around my throat. 'Our conditioning. It takes practice, you know?' She began to tighten her grip; blood rushed to my face. I placed my hands over hers, tried to prise them off me.

'Sylvie?'

She looked me over like an object, muttering between breaths. The rumours were like walls built around her persona, protecting what lay within.

'Sylvie,' I said again. 'Please. I can't breathe.'

She loosened her fingers as though waking from a dream. Pain throbbed at my temples, swirls of black obscured my vision.

'Fuck you,' she said quietly and began to sob. 'Fuck Quinn. Fuck Yates. Fuck the lot of you.'

She fell against me, and I could breathe again. The ringing stopped and the elevator began to descend. I eased her to the floor, kneeled beside her and placed a hand on the small of her back. It had been one of the first things we'd been taught as first years. How to heal one another. I'd forgotten.

The elevator doors opened. A mingling of companies had gathered. Quinn pushed through them and lifted Sylvie to her feet. 'Disgraceful,' she slung at me. With that, the second and third years dispersed, shaking their heads, rolling their eyes. They'd seen versions of this before. But the first years loitered and observed the scene like any other they'd witnessed in the performance spaces above.

'What's disgraceful is your misuse of her,' I responded quietly.

Quinn moved towards me briskly, her small frame engorged with rage. 'Bite your tongue,' she said. 'I sense your yearning.'

'Do you?' I asked uncertainly.

'If only you would *comply*.'

'Like Sylvie?'

Quinn became sardonic. 'Yes. Like Sylvie.'

And I was drawn in, compelled by the strength of her scrutiny. It's what I'd wanted for so long, for my potential to be acknowledged.

'It's not *use* if one consents,' she continued. 'If one desires it. It's what I like to think of as a contribution.'

I became suddenly aware of Quinn's nails on my forearm. She looked at her hand and let go. Tiny crescent moons marked my skin.

'And what a gift that is to the world,' she finished.

'I don't know if I want to make that kind of contribution,' I said, thinking of Barbara, of Ford, of the care they took with their actors.

Quinn laughed. 'You already have.'

The truth struck me. '*Miss Julie.*'

She warmed with my defeat. 'Yates said you did so well. Art and sacrifice go hand in hand, my dear. Don't waste your ability to go the distance.'

And I was discarded.

Quinn tapped Sylvie beneath her chin, like waking a living doll, and led her discreetly to the reception counter.

'For goodness sake,' Genevieve called in a singsong voice intended to mask her annoyance at the disruption. 'We're not at the circus!'

'Aren't we?' a disembodied voice replied.

Genevieve scolded me. Behind her, four firefighters were waiting, but there had been no emergency. 'A waste of resources,' she said, 'to be experimenting like that.' With language, with the space. With ourselves.

Genevieve clapped her hands and the students scattered. I stood alone by the elevator and focused on my breathing. The agents' day celebrations continued.

Sylvie and Quinn remained by reception, speaking in animated whispers. I looked across the foyer. No one else seemed to have noticed.

'*Please,*' Quinn said.

Sylvie lifted her voice, '*If you only knew how hard it is for me to go,*' she replied, taking up Nina's text again.

Quinn glanced behind her quickly before answering, '*Someone ought to see you home, little one.*'

Sylvie nodded and allowed Quinn to walk her outside.

It was beautiful and utterly devastating; a Chekhovian moment made real. *Allow it to pass through you,* Judith had said once. But the process marked each of us differently. Autonomy was difficult to grasp.

I called Sylvie's name, concerned. When she didn't respond, I tried another. 'Nina!'

She whipped around to face me, but the short walk to the entrance seemed to have drained her of all character. An empty vessel stood in her place.

'Are you okay?' I asked.

Sylvie looked at me quizzically. 'I—'

'Absolutely,' Quinn interjected.

'Yes, absolutely,' Sylvie echoed.

Quinn took her hand and led her away.

—

I was carried by a wave of students funnelling into Studio One for the final assembly of the year. Quinn's empty chair drew focus. My peers looked to me for the meaning of her absence. Loyal to Sylvie, privy to the cost of her art, I remained silent.

The students were unsettled, mentally elsewhere—at the Malthouse already with glasses full of drink. Ford took to the floor between the row of faculty and the seating bank of students, quietening us with a raised hand.

'From the top,' he said, bringing us back to the reason we'd been called together: to say goodbye to the third years and to thank them for their work.

Ford recapped the year, reeling off highlights from various productions. There were tears and shouts of encouragement for characters to be played, if only for a line or two. So intertwined were the plays, the company members and the staff that to simply leave seemed impossible, and incredibly sad. And yet we'd all wanted to get through it at one time or another, to the end of class, the end of a performance, the end of a term. To prove that we were capable in another form, another text, exhausted with our present selves. But outside the walls of the drama building there was no one from whom to seek support—no faculty, no company—and that seemed unsatisfactory in light of what we'd experienced. You were alone out there. We'd been spoiled.

'For those of you continuing with your training,' Ford began, as though it were our choice, 'it will be without our head of school. Quinn will be coaching a colleague in Ireland for the better part of next year. She wanted to share the news with you herself but is currently tending to the needs of a student. So it has fallen to me, and may I say how honoured I am to be stepping into her role.'

Applause filled the space.

Ford smiled. 'I will release you to the wild in a moment,' he said, 'but before I do, may I remind you of something very important.' His gaze roamed over the assembled students, settling finally on my face. 'Trust your instincts. After all, that is what drew us to you in the first place.'

EPILOGUE

Dried leaves whipped my ankles. The heat pounded overhead. When I found them, I felt nostalgic for a time not yet passed. They were like a picture, my friends, lying languid against the green of Edinburgh Gardens. I squinted, determined to imprint them on memory. A beautiful motley of denim, polka dot and burgundy. Richard, Imogen, Emmet and Dylan.

'Get over here!' Richard called, and I tripped over my feet to get closer. The bottle of red was taken first, then I was pulled onto the rug, kissed, and the reason for my tardiness interrogated. *Packing*, I exclaimed, but they disregarded my excuse, and I was thrust directly into a conversation about Emmet's new director at the Sydney Theatre Company.

'He's brilliant,' Dylan said, 'a wunderkind.'

'He's a hack!' Richard replied.

Emmet arched an eyebrow. 'Jealous, mate?'

'Only of the possibility of a little tete-a-tete,' Richard said.

'Not learned your lesson, then?' Imogen asked.

Richard scowled. 'Come on, now.'

'I'll report back,' Emmet said and winked.

I stifled my laughter. The affair with Judith was a sore point. Richard had not been the only one. He was heartbroken, pining for his teacher and Vivien both. To imagine all three in a room together, on the floor in our second year, was difficult. But likely. It happened all the time in the industry.

'Here,' Richard said and handed me a photograph. 'Vivien wanted you to have this.' It was an image of a woman caught between a phrase and a smile. Fire behind the eyes, determination.

Imogen snatched the photograph and held it up to the sky. The woman shook in the wind; like a still from a projector, she flickered.

'Viv really caught you, didn't she?' Imogen said.

My heart fluttered at the transformation. At the acknowledgement. At the proof between Imogen's fingertips of my ability. Me, as Alice in *Closer*.

'Strong, no?' Richard added, and the photograph was passed between us.

Emmet held it the longest and returned it to me with a nod. 'You kept going.'

I had.

My vision blurred from the alcohol, but I was content, no longer afraid to drink too little or too much. I had an hour to enjoy with my friends before I left for the airport to travel home for the summer. They loaded me up with recommendations of novels to read and films to watch, to be discussed when we returned—though none of us could be certain we'd make it to our second year.

'Here he is!' Richard yelled.

Saxon opened his arms to the party. We applauded. He shook the hands of the men, kissed Imogen's cheek and kneeled before me, shading his eyes from the sun.

'Maeve.'

Yes, I thought. *That's who I am.*

We breathed one another in.

I saw the possibilities, then, of the characters we'd play and the spaces we'd fill. Saxon and me: cast members, allies, equals.

Breath is imagination.

ACKNOWLEDGEMENTS

First Year would not exist without Sullivan and Bo Valor. My boys, thank you for being nothing but your most authentic selves and for teaching me to embrace mine.

Thank you to the wonderful team at Allen & Unwin. To my publisher, Annette Barlow—my gratitude is boundless. To my editor, Christa Munns, and my copyeditor, Ali Lavau, thank you for sharing your expertise with me, *First Year* is far stronger for it.

To my first reader, Tenille Duncan, thank you for your kind encouragement and enthusiasm for the story. And thank you to Kate Bird, for being in my corner, always.

Thank you to my family—Mum, Matthew, Carly and Craig—your support means the world. Thank you also to Mormor, for your unwavering belief in me.

To my husband, Tim Ross, I am grateful every day for the life we have made together. You and the boys are my home.

Finally, while *First Year* is a work of fiction, I would like to acknowledge the actors I trained alongside. Your courage and commitment to the craft has inspired me over the years to strive to create work that is more passionate and uncompromising in its vision. I have been fortunate enough to translate that into producing projects with some of you; the most intelligent, talented and open-hearted alumni. What a privilege, thank you.